Western Roundup

THE MACMILLAN COMPANY
NEW YORK · CHICAGO
DALLAS · ATLANTA · SAN FRANCISCO
LONDON · MANILA

IN CANADA
BRETT-MACMILLAN LTD.
GALT, ONTARIO

Western Roundup

by Members of the Western Writers of America

edited by Nelson Nye

with an introduction by Paul I. Wellman

THE MACMILLAN COMPANY   NEW YORK   1961

First Printing

Permission to quote copyrighted material is acknowledged as follows: "That 7X Bull," by Elmer Kelton, copyright 1954 by Better Publications, Inc., and originally published in *Texas Rangers*, July, 1954; "Shiftless Slow," by Leslie Ernenwein, copyright 1952 by Best Books, Inc., and originally published in *Ranch Romances*, 2nd May issue, 1952; "Smart," by Wayne D. Overholser originally published in *Argosy Magazine* as "The Law-Abiding Outlaw," copyright 1959 by Popular Publications, Inc.; "The Marshal of Indian Rock," by Fred Grove, originally published in *Max Brand Western* as "Town of No Return," copyright 1953 by New Publications, Inc.; "Way of the Law in Calico," by John B. Prescott, originally published in *The Saturday Evening Post* as "The Landlady's Daughter," copyright 1956 by the Curtis Publishing Company; "High-Carded," by Lewis Patten, originally published in *Western Short Stories* as "Fast Draw Feud," copyright, 1950 by Lewis B. Patten; "Due Process," by Steve Frazee, first published in *Ellery Queen's Mystery Magazine*, © March, 1960; "Jackass Judgment," copyright by Kenneth Fowler, first published in *Esquire*, July, 1952; "Hired Gun," by William R. Cox, originally published in *Argosy Magazine*, copyright 1951 by Popular Publications, Inc.; "Timber Tough," by Noel Loomis, originally published in *Argosy Magazine*, copyright 1949 by Popular Publications, Inc.

The Macmillan Company, New York
Brett-Macmillan Ltd., Galt, Ontario

Printed in the United States of America

Library of Congress catalog card number: 61-17161

Note

The Western Writers of America is an organization of professional authors whose aims are to promote their common interests, encourage the writing of better quality Westerns, and bring them more effectively to the attention of the reading public. One part of WWA's extensive program has been the publication of an annual collection of stories by its member writers. Eight such volumes have preceded this one: *Bad Men and Good, Holsters and Heroes, The Fall Roundup, Branded West, Hoof Trails and Wagon Tracks, Wild Streets, Frontiers West,* and *Spurs West*. WWA has also published a series of juvenile anthologies, and annually sponsors the SPUR AWARDS (open to the world) with an $1100 purse for bests in five categories. WWA sponsors additionally the COVER ART AWARDS for publishers and artists in both soft and hard covers.

Introduction

by Paul I. Wellman

WHAT IS THE WEST? One of the difficulties in answering that question is the inexplicit nature of the borders both of territory and time. Indeed, one sometimes wonders if the West is not a state of mind, as much as an area, or even an era.

Today horsemen still ride the mountains and deserts with their horn-spiked herds, but they do not of necessity wear six-shooters. Their land, once lonely, is now crisscrossed by ribbons of concrete, and they have and use the speeding car, the air strip, the telephone, the radio, even the television (where they see themselves sometimes ridiculously maligned).

Does this argue that romance has departed from the West? Indeed not. There are today dude ranches almost in the suburbs of some of the great cities of the Atlantic Coast, where the wide sombrero, the high-heeled boot, the stock saddle, yes, even the chaps, are much affected and people (for a fee) may at least imagine themselves living in the far untrammeled range. Romance has by no means been lost in the land of mighty distances and magnificent scenery, else why would it be synthetically offered to the denizens of the East?

Most distinctive of all the American scenes was the old West. Across it rode the cowboys, a unique cavalry, weaponed, humorous, unstable, sometimes murderous. Its trail towns fermented, festering and boiling over with energy and evil. Its distances were mighty, its vistas magnificent. The Indians of this country attained a spectacularness, both of appearance and deed, unmatched. There was in the West opportunity for endless excitement and tragedy, gambling for great stakes in money or lives, heroism and cowardice, honor and treachery, generosity and greed; above all, a keyed-up dangerous existence.

The cattleman's garb of the West is perhaps the one distinctive and universally recognized regional costume this nation has evolved. The skills, the vernacular, the humor, the deeds of the West have imprinted themselves indelibly on the traditions of our country. It would, indeed, hardly be overstating it to say that the West was and is the most essentially American part of all America.

Out of such materials a rich and varied literature inevitably has grown. It possesses a great tradition, for names like those of Mark Twain, Bret Harte, Owen Wister, Alfred Henry Lewis, Stewart Edward White and their notable followers, march with it.

This volume contains an anthology of the best current Western stories. They are for the reader who takes pride in the history and the legends of his country, for the reader who enjoys rich color and salty character, for the reader whose pulse responds to adventure— for adventure is inherent in any tale of the West.

Sample these stories. You will find them as stimulating as the tangy air blowing off sagebrush flats, or a keen whiff of cedar smoke from a campfire on a frosty mountain morning.

Contents

Only Good Ones

by Elmore Leonard

Author of five or six novels and several short stories, "Dutch" Leonard, a Louisianan by birth, lives at Lathrup Village, Michigan, works in Detroit and writes in whatever time is left over. "Only Good Ones" is an original story giving a dependable example of the kind of work one can expect from his pen.

🌿 🌿 🌿

PICTURE THE GROUND RISING on the east side of the pasture with scrub trees thick on the slope and pines higher up. This is where everybody was. Not all in one place but scattered in small groups: about a dozen men in the scrub, the front line men, the shooters who couldn't just stand around. They'd fire at the shack when they felt like it or, when Mr. Tanner passed the word, they would all fire at once. Other people were up in the pines and on the road which ran along the crest of the hill, some three hundred yards from the shack across the pasture. Those watching made bets whether the man in the shack would give himself up or get shot first.

It was Saturday and that's why everybody had the time. They

would arrive in town that morning, hear about what had happened and, shortly after, head out to the cattle company pasture. Almost all of the men went out alone, leaving their families in town; though there were a few women who came. The other women waited. And the people who had business in town and couldn't leave waited. Now and then somebody came back to have a drink or their dinner and would tell what was going on. No, they hadn't got him yet. Still inside the line shack and not showing his face. But they'd get him. A few more would go out when they heard this. Also a wagon from De Spain's went out with whisky. That's how the saloon was set up in the pines overlooking the pasture and why nobody went back to town after that.

Barely a mile from town those going out would hear the gunfire: like a skirmish way over on the other side of a woods, thin specks of sound, and this would hurry them. They were careful, though, topping the slope, looking across the pasture, getting their bearings, then peering to see who was present. They would see a friend and ask about this Mr. Tanner and the friend would point him out.

The man there in the dark suit: thin and bony, not big but looking like he was made of gristle and hard to kill, with a mustache and a thin nose and a dark dusty hat worn square over his eyes. That was him. Nobody had ever seen him before that morning.

They would look at Mr. Tanner, then across the pasture again to the line shack three hundred yards away. It was a little bake-oven of a hut, wood framed and made of sod and built against a rise where there were pines so the hut would be in shade part of the day. There were no windows in the hut, no gear lying around to show anybody lived there. The hut stood in the sun now with its door closed, the door chipped and splintered by all the bullets that had poured into it and through it.

Off to the right where the pine shapes against the sky rounded and became willows, there in the trees by the creek bed, was the man's wagon and team. In the wagon were the supplies he had bought that morning in town before Mr. Tanner spotted him.

Out in front of the hut about ten or fifteen feet was something on the ground. From the slope three hundred yards away nobody could tell what it was until a man came who had field glasses. He looked up and said, frowning, it was a doll: one made of cloth scraps, a stuffed doll with buttons for eyes.

The woman must have dropped it, somebody said.

The *woman?* the man with the field glasses said.

A Lipan-Apache woman who was his wife or his woman or just with him. Mr. Tanner hadn't been clear about that. All they knew was she was in the hut with him and if the man wanted her to stay and get shot that was his business.

Bob Valdez, twenty years old and town constable for three weeks, carrying a shotgun and glad he had something to hold onto, was present at the Maricopa pasture. He arrived about noon. He told Mr. Tanner who he was, speaking quietly and waiting for Mr. Tanner to answer. Mr. Tanner nodded but did not shake hands and turned away to say something to an R. L. Davis who rode for Maricopa when he was working. Bob Valdez stood there and didn't know what to do.

He watched the two men. Two of a kind, uh? Both cut from the same stringy hide and looking like father and son: Tanner talking, never smiling, hardly moving his mouth; R. L. Davis standing hip-cocked, posing with his revolver and rifle and a cartridge belt over his shoulder and the funneled, pointed brim of his sweaty hat nodding up and down as he listened to Mr. Tanner, smiling at what Mr. Tanner said, laughing out loud while still Mr. Tanner did not even show the twitch of a lip. Bob Valdez did not like R. L. Davis or any of the R. L. Davises he had met. He was civil, he listened to them, but God there were a lot of them to listen to.

A Mr. Beaudry who leased land to the cattle company was there. Also Mr. Malsom, manager of Maricopa, and a horsebreaker by the name of Diego Luz, who was big for a Mexican but never offensive and he drank pretty well.

Mr. Beaudry, nodding and also squinting so he could picture the man inside the line shack said, "There was something peculiar about him. I mean having a name like Orlando Rincon."

"He worked for me," Mr. Malsom said. He was looking at Mr. Tanner. "I mistrusted him and I believe that was part of it, his name being Orlando Rincon."

"Johnson," Mr. Tanner said.

"I hired him two, three times," Mr. Malsom said. "For heavy work. When I had work you couldn't kick a man to doing."

"His name is Johnson," Mr. Tanner said. "There is no fuzzhead by the name of Orlando Rincon. I'm telling you this one is a fuzzhead from the Fort Hauchuca Tenth fuzz-head cavalry and his name was Johnson when he killed James C. Baxter a year ago and nothing else."

He spoke as you might speak to young children to press something into their minds. This man had no warmth and he was probably not very smart. But there was no reason to doubt him.

Bob Valdez kept near Mr. Tanner because he was the center of what was going on here. They would discuss the situation and decide what to do. As the law enforcement man he, Bob Valdez, should be in on the discussion and the decision. If someone was to arrest Orlando Rincon or Johnson or whatever his name was, then he should do it; he was town constable. They were out of town maybe, but where did the town end? The town had moved out here now; it was the same thing.

Wait for Rincon to give up. Then arrest him.

If he wasn't dead already.

"Mr. Malsom." Bob Valdez stepped toward the cattle company manager who glanced over but looked out across the pasture again, indifferent.

"I wondered if maybe he's already dead," Valdez said.

Mr. Malsom, standing heavier and taller and twenty years older than Bob Valdez, said, "Why don't you find out?"

"I was thinking," Valdez said, "if he was dead we could stand here a long time."

R. L. Davis adjusted his hat, which he did often, grabbing the funneled brim, loosening it on his head and pulling it down close to his eyes again and shifting from one cocked hip to the other. "This constable here's got better things to do," R. L. Davis said. "He's busy."

"No," Bob Valdez said. "I was thinking of the man, Rincon. He's dead or he's alive. He's alive maybe he wants to give himself up. In there he has time to think, uh? Maybe—" He stopped. Not one of them was listening. Not even R. L. Davis.

Mr. Malsom was looking at the whisky wagon; it was on the road above them and over a little ways with men standing by it, being served off the tailgate. "I think we could use something," Mr. Malsom said. His gaze went to Diego Luz the horsebreaker and Diego straightened up; not much, but a little. He was heavy and very dark and his shirt was tight across the thickness of his body. They said that Diego Luz hit green horses on the muzzle with his fist and they minded him. He had the hands for it; they hung at his sides, not touching or fooling with anything. They turned open, gestured, when Mr. Malsom told him to get the whisky and as he moved off, climbing the slope, one hand held his holstered revolver to his leg.

Mr. Malsom looked up at the sky, squinting and taking his hat off and putting it on again. He took off his coat and held it hooked over his shoulder by one finger, said something, gestured, and he and Mr. Beaudry and Mr. Tanner moved a few yards down the slope to a hollow where there was good shade. It was about two or two-thirty then, hot, fairly still and quiet considering the number of people there. Only some of them in the pines and down in the scrub could be seen from where Bob Valdez stood wondering whether he should follow the three men down to the hollow. Or wait for Diego Luz who was at the whisky wagon now where most of the sounds that carried came from: a voice, a word or two that was suddenly clear, or laughter, and people would look up to see what was going on. Some of them by the whisky wagon had lost interest in the line shack. Others were still watching though: those farther along the road sitting in wagons and buggies. This was a day, a date, uh? that people would remember and talk about. Sure, I was there, the man in the buggy would be saying a year from now in a saloon over in Benson or St. David or somewhere. The day they got that army deserter, he had a Big-Fifty Sharps and an old Walker and I'll tell you it was ticklish business.

Down in that worn-out pasture, dusty and spotted with desert growth, prickly pear and brittlebush, there was just the sun. It showed the ground cleanly all the way to just in front of the line shack where now, toward mid-afternoon, there was shadow coming out from the trees and from the mound the hut was set against.

Somebody in the scrub must have seen the door open. The shout came from there and Bob Valdez and everybody on the slope was looking by the time the Lipan-Apache woman had reached the edge of the shade. She walked out from the hut toward the willow trees carrying a bucket, not hurrying or even looking toward the slope.

Nobody fired at her; though this was not so strange. Putting the front sight on a sod hut and on a person are two different things. The men in the scrub and in the pines didn't know this woman. They weren't after her. She had just appeared. There she was; and no one was sure what to do about her.

She was in the trees a while by the creek, then she was in the open again, walking back toward the hut with the bucket and not hurrying at all: a small figure way across the pasture almost without shape or color, with only the long skirt reaching to the ground to tell it was the woman.

So he's alive, Bob Valdez thought. And he wants to stay alive and he's not giving himself up.

He thought about the woman's nerve and whether Orlando Rincon had sent her out or she had decided this herself. You couldn't tell about an Indian woman. Maybe this was expected of her. The woman didn't count; the man did. You could lose the woman and get another one.

Mr. Tanner didn't look at R. L. Davis. His gaze held on the Lipan-Apache woman, inched along with her toward the hut; but he must have known R. L. Davis was right next to him.

"She's saying she don't give a goddamn about you and your rifle," Mr. Tanner said.

R. L. Davis looked at him funny. Then he said, "Shoot her?" Like he hoped that's what Mr. Tanner meant.

"Well, you could make her jump some," Mr. Tanner said.

Now R. L. Davis was on stage and he knew it and Bob Valdez could tell he knew it by the way he levered the Winchester, raised it and fired all in one motion and as the dust kicked behind the Indian woman who kept walking and didn't look up, R. L. Davis fired and fired and fired as fast as he could lever and half aim and with everybody watching him, hurrying him, he put four good ones right behind the woman. His last bullet socked into the door just as she reached it and now she did pause and look up at the slope, staring up like she was waiting for him to fire again and giving him a good target if he wanted it.

Mr. Malsom laughed out loud. "She still don't give a goddamn about your rifle."

It stung R. L. Davis, which it was intended to do. "I wasn't aiming at her!"

"But she doesn't know that." Mr. Malsom was grinning, turning then and reaching out a hand as Diego Luz approached them with the whisky.

"Hell, I wanted to hit her she'd be laying there, you know it."

"Well now you go tell her that," Mr. Malsom said, working the cork loose, "and she'll know it." He took a drink from the bottle and passed it to Mr. Beaudry who drank and handed the bottle to Mr. Tanner. Mr. Tanner did not drink; he passed the bottle to R. L. Davis who was standing, staring at Mr. Malsom. Finally R. L. Davis jerked the bottle up, took a long swallow and that part was over.

Mr. Malsom said to Mr. Tanner, "You don't want any?"

"Not today," Mr. Tanner answered. He continued to stare out across the pasture.

Mr. Malsom watched him. "You feel strongly about this army deserter."

"I told you," Mr. Tanner said, "he killed a man was a friend of mine."

"No, I don't believe you did."

"James C. Baxter of Fort Huachuca," Mr. Tanner said. "He come across a tulapai still this nigger soldier was working with some Indians. The nigger thought Baxter would tell the army people so he shot him and ran off with a woman."

"And you saw him this morning."

"I had come in last night and stopped off, going to Tucson," Mr. Tanner said. "This morning I was getting ready to leave when I saw him; him and the woman."

"I was right there," R. L. Davis said. "Right, Mr. Tanner? Him and I were on the porch by the Republic and Rincon goes by in the wagon. Mr. Tanner said, 'You know that man?' I said, 'Only that he's lived up north of town a few months. Him and the woman.' 'Well, I know him,' Mr. Tanner said. 'That man's a army deserter wanted for murder.' I said, 'Well let's go get him.' He had a start on us and that's how he got to the hut before we could grab onto him. He's been holed up ever since."

Mr. Malsom said, "Then you didn't talk to him."

"Listen," Mr. Tanner said, "I've kept that man's face before my eyes this past year."

Bob Valdez, somewhat behind Mr. Tanner and to the side, moved in a little closer. "You *know* this is the same man, uh?"

Mr. Tanner looked around. He stared at Valdez. That's all he did—just stared.

"I mean, we have to be sure," Bob Valdez said. "It's a serious thing."

Now Mr. Malsom and Mr. Beaudry were looking up at him. "*We*," Mr. Beaudry said. "I'll tell you what, Roberto. We need help we'll call you. All right?"

"You hired me," Bob Valdez said, standing alone above them. He was serious but he shrugged and smiled a little to take the edge off the words. "What did you hire me for?"

"Well," Mr. Beaudry said, acting it out, looking up past Bob Valdez and along the road both ways. "I was to see some drunk Mexicans I'd point them out."

A person can be in two different places and he will be two different people. Maybe if you think of some more places the person will be more people, but don't take it too far. This is Bob Valdez standing by himself with the shotgun and having only the shotgun to hold onto. This is one Bob Valdez. About twenty years old. Mr. Beaudry and others could try and think of a time when Bob Valdez might have drunk too much or swaggered or had a certain smart look on his face, but they would never recall such a time. This Bob Valdez was all right.

Another Bob Valdez inside the Bob Valdez at the pasture that day worked for the army one time and was a guide when Crook chased Chato and Chihuahua down into the Madres. He was seventeen then, with a Springfield and Apache moccasins that came up to his knees. He would sit at night with the Apache scouts from San Carlos, eating with them and talking some as he learned

Chiricahua. He would keep up with them all day and shoot the Springfield one hell of a lot better than any of them could shoot. He came home with a scalp but never showed it to anyone and had thrown it away by the time he went to work for Maricopa. Shortly after that he was named town constable at twenty-five dollars a month, getting the job because he got along with people: the Mexicans in town who drank too much on Saturday night liked him and that was the main thing.

The men with the whisky bottle had forgotten Valdez. They stayed in the hollow where the shade was cool watching the line shack and waiting for the army deserter to realize it was all up with him. He would realize it and open the door and be cut down as he came outside. It was a matter of time only.

Bob Valdez stayed on the open part of the slope that was turning to shade, sitting now like an Apache and every once in a while making a cigarette and smoking it slowly as he thought about himself and Mr. Tanner and the others, then thinking about the army deserter.

Diego Luz came and squatted next to him, his arms on his knees and his big hands that he used for breaking horses hanging in front of him.

"Stay near if they want you for something," Valdez said. He was watching Beaudry tilt the bottle up. Diego Luz said nothing.

"One of them bends over," Bob Valdez said then, "you kiss it, uh?"

Diego Luz looked at him, patient about it. Not mad or even stirred up. "Why don't you go home?"

"He says get me a bottle you run."

"I get it. I don't run."

"Smile and hold your hat, uh?"

"And don't talk so much."

"Not unless they talk to you first."

"You better go home," Diego said.

Bob Valdez said, "That's why you hit the horses."

"Listen," Diego Luz said, scowling a bit now. "They pay me to break horses. They pay you to talk to drunks on Saturday night and keep them from killing somebody. They don't pay you for what you think or how you feel, so if you take their money keep your mouth shut. All right?"

Diego Luz got up and walked away, down toward the hollow. The hell with this kid, he was thinking. He'll learn or he won't learn, but the hell with him. He was also thinking that maybe he could get a drink from that bottle. Maybe there'd be a half inch left nobody wanted and Mr. Malsom would tell him to kill it.

But it was already finished. R. L. Davis was playing with the bottle, holding it by the neck and flipping it up and catching it as it came down. Beaudry was saying, "What about after dark?" Looking at Mr. Tanner who was thinking about something else and didn't notice. R. L. Davis stopped flipping the bottle. He said, "Put some men on the rise right above the hut; he comes out, bust him."

Well, they should get the men over there, Mr. Beaudry said, looking at the sky. "It won't be long till dark."

"Where's he going?" Mr. Malsom said.

The others looked up, stopped in whatever they were doing or thinking by the suddenness of Mr. Malsom's voice.

"Hey, Valdez!" R. L. Davis yelled out. "Where you think you're going?"

Bob Valdez had circled them and was already below them on the slope, leaving the pines now and entering the scrub brush. He didn't stop or look back.

"Valdez!"

Mr. Tanner raised one hand to silence R. L. Davis, all the time watching Bob Valdez getting smaller, going straight through the scrub, not just walking or passing the time but going right out to the pasture.

"Look at him," Mr. Malsom said. There was some admiration in his voice.

"He's dumber than he looks," R. L. Davis said. Then jumped a little as Mr. Tanner touched his arm.

"Come on," Mr. Tanner said. "With the rifle." And started down the slope, hurrying and not seeming to care if he might stumble on the loose gravel.

Bob Valdez was now halfway across the pasture, the shotgun pointed down at his side, his eyes not leaving the door of the line shack. The door was probably already open enough for a rifle barrel to poke through. He guessed the army deserter was covering him, letting him get as close as he wanted; the closer he came the easier to hit him.

Now he could see all the bullet marks in the door and the clean inner wood where the door was splintered. Two people in that little bake-oven of a place. He saw the door move.

He saw the rag doll on the ground. It was a strange thing, the woman having a doll. Valdez hardly glanced at it but was aware of the button eyes looking up and the discomforted twist of the red wool mouth. Then, just past the doll, when he was wondering if he would go right up to the door and knock on it and wouldn't that be a crazy thing, like visiting somebody, the door opened and the Negro was in the doorway, filling it, standing there in pants and boots but without a shirt in that hot place and holding a long-barreled Walker that was already cocked.

They stood ten feet apart looking at each other, close enough so that no one could fire from the slope.

"I can kill you first," the Negro said, "if you raise that."

With his free hand, the left one, Bob Valdez motioned back over his shoulder. "There's a man there said you killed somebody a year ago."

"What man?"

"Said his name is Tanner."

The Negro shook his head, once each way.

"Said your name is Johnson."

"You know my name."

"I'm telling you what he said."

"Where'd I kill this man?"

"Huachuca."

The Negro hesitated. "That was some time ago I was in the Tenth. More than a year."

"You a deserter?"

"I served it out."

"Then you got something that says so."

"In the wagon, there's a bag there my things are in."

"Will you talk to this man Tanner?"

"If I can hold from hitting him one."

"Listen, why did you run this morning?"

"They come chasing. I don't know what they want." He lowered the gun a little, his brown-stained looking tired eyes staring intently at Bob Valdez. "What would you do? They come on the run. Next thing I know they is firing at us. So I pop in this place."

"Will you come with me and talk to him?"

The Negro hesitated again. Then shook his head. "I don't know him."

"Then he won't know you, uh?"

"He didn't know me this morning."

"All right," Bob Valdez said. "I'll get your paper says you were discharged. Then we'll show it to this man, uh?"

The Negro thought it over before he nodded, very slowly, as if still thinking. "All right. Bring him here I'll say a few words to him."

Bob Valdez smiled a little. "You can point that gun some other way."

"Well . . ." the Negro said, "if everybody's friends." He lowered the Walker to his side.

The wagon was in the willow trees by the creek. Off to the right. But Bob Valdez did not turn right away in that direction. He backed away, watching Orlando Rincon for no reason that he knew of. Maybe because the man was holding a gun and that was reason enough.

He had backed off six or seven feet when Orlando Rincon shoved the Walker down into his belt. Bob Valdez turned and started for the trees.

This was when he looked across the pasture. He saw Mr. Tanner and R. L. Davis at the edge of the scrub trees but wasn't sure it was them. Something tried to tell him it was them, but he did not accept it until he was off to the right, out of the line of fire, and by then the time to yell at them or run toward them was past for R. L. Davis had the Winchester up and was firing.

They say R. L. Davis was drunk or he would have pinned him square. As it was the bullet shaved Rincon and plowed past him into the hut.

Bob Valdez saw him half turn, either to go inside or look inside, and as he came around again saw the man's eyes on him and his hand pulling the Walker from his belt.

"They weren't supposed to," Bob Valdez said, holding one hand out as if to stop Rincon. "Listen, they weren't supposed to do that!"

The Walker was out of Rincon's belt and he was cocking it. "Don't!" Bob Valdez yelled. "Don't!" Looking right in the man's eyes and seeing it was no use and suddenly hurrying, jerking the shotgun up and pulling both triggers so that the explosions came out in one big blast and Orlando Rincon was spun and thrown back inside.

They came out across the pasture to have a look at the carcass, some going inside where they found the woman also dead, killed by a rifle bullet. They noticed she would have had a child in a few months. Those by the doorway made room as Mr. Tanner and R. L. Davis approached.

Diego Luz came over by Bob Valdez who had not moved. Valdez stood watching them and he saw Mr. Tanner look down at Rincon and after a moment shake his head.

"It looked like him," Mr. Tanner said. "It sure looked like him."

He saw R. L. Davis squint at Mr. Tanner. "It ain't the one you said?"

Mr. Tanner shook his head again. "I've seen him before though. Know I've seen him somewheres."

Valdez saw R. L. Davis shrug. "You ask me they all look alike." He was yawning then, fooling with his hat, and then his eyes swiveled over at Bob Valdez standing with the empty shotgun.

"Constable," R. L. Davis said. "You went and killed the wrong coon."

Bob Valdez started for him, raising the shotgun to swing it like a club, but Diego Luz drew his revolver and came down with it and Valdez dropped to the ground.

Some three years later there was a piece in the paper about a Robert Eladio Valdez who had been hanged for murder in Tularosa, New Mexico. He had shot a man coming out of the Regent Hotel, called him an unprintable name and shot him four times. This Valdez had previously killed a man in Contention and two in Sands during a bank holdup, had been caught once, escaped from jail in Mesilla before trial and identified another time during a holdup near Lordsburg.

"If it is the same Bob Valdez used to live here," Mr. Beaudry said, "it's good we got rid of him."

"Well, it could be," Mr. Malsom said. "But I guess there are Bob Valdezes all over."

"You wonder what gets into them," Mr. Beaudry said.

That 7X Bull

by Elmer Kelton

Born on a big Texas ranch where his father was foreman, Elmer Kelton is a reporter and columnist on the San Angelo *Standard-Times*. A Spur Award winner in 1957, his book *Buffalo Wagons* was named Best Western Novel of the Year.

❧ ❧ ❧

THAT OLD MOTLEY-FACED bull bellowing his arrogant way up and down the caprock country was about all that was left to show for the sprawling 7X outfit. The 7X had been burned onto his roan-colored hip in the last fall branding before the receivers took over. They sold the rest of the cattle and scattered them all over hell and half of Texas. But nobody ever smeared a loop on old 7X again. His horns were mossy now from age, and his red-flecked hide was scarred from scores of fights which had all ended the same way.

Old 7X was a holdout of the Longhorn strain. True, his sire had been a whitefaced Hereford brought in to deepen the bodies and shorten the legs of the rangy Texas cattle. But 7X had taken after his mammy, a waspy old outlaw long of horn and leg, short of patience and temper.

I said the bull was *about* all there was left. Dodge Willingham was still around, too. He was on the off side of sixty now, spare and dried as a strip of jerked beef. He'd been with the 7X outfit ever since they'd trailed their first Longhorn cattle up from the South Texas brush country. There hadn't been any barbed wire then, and a man whose luck played out could still lose his scalp under a bloody Comanche moon.

After the bustup, Dodge had stayed on with the new Bar J, which had bought out the headquarters division of the 7X.

Dodge and the big bull had a right smart in common. They were both throwbacks to a time that was gone. And they were fighters, the both of them. Every so often an old restlessness got to riding Dodge, like the time in Midland he decided a saloon was too quiet for his taste. He hollered disgustedly, "What is this, a church?" and tipped a table full of cards and poker chips into the player's laps. They beat the whey out of him. Dodge had a wonderful time.

He was an old hand when I first knew him. I was just a raw young kid who wanted to walk in his footsteps, but mostly he acted like he didn't even know I was there.

I'll never forget the spring day the Bar J foreman dropped in at our dugout line camp. Ellison Finch was Old Man Johnson's son-in-law. Finch was the kind who never wanted you to forget who the boss was. He jerked his thumb at Dodge's .30-.30 rifle on its pegs over the door.

"Dodge," he said, "I've took all I'm goin' to from that old red roan bull. He's killed a dozen of my . . . of the ranch's good bulls, and he's chased off plenty more. He's sired more wild scrawny calves than you and me could both count. Now I want you to take that gun and go find him. Spend a week if you got to, but find him. And be almighty sure he's dead before you ride away."

Dodge's pale gray eyes seemed to glisten as he looked up at the gun. His horny fist knotted up hard as a liveoak stump.

"Looky here, Finch," he spoke after a long minute, "old 7X has been around a long time. He ain't got much longer to go. Why don't you just leave him be?"

When he had been an ordinary thirty-a-month cowboy, Finch had stood in awe of Dodge like everybody else had. Now he glared a hole through the aging cowpuncher.

"That old bull has outlived his time," Finch said. "He's a nuisance, even a hazard. If you won't kill him, I'll get me somebody that will."

After Finch left, Dodge walked out to the barn to sit and brood. He stayed there till dark, and I knew better than to go bother him. In my own mind I was already grown. But to Dodge Willingham I was still just a button and was supposed to keep quiet. Next morning he took the .30-.30 and rode out. About suppertime he was back, his mouth a straight, hard line. He barely spoke a word for a week.

Old 7X was never mentioned again until the fall roundup. The wagon was camped at Comanche Wells on the caprock the day Dodge failed to come in on drive. We went on with the branding and cutting out of long-age cattle to push to the railroad. But all the time we kept looking over our shoulders. Late in the afternoon we saddled fresh horses and started out to search.

We met Dodge walking in, a mile from camp. His clothes were torn and smeared with blood. The side of his face was skinned like he'd slid down a mountain on his ear.

"That old dun stumbled on a slope and broke his neck," he told Finch. "Took me an hour to work my saddle loose. I carried it a good ways and left it where I could find it again."

I noticed that Dodge looked at the ground as he talked. He had always been able to stare the devil straight in the eye and spit on him. Something in his voice didn't ring true. I knew. But Finch took Dodge at his word. That is, till we got the old puncher back to the wagon and stretched him out on his tarp-covered bedroll. We took the blood-smeared shirt off of him. Finch stared in wonder at Dodge's wound. Then anger boiled into Finch's sun-blistered face.

"That gash you've got there . . . I know a horn rip when I see one. Did you shoot that 7X bull like I told you to?"

Dodge knew he was caught. You could tell by the sick look that wiped across his stubbled face.

Finch bent over him, his fingers stuck out stiff as wagon spokes. "I ought to fire you, Dodge. I would, if I didn't know the old man'd raise hell about it. Now that bull's sired him another crop of mean, scrubby calves. You ought to've shot him. We'll bring him in now. We'll tie a clog to his foot and drag him in if we have to. He'll go to market with the steers and wind up as sausage. Before it's over you'll wish you'd killed him."

Anybody else would have just sent another cowboy out to kill the bull and said nothing more. But Finch wanted Dodge to know who the boss was.

Dodge didn't seem to be worried much. I guess he knew the old outlaw too well. "I jumped 7X up there close to the bluffs," he told us later. "I thought I'd run him off away from the drive, so nobody would see him. But before I could hardly move, he'd rammed a horn right through that dun. I like to've not got away from there myself."

Even then you could hear the pride in Dodge's voice. "What I mean, boys, he's a fighter. There ain't many of us left."

For the next few days Finch would detail a few punchers to go and try to bring old 7X in. The results were always the same. Some of the cowboys never got close enough to see anything of the bull except his south end going north. Others caught up with him and wished they hadn't. The rest of us went on with the regular roundup. Finch had taken Dodge out of the saddle and put him to swamping for the wagon cook—washing up the utensils, shagging in the wood.

One day two cowboys came walking in from the bluffs, leading their half-crippled horses. Finch blew up and left camp, talking to himself. When he came back two days later, he brought two mean-looking dogs with him.

"Cow dogs," he said, his gloating eyes resting on Dodge.

Dodge snickered. "Old 7X'll tear up them pups like a lobo wolf does a jackrabbit."

Finch shook his head, grinning mean. "You're goin' with us to-morrow, Dodge. I want you to see this."

I felt sorry for Dodge as I watched Finch walk out toward the remuda, still snickering. He'd never seen cow dogs work. I had. I'd been rep for the Bar J one time when the Rafter Ds had been using them to jump outlaw cattle down out of the rough country.

We quartered north from camp next morning and came upon a wild steer that we had missed somehow.

"Watch this, Dodge," Finch said. He spoke to the trailing dogs. They went bounding after the steer, faster than a horse could run. It went so quick we hardly saw how it happened. The biggest dog darted in and grabbed the steer's nose with his teeth. Somehow he swung his body between the animal's forelegs. The steer went crashing to the grass-matted ground. He got up and ran again, only to be thrown once more.

For the first time, the confidence began to drain out of Dodge's face. Worry settled into his smoke-gray eyes.

The bluffs and the rough, broken country around them had been old 7X's favorite running grounds ever since his snaky mammy had first stood over him, licking him clean and giving him his first belly-ful of warm milk to steady those wobbly legs. There, except for the year he had been a calf, he had showed his heels to cowboys every time they ever went after him.

Strange tales about him had grown by the dozen. And a bright light always flickered in the eyes of old cowboys like Dodge Willingham as they told those tales around crackling mesquite campfires, or by dancing yellow lamplight in a smoky bunkhouse.

We found where the big roan bull had been watering in a low swale which always caught the runoff from the rains. Tracks showed there might be a couple of cows with him. Excitement began to flush Finch's heavy face. His hands kept rubbing against his leather chaps as we worked along the edge of the bluffs.

We rode up on one of the cows first. She was a rangy, high-tailed old sister that showed her Hereford blood only in her markings. Her long legs carried her clattering down a slope with the speed of an antelope. One of the cowboys spurred after her. Finch called him back.

"Let her go. It's the bull we want."

Old 7X spotted us first. We saw him break from a small clump of mesquite and take out in a high lope for the broken ground that lay to the south. Whatever else his age might have done, it hadn't slowed his speed.

Finch hollered like a half-grown kid and socked spurs to the sorrel horse he rode. We fell in behind him. Even Dodge, reluctant as he was, stayed right up with the bunch. We didn't get within shouting distance of old 7X till he went sliding down the steep side of a hill, taking a shower of small rocks with him.

Down past the crest of the next hill waited the bluffs. It wasn't but a minute or two till we had old 7X ringed in. The only way out for him was down the face of a cliff. He stood looking at us in anger and contempt, his long tail arched, his horned head proud and high, jerking from one of us to the other. Then he decided the foolishness had gone on long enough. He lowered that great head and came charging like the locomotive on a Santa Fe freight. Every one of us except Dodge had our ropes down and our cinches hauled up tight. But the sight of that snorting old bull bearing down on us made us forget everything except to get out of his way. We could hear Finch shouting at us, but he didn't sound nearly as mean as that bull.

Old 7X roared through the line and kept going. I wouldn't have given a plugged nickel for anybody's chance of ever catching him.

But Finch didn't quit. He sicked the dogs after the old roan. They must have run a quarter of a mile before they finally caught up with him. He slid to a sudden stop and turned to face them, those sharp horns down. He made a quick pass at the smaller of the dogs. I heard the dog yelp as a horn glanced off his lanky rump.

The older dog knew his business. He jumped in and clamped his sharp teeth on 7X's long ear. The bull roared and shook his head violently. The dog had to let go. The bull lunged at him, but the dog scooted out of the way. The younger dog leaped in and tried at 7X's other ear but missed. Then the big dog got hold of the bull's nose. The smaller dog tried again, and this time he grabbed the ear.

Old 7X pitched and bellowed, the dogs staying with him. The two were trying to pull him down, but he was too heavy.

We reined up and watched, hardly knowing whether to believe it or not. Even as 7X fought his hardest, we knew he was licked.

Old Dodge was licked too. Never had I seen the hopelessness that had sunk into his wind-carved face. I wished I could help him. But what was there a button could say?

Cruel pleasure glowed in Finch's face. His eyes fairly glittered with the pride of doing something nobody else had ever done.

"For God's sake, Finch," Dodge pleaded, "call them dogs off of him. Ain't you got a drop of human blood left in you?"

"We'll call off the dogs when we get our ropes on that old hellion."

Finch rode in close and dropped a small loop over the outlaw's horns. "Somebody else tie on too," he said. "We don't want him bustin' our ropes loose."

Johnny Tisdale dabbed another loop over 7X's horns. A third rider worked around and heeled the bull. They rode off in opposite directions. Stretched out, the old roan fought for balance, then heaved over onto his side with the solid thump of a boulder smacking into mud. The dogs let go. They moved off and faced around to watch, their lank sides heaving, their tongues lolling out.

Finch turned his horse over to another cowboy to keep the rope tight. He swung down, his big Chihuahua spurs jingling. He cut his grinning eyes toward Dodge, then away again. He was taking his time, letting Dodge get the full benefit of this. Finch walked to a mesquite tree and whittled off a limb to about three feet in length. Notching one end of it, he tied it to the bull's huge right forefoot with a pigging string.

"Now, old bull," he said, "let's see how you run with this clog on you."

Finch trotted back to his horse. The moment the bull felt the ropes slacken, he jumped to his feet, his head down in challenge. He tried to paw dirt and felt the clog drag. He shook the foot, but the long stick still hung there.

With a bellow he charged at one of the horses. The first long step shook the heel rope off his hind feet, but two ropes were still fastened around his horns. He tripped on the clog and plunged to the ground. He got up again, shaking his head. It was then that I noticed for the first time that his left eye was gone. He had probably lost it in some bruising battle here among these bluffs.

Old 7X tried to charge again, but the same thing happened to him. Time and again he would get up, hind feet first, and once more the clog would send him crashing down. Finch would let the dogs rush in and grab him to add to the bull's misery.

Feeling humiliated myself, I knew how this must be affecting Dodge. "Come on, Dodge," I said, pulling my horse around. "What do you say we ride back to the wagon?"

He shook his head, anger building in his eyes.

Old 7X gave up at last, his muscles quivering from fatigue. "All right, boys," said Finch, "let's take him in."

Ropes still on his horns, they started him toward the wagon. Every time he faltered, the dogs grabbed at his heels. Every time he tried to run, the clog stopped him. Finch had won.

As we rode in we found the rest of the hands working the day's gather in the plank corrals. The roan bull began to bellow at the sight and sound of the other cattle. Finch and Johnny led him through a gate. Finch pulled up and grinned in triumph.

"Here you are, you old scorpion. Next stop's a sausage grinder."

They had to heel him and throw him down again to get the ropes off. Then Finch left him in a tiny pen with a bunch of long-age steers and gave us all plenty to do. The last I saw of old 7X for a while, he was hooking irritably at the unlucky steers that had to share the small space with him. If it weren't for the clog, he would go over that fence like it wasn't there and be back in the bluffs by the middle of the afternoon.

After we ate dinner we went to the corrals to brand the calves that had been dropped since the last roundup. Catching my breath while waiting for a heeler to drag up another calf, I sighted Dodge slipping around behind the corral where old 7X was. The bull had quieted down and stood beside the plank fence. I saw Dodge look around quickly, then take a knife out of his pocket, kneel down and reach under the bottom plank. In a moment he came bowlegging it back, satisfaction in his grizzled face.

After the branding, Finch sent most of the cowboys out to push the herd far back onto the south end of the ranch. That way the freshly worked cattle weren't so apt to get caught again in the next few day's gather. Most of the outfit gone, Finch walked over to the small corral where 7X was. "Turn him out in the trap with the steers," he said. "He ain't a-goin' to do much with that clog on him."

Johnny Tisdale opened the gate to let the steers out of the little pen into a bigger one. Old 7X waited until the rest of the cattle were out before he budged. Then, resignedly, he moved slowly toward the gate.

Suddenly he stopped and shook his right forefoot. The clog was gone. He stood there as if he was trying to puzzle the thing out. Then he shook that great head, lowered it and came on the run.

Finch just had time to let out a startled yelp and hit the fence. He climbed it three planks at a time. The rest of us weren't far behind him. I glimpsed Dodge standing off to one side, laughing fit to kill. The bull made a beeline for the outside gate. He tried to jump it but splintered the top two planks like matchsticks.

All our horses were tied outside, up and down the fence. At the sight of that monster of a bull bearing down upon them, they snorted in panic and popped bridle reins right and left. In seconds every horse was loose, and every one of us was left afoot. Unable to move, we just stood there and watched while old 7X headed for the bluff country in a high lope.

A mule driver would have blushed if he could have seen Finch tear the hat from his head and stomp on it and could have heard the things Finch said. When he finally ran out of cusswords in English and had used up the few Spanish ones he knew, Finch walked over and picked up the clog. His wide mouth dropped open as he fingered the end of the pigging string. Anybody could tell it had been cut. He stomped out of the pen, his raging eyes fixed on Dodge. His fists were knotted, and his jaws bulged out.

"You damned old reprobate, you'll wish you'd left this country ten years ago!"

Dodge didn't back away from Finch. When I saw Finch was going to hit him, I stepped between them. I was getting mad myself. "Better take a dally on that temper, Finch," I said. "Lay a hand on Dodge and you'll have to whip me too."

Dodge caught my shoulder and roughly pushed me aside. "Keep out of it, button!"

I stood uncertainly, my feelings hurt by the old man's rebuff. Finch's eyes brimmed with fury. "You're fired, the both of you, and I don't care what old Johnson says about it. Either I'm the boss here or I ain't."

Dodge just shrugged. "I'd done decided to quit anyhow." This is no place for a *man* to work."

We stayed there that night because it was too late to leave the wagon. All Dodge would say to me was, "You sure ripped your britches, boy."

Next morning we watched the cowboys rope their horses out of the remuda. Finch was taking about half the crew to the bluffs. He swore he was going to get that bull today and get him alive. He stopped for one last dig at Dodge.

"He won't get away this time, Dodge. We'll use the dogs again. And once we catch him, he'll tame down quick. I'm goin' to take the pride out of him."

He pulled out his knife, holding it up for Dodge to see.

Dodge's ears flared red. He brought up his gnarled fist and drove it into Finch's face. A trickle of blood worked down from Finch's nose. Dodge crouched to do it again, but I caught his arm. Finch brought up his fists, looking first at Dodge and then at me. He turned around, climbed into the saddle and led out in a stiff trot, his back arrow straight.

We watched the riders move away as daylight fanned out across the rolling short-grass country. Dodge saddled his horse, jerking at the cinch harder than was necessary. Finished, he led him toward the chuckwagon. Grim purpose came into his face as he wrapped the reins around a mesquite limb a proper distance from the cookfire. He reached up into the wagonbed and pulled out a rifle that the cook kept there.

The cook's jaw sagged. "Good God, Dodge, they'll hang you!"

The same thought had hit me, and the pit of my stomach was like ice.

Dodge shook his head. "I ain't after Finch. He ain't worth what it'd cost me." Sadness settled over him. "Looks like old 7X has finally got to go. But he deserves better than what Finch'll give him. At least he ought to be allowed to die respectable." He turned to me. "Comin', boy?"

Dodge swung into the saddle and spurred out in the lead, rifle across his lap. We skirted east a ways, to be out of sight of Finch and the other punchers. Then we moved into an easy lope and held it. After a while we knew we were ahead, for even in anger Finch would keep his horses in a sensible trot to save their strength.

When we got to the bluffs we climbed up high and looked behind us. We saw no sign of Finch. That gave us a little time to find old 7X first. We needed it. It took us the better part of an hour before we finally saw the old patriarch trying to hide himself in a clump of mesquite brush. We eased down toward him, our horses alert, their ears poking forward like pointing fingers. Seeing that we had spotted him, 7X bolted out of the thicket, popping brush like a buffalo stampede. But there was a bad limp to his right forefoot.

"Damned clog done that to him," Dodge muttered. He spurred up. The bull saw he couldn't outrun us, and he faced around. He tossed his head.

I saw Dodge's Adam's apple working up and down as he levered a cartridge into the chamber. He raised the rifle to his shoulder, held it there a moment, then slowly let it down. His hands trembled.

"I can't do it. I'd sooner put a bullet in Finch."

Right then old 7X decided to fight his way out. He charged. Dodge whipped the rifle up, but panic had grabbed hold of his horse. The big gray boogered to one side, and Dodge tumbled out of the saddle. The rifle roared. The bullet exploded a brown puff of dust from the ground.

My heart was in my mouth. Old 7X was almost upon Dodge, and there wasn't any place for the old puncher to jump. I spurred up beside Dodge and grabbed at his shoulders. In desperation he dug his fingers into my leg, trying to pull up beside me. I managed to swing my horse around to protect Dodge. But old 7X's huge head plowed into my dun's haunches. The horse fell.

I landed on top of Dodge. We both jumped to our feet, but we were too late to grab the bridle reins. My horse had run away. We stood there with our backs to the steep bluff. Not a solitary thing to grab onto or a place to climb.

As old 7X whirled around to fasten his good eye upon us again, I saw Dodge's rifle lying in the dust. So scared I could hardly breathe, I grabbed it up. Somehow I managed to lever another cartridge into place as the great roan bull bellowed and came at us.

There wasn't time to aim. I jammed the riflebutt to my shoulder and squeezed the trigger, my teeth biting halfway through my lip. Old 7X went down on his knees. The bullet had glanced off just above the right eye. He staggered to his feet again. He stood shaking that huge head in pain. Blood trickled down from the wound.

Dodge saw the trouble as soon as I did. "By George, that blood has blinded him."

Hearing Dodge's voice, the bull stopped shaking his head. In one last brave charge, he lunged blindly at the sound of the man he hated. We jumped out of his way, and he kept running.

At the edge it seemed he stopped dead still for a second. Then he was gone, plunging down off the sheer face of the bluff. I heard Dodge gasp. From below came the crashing sound of impact.

It took us a while to catch our boogered horses and work our way down to the base of the bluff. We found the mossy-horned old bull lying there just as he had landed. Life was gone from the battle-scarred body. I saw the glistening in Dodge's gray eyes. The old puncher knelt and traced with his finger the dim outline of an ancient 7X brand on the roan hip.

"I put that brand there myself, a long time ago." He was silent a while, remembering. "But times change, and things that won't change have got to go. Old 7X and me, we stayed beyond our day." He straightened and gazed a long while across the rolling short-grass country to the south of us, the old 7X range. "He went out in a way that was fittin to him. He fought to the last."

I held my silence as long as I could. Finally I said, "We better be movin' on, Dodge. Finch'll be along directly."

Dodge squatted stiffly on his spurred heels and began rolling a cigarette, making it plain he was going to wait. "Old 7X left here a-fightin'. So will I."

"But you don't really think you can whip Finch, do you?"

Dodge shrugged. "I'll never know unless I try." He turned up his tough old face and glanced at me with that brimstone look in his eyes. "If it turns out *I* can't whip him, I expect *you're* man enough to."

I knew then that I wasn't just a button anymore.

Shiftless Slow

by Leslie Ernenwein

"Ernie" for the past seven years has been Editor of *The Roundup*, WWA's slick-paper monthly ambassador to the world of books and he has also served on the Board. He is the author of more than three hundred short stories and twenty-seven novels, one of which—*High Gun*—won the Spur for Best Western Novel of 1956.

❧ ❧ ❧

SHERIFF ED SHEFFLIN was playing checkers with Joe Pruitt at the Palace Livery when a barefooted boy ran across Main Street's wide dust and announced, "They want you at the jail, Sheriff Ed!"

Shefflin's bushy-browed eyes remained focused on the checkerboard in squinting thoughtfulness for a moment before he moved a checker. Then he looked up and asked, "Who's they, son?"

"Sam Garland, Frank Borden and County Attorney Morris. Mr. Garland rode in from the Yellows. He says old Burro Beal has been murdered."

"So?" Shefflin mused.

And Joe Pruitt blurted, "Who would murder that harmless old desert rat?"

Even now, pushing back his chair and getting up, Ed Shefflin didn't hurry. There were those in Junction City who said Big Ed Shefflin hadn't made a fast move during all the years he'd worn a sheriff's badge.

He gave the checkerboard a final glance and suggested, "Just set the board on that shelf, Joe, so's we can finish the game later on."

That was another thing they said about Big Ed—that he couldn't abide quitting a thing once he got started. Like the time he trailed Spanish Bill clean across the Mexican border and captured him five miles into Sonora. The county attorney had complained that it wasn't legal for Ed to do that, and might cause trouble with the Mexican government. But Big Ed had grinned and said, "If they want Spanish Bill's body we'll tote it back to them."

Now, as he quartered across Main Street with the boy, Shefflin moved with an old man's reluctance. He was a big man. Not fat, but big all over. And he walked the way most saddle-bred men do, as if it was a chore.

The barefooted boy kept getting ahead. He stopped to wait, and asked, "Are you going to swear in a posse, Sheriff Ed?"

"Don't reckon so," Shefflin said. "They mostly get in each other's way."

He tipped his hat to Flossie Eggleston and asked, "How's the sick daughter, ma'am?"

"Much better," Mrs. Eggleston said. "Doctor Blake predicts she'll be up and around within a week."

"Why, that's fine!" Big Ed exclaimed. "Just fine!"

Walking on with the boy, he said in a pleased voice, "That little girl was pitiful sick, and now she's going to be all right."

He waved to Tate Malone who was tooling his ranch wagon up to the loading platform at the Mercantile, and called, "How's things in the Kettle Drums, Tate?"

"Dry," Malone said. "Awful dry."

When Shefflin slowed down as if to talk, the boy said impatiently, "They're a-waiting on you, Sheriff Ed. There's Frank Borden bringing his Winchester from home already. He said you'd need a posse sure."

Big Ed chuckled, and asked, "Did he say why I'd need one, son?"

"Well, Frank said you was too slow to track down a murderer."

"So," Shefflin mused, remembering that young Borden would be his opponent in the coming election.

That didn't bother Bid Ed much. Folks wouldn't be fooled by Frank's chin chatter about the county needing a younger sheriff. Not the ranch folks, anyway. Frank was town raised and town green about most things.

Seeing the crowd that awaited him at the jail, Big Ed frowned and said to the boy, "Beats hell how fast bad news gets around."

As Shefflin walked through the crowd, Sam Garland asked slyly, "Did we interrupt your checker game, Ed?"

Some of the men laughed, and Frank Borden said, "Swear in some of us as deputies and we'll go saddle up."

Big Ed ignored that suggestion. He walked up to Sam Garland whose black eyes seemed buckshot small in so lardy a face. "What happened to Beal?" he inquired.

"Well, all I know is that somebody crushed his skull with Burro's own pickax and left him lying there dead. On my way to town this morning I saw some buzzards circling low over in the roughs just west of the Pantano Wash fork. Figured it might be one of my cows and went to look. There was Burro, dead."

There was a rising babble of conversation in the crowd—men recalling how harmless and likeable Burro Beal had been, and forgetting all the times they'd made fun of him for his endless treasure hunting.

Big Ed asked, "Any sign—hoofprints or anything?"

"Sure," Garland said. "Somebody rode into Burro's camp and rode out again. I followed the tracks for a ways, but they petered out on that malpais ridge south of the new homesteader's shack."

"You mean the tracks were headed toward Cecil Melrose's place?" Frank Borden asked importantly.

Garland nodded.

"Well, I thought there was something odd about Melrose the

first time I saw him. Why should a man from St. Louis stake out a homestead in the Yellows?"

County Attorney Morris said skeptically, "Melrose told me he had to live in a dry climate."

Big Ed gave Garland his strict and unwavering attention. He asked, "You see anything else that would help me, Sam?"

"Well, what footprints I saw near Burro's body was shoe prints. Not made by boots, but by shoes."

He spoke hesitantly, as if reluctant to say this, which seemed odd to Big Ed. For there was no doubt who Garland's suspicions were pointing to, and it was well known that he'd had trouble with Cecil Melrose whose fence kept Garland's cows away from Pot Hole Spring.

Now Frank Borden exclaimed, "There's only one man in the Yellows who wears shoes instead of boots. Cecil Melrose!"

"The new homesteader must've done it!" a man exclaimed. "He must be the murderer!"

Big Ed asked, "Anybody used the west trail past your place lately, Sam?"

And when Garland shook his head, Shefflin asked, "How about that drifter I sent out your way last week looking for a job?"

"He kept going," Garland said. "Just stayed overnight and went on the next morning."

Frank Borden asked impatiently, "You want me to ride out to Melrose's with you, Ed?"

"Reckon not," Big Ed said. "I want to look around a little first."

"What for?" Borden demanded. "Sam has told you where to find the killer."

Big Ed nodded agreement to that. But he said, "I want to look around, regardless. Rushing this thing now won't help poor Burro none at all."

Garland complained sourly, "I almost foundered a good horse hurrying here with the news."

County Attorney Morris sounded impatient as he asked, "Hadn't you better get started, Ed?"

Shefflin shrugged and walked back toward the Palace Livery.

Just because a sheriff didn't swear in a big posse and go through a lot of hustle and bustle, some folks reckoned he was wasting time. But a lawman had to figure out the angles before he went hightailing out into the brush. He had to shape up some sort of a pattern in his mind and make every move count for something. . . .

When he passed the Mercantile, Big Ed turned to the platform where Tate Malone was loading sacked flour. "Anybody used the west trail past your place in the past week?" Shefflin asked.

Malone shook his head. "Ain't saw a soul out there for upwards of a month. Gets downright lonesome, Ed."

"Shouldn't wonder," Shefflin agreed, tallying that information and placing a certain value on it.

Presently, as Sheffllin angled across Main Street, he waited for Flossie Eggleston's buckboard. When she came abreast of him he asked, "Any travel up the north trail lately?"

"No, Ed. Seems like folks don't cross the Yellows in this hot weather. They got better sense."

He thanked Flossie and went on into the livery stable where Joe Pruitt asked, "You going law-dogging, or do we finish that game of checkers?"

"I'll be back about day after tomorrow, looks like," Big Ed said, taking his bridle from a peg in the harness room. "Burro's body is in the roughs just west of the Pantano Wash fork. I hope you can get out there with a wagon before the buzzards gobble him up."

Half an hour later, with his saddlebags well loaded and a blanket roll behind his saddle, Big Ed rode out of Junction City at a leisurely jog trot. When he crossed the Long Arroyo bridge he turned off the road and headed due south, which would have seemed mighty odd to Frank Borden if he had been watching.

Big Ed had a lonely man's habit of talking to his horse. He said, "Saber, there's only two ways a man could cross the Yellows from Junction City. One would be by Malone's ranch and the other by Eggleston's. He'd stop for water either way."

It was upwards of an hour later when Sheffllin's questing eyes observed horse tracks in the dust. Studying them he said, "Not more'n a couple hours old," and expressed satisfaction by bragging, "Just like I reckoned, by grab."

It occurred to Big Ed now that Saber, being fresh, could probably overtake the other horse before dark if he was pushed a trifle. But the sun was blazing hot and Saber was getting along in years.

"Like me," Big Ed reflected. "Shiftless slow."

Afterward, when he crossed a wide dry wash, Shefflin stopped to contemplate the scooped-out place in the sand where a man had dug for water and found it.

"Don't know the country," Shefflin mused. "There's good water not more'n three miles ahead of him and a trifle south."

It was coming dusk now, and so Big Ed angled south of the tracks to Concho Spring. Cows had watered here today, but no horses. That fact amused him, thinking how the fellow he was following had gone to the trouble of digging for water.

With Saber hobbled and foraging for sparse grass, Big Ed gathered dead mesquite branches for his supper, arranging the dry sticks spoke fashion so they'd produce a maximum of heat without much smoke. There was no telling how near that other jigger had camped for the night. A man who didn't know where water was might camp most any place. Soon as the coffee boiled Ed scooped sand onto the fire and put it out.

Eating one of the dried beef sandwiches he had brought along, Big Ed thought about Burro Beal who had dreamed of finding the Curly Bill cache of Wells Fargo gold which the outlaw had hidden somewhere in this part of Arizona Territory.

Old Burro had dug a thousand holes in the Yellow Hills where he was convinced the treasure was hidden. No matter how much folks funned at him he had kept right on digging, year after year. It seemed downright odd that anyone would have killed him—unless Burro had discovered the buried gold.

Recalling Garland's recital, Big Ed remembered how the rancher's talk had convinced Frank Borden that Melrose was the murderer. Young Borden was too quick with his guessing. Of course it could have been Melrose. He was an odd jigger—a big city man trying to be a homesteader and knowing nothing about the country.

Suddenly Shefflin thought: *The man I'm trailing didn't know about this spring.*

Maybe Frank Borden had guessed right about Melrose being the murderer. That homesteader might be high-tailing for the tules. But even so, the sheriff had thought of heading southward to cut his trail.

Big Ed felt better then. He grinned, remembering how Joe Pruitt had warned him that the Junction City *Weekly Gazette* was going to back Borden in the election. "They're going to run a big story saying that you're too old and too slow for the job. They're going to nickname you Shiftless Slow Shefflin," Pruitt had said.

But Big Ed knew it took more than a newspaper story to make a good sheriff.

Up early, Shefflin drank his coffee beside a frugal fire and was asaddle when first daylight came. Picking up the horse tracks of yesterday, he kept Saber at a walk until the old gelding was well loosened up, then urged him to a lope.

The sun had barely rimmed the eastern hills when Big Ed came to the remains of a dead campfire. Dirt had been scooped on, so that it looked like the bulging hub of a rimless wheel.

Big Ed dismounted, put a palm on the mound and felt its heat. "Not more'n half an hour ahead of us," he told Saber.

Whereupon Shefflin did an odd thing. Deserting the hoofprints he had been following, he rode directly south for upwards of two hours at a fast clip, climbed a long ridge and angled eastward until the crest tapered off into a brush-fringed pass. Here he dismounted, tied Saber to a scrub oak and walked into the pass. Observing no hoofprints, he sat down behind a boulder and waited.

There wasn't any doubt in Big Ed's mind now. All men, he had observed, followed a set pattern, whether they were ranchers, greenhorns or murderers. Every man revealed what he was by the way he did certain things.

Take Frank Borden, for instance. You could tell what he was just by listening to him talk. A glory rider, wanting to look smarter and more important than other folks. And this fellow heading toward

Mexico was following a pattern that could be identified and understood if a man just put his mind to it.

Which was why Big Ed wasn't at all surprised when he heard hoofbeats coming along the pass, nor when he saw who the rider was. A sheriff who had worn a law badge for upwards of fifteen years got so he could read signs pretty well. . . .

It was noon of the third day when Joe Pruitt saw Big Ed ride up to the stable doorway, leading a horse that had a man's body lashed to the saddle. "Who in hell you got there?" Joe demanded.

"A murderer, or a witness," Shefflin announced wearily. "Don't know which, yet."

He dismounted with unusual caution because his right arm was in a sling. Seeing the bloodstains now, Pruitt blurted, "You got yourself shot!"

Big Ed nodded. He asked, "Is Sam Garland in town?"

"Hell yes, and almost everybody else. Frank Borden got himself deputized by the county attorney. He arrested Melrose and they're going to have a hearing right after noon meal. They're over to the Elite Café now."

Sheriff Shefflin thought about that for a long moment. Then he said, "Listen close, Joe. If you do just like I say we might prove who killed Burro Beal."

Afterward he walked toward the jail, meeting no one until he was almost to the doorway. Then the same boy who had fetched him two days ago, ran up and asked, "Did you hear about Sam arresting Cecil Melrose?"

Shefflin nodded. He used his left hand to take a quarter from his pocket, and handed the silver piece to the boy. "Go tell the county attorney I brought in a prisoner—the man who murdered Burro Beal. You'll find Morris at the Elite."

Then, as the boy ran toward the café, Big Ed went into his office and sat down. This deal hadn't worked out quite like he had hoped it would. Instead of surrendering peacefully, the drifter had grabbed for his gun. It was a darn fool thing to do, and he had been dead when he fired the bullet that broke Shefflin's arm.

Big Ed swore softly. It had been a tedious chore, loading the body one-handed, and his arm had ached all the way in. It still did. He'd have to go see Doc Blake directly.

Big Ed heard Frank Borden's excited voice before he saw him. The young would-be sheriff was hurrying across Main Street with Morris, Garland and three other men. Ed frowned, understanding how this would have to be handled—understanding also that he might be a laughing stock in this town if his calculations were wrong.

He grimaced, visualizing how that would be, with folks calling him Shiftless Shefflin behind his back. But none of that worry showed in his face when Borden, Morris and Garland came hurrying into the office.

"What's this I hear about you bringing in a prisoner?" Morris demanded.

Big Ed nodded. "The drifter who rode through here a week ago," he said quietly and watched Sam Garland's face.

"But we've got Melrose in jail charged with Burro's murder!" Frank Borden exclaimed. "You've arrested the wrong man!"

Big Ed shook his head. He glanced out the side window as if there was no hurry about settling this thing. He noticed that a board was missing from the wooden awning in front of the Mercantile and sunlight made one bright slash on the otherwise shaded sidewalk. He could remember when that awning was built, the boards mill-new and resinous. Now the awning was old and dried out and falling apart.

"What makes you think the drifter had anything to do with it?" Garland asked impatiently.

Big Ed looked at him. "I guess you know the answer to that," he said sharply. "You're under arrest."

"Me? What in hell for?"

And County Attorney Morris asked quickly, "You drunk, Ed?"

Shefflin ignored that. He said to Garland, "I'm charging you with the murder of Burro Beal."

Garland's eyes popped open wider than Big Ed had ever seen them. "How could you suspicion me?" he demanded.

"Well, you said the drifter just stayed overnight. But he stayed a week—until you found out that Burro had discovered Curly Bill's cache. Then you made a deal with the drifter, share and share alike if he'd kill Burro and hightail for Mexico."

"You're a liar!" Garland shouted. "I never saw no treasure!"

Big Ed had never done much lying, and it came hard to him now. But there was an innocent man in jail, and so he said, "The drifter says you got half. The biggest half. But he doesn't know where you hid it."

Then Shefflin asked coaxingly, "Where'd you hide it, Sam?"

The old sheriff acted surprised when Garland drew his gun and snarled, "You'll never know, lawdog!"

Big Ed glanced at his broken arm as if to make sure he was too crippled for a try at drawing his gun. Morris and Borden gawked at Garland in bug-eyed astonishment as the rancher bragged, "None of you will ever see that gold."

He backed toward the door, waggling the gun at them.

Big Ed said morosely, "Well, you told the truth about one thing. You said the murderer wore shoes instead of boots. That's what the drifter was wearing—shoes."

Garland laughed at him. "Smart, ain't you, Shefflin. But I'll tote the gold across the line so fast you won't even see my dust."

Shefflin shrugged. He looked downright dejected as he said, "All right, Joe."

Which was when Joe Pruitt poked the muzzle of Big Ed's Winchester into Garland's back and said, "Hoist 'em!"

Sheriff Ed Shefflin was playing checkers with Joe Pruitt one-handed when Frank Borden came into the stable and announced, "I'm not running against you in the election."

Big Ed didn't look up until he had made a move. Then he said, "That's just fine, Frank—just fine."

"What I can't figure out is how you knew you were trailing the drifter and not Melrose," Borden said wonderingly.

Big Ed grinned. "Why that was simple, son. Melrose is a greenhorn. He wouldn't have enough savvy to dig in a dry wash for water, nor to build his fire spoke fashion so's it wouldn't make much smoke."

"But if you killed the drifter before he had a chance to talk, how'd you know Garland was in cahoots with him?" Borden insisted.

"That was simple also," Big Ed explained. "Most folks follow a certain pattern. Garland lied when he said the drifter just stayed overnight. I knew he was lying because both Tate Malone and Flossie Eggleston said no one went by their places lately. So I figured Sam had some reason for lying, and that the drifter was heading south with his share of the loot."

Young Borden shook his head. "How would a man figure out all those angles ahead of time?" he muttered, plainly bewildered.

"By being shiftless slow, I reckon," Big Ed said, and winked at Joe Pruitt.

The Streets of Laredo

by Will Henry

Will Henry, born Henry W. Allen, won the 1960 Spur for Best Western Historical Novel and the Levi Strauss Golden Saddleman Sweepstakes for *From Where the Sun Now Stands*. This present story, not previously published, marks Allen's second appearance in a WWA anthology. "Hank" is a Californian.

❦   ❦   ❦

CALL HIM McCOMAS. Drifter, cowboy, cardsharp, killer. A man already on the road back from nowhere. Texas of the time was full of him and his kind. And sick with the fullness.

McComas had never been in Laredo. But his shadows, many of them, had been there before him. He knew what to expect from the townsfolk when they saw him coming on, black and weedy and beardgrown, against the late afternoon sun. They would not want him in their town, and McComas could not blame them. Yet he was tired, very tired, and had come a long, tense way that day.

He steeled himself to take their looks and to turn them away as best he might. What he wanted was a clean bed, a tub bath, a hotel meal and a short night's sleep. No women, no cards, no whisky. Just six hours with the shades drawn and no one knocking at the door. Then, God willing, he would be up in the blackness before the dawn. Up and long gone and safe over the border in Nueva Leon, Old Mexico, when that Encinal sheriff showed up to begin asking questions of the law in Laredo. The very last thing he wanted in Texas was trouble. But that was the very last thing he had ever wanted in any place, and the very first he had always gotten. In Laredo it started as it always started, everywhere, with a woman.

Still, this time it was different. This time it was like no trouble which had ever come to him before. Somehow, he knew it. He sensed it before his trim gelding, Coaldust, set hoof in the streets of Laredo.

Those border towns were all laid out alike. Flat as a dropped flapjack. One wide street down the middle, running from sagebrush on one end to the river on the other. Some frame shacks and adobes flung around in the mesquite and catclaw, out where the decent people did not have to look at them. Then, the false fronts lining the main street. And, feeding off that, half a dozen dirt allies lying in two lines on either side like pigs suckling a sow asleep in the sun. After these, there were only the church, school, and cemetery. It was the latter place, clinging on the dryhill flanks of the town, where the land was even too poor for the Mexican shacks, that McComas and Coaly were presently coming to.

It lay to their left, and there was a burying party moving out from town, as they moved in. McComas had to pull Coaly off the road to let the procession pass. For some reason he felt strange, and hung there to watch the little party. It was then he saw the girl.

She was young and slim, with a black Spanish *reboza* covering her head. As the buggy in which she was riding with the frock-coated parson drew abreast of McComas, she turned and stared directly at him. But the late sun was in his eyes and he could not see her features. Then, they were gone on, leaving McComas with a peculiar, unpleasant feeling. He shook as to a chill. Then, steadied himself. It was no mystery that the sight had unsettled him. It was a funeral, and he had never liked funerals.

They always made him wonder though.

Who was it in the coffin? Was it a man or woman? Had they died peaceful or violent? What had they done wrong, or right? Would he, or she, be missed by friends, mourned by family, made over in the local newspaper, maybe even mentioned in the San Antonio and Austin City papers?

No, he decided. Not this one. There were no family and friends here. That girl riding in the preacher's rig wasn't anybody's sister. She just didn't have the look. And the two roughly dressed Mexican laborers sitting on the coffin in the wagon ahead of the buggy were certainly not kith or kin of the deceased. Neither was the seedy driver. As for the squarebuilt man on the sorrel mare heading up the procession, he did not need the pewter star pinned on his vest to tag him for McComas. The latter could tell a deputy sheriff as far as he could see one, late sun in the eyes, or not.

The deputy could tell McComas too. And he gave him a hard looking over as he rode by. They exchanged the usual nods, careful and correct, and the deputy rode on, as any wise deputy would.

Directly, he led the buggy and the wagon into the weed-grown gate of the cemetery, and creaking up the rise to a plot on the crown of the hill. There, the drivers halted their horses, let down their cargoes. Still, McComas watched from below.

The two Mexicans strained with the coffin. It was a long coffin, and heavy. A man, McComas thought. A young man, and standing tall. One who had been taken quick, with no warning, and not long ago. No, this was no honored citizen they were putting under. Honored citizens do not come to boothill in the late afternoon with the town deputy riding shotgun over the ceremony. Nor with only a lantern-jawed, poorbones preacher and a leggy young girl in a black Mexican shawl for mourners. Not by considerable.

McComas might even know the man in that coffin. If he did not, he could describe him perilously close. All he had to do was find the nearest mirror and look into it.

Again, he shivered. And again controlled himself.

He was only tired and worn down. It was only the way he felt about funerals. He always felt dark in his mind when he saw a body going by. And who didn't, if they would be honest enough to admit it? Nobody likes to look at a coffin, even empty. When there is somebody in it and being hauled dead-march slow with the wagon sounding creaky and the people not talking and the cemetery gates waiting rusty and half-sagged just down the road, a man does not need to be on the dodge and nearly drunk from want of sleep to take a chill and to turn away and ride on feeling sad and afraid inside.

In town, McComas followed his usual line. He took a room at the best hotel, knowing that the first place the local law will look for a man is in the second and third-rate fleatraps where the average fugitive will hole up. Laredo was a chancey place. A funnel through which poured the scum of bad ones down into Old Mexico. If a man did not care to be skimmed off with the others of that outlaw dross, he had to play it differently than they did. He didn't skulk. He rode in bold as brass and bought the best. Like McComas and Coaly and the Border Star Hotel.

But, once safely in his room, McComas could not rest. He only paced the floor and peeked continually past the drawn shade down into the sun haze of the main street.

It was perhaps half an hour after signing the register, that he gave it up and went downstairs for just one drink. Twenty minutes more and he was elbows-down on the bar of the Ben Hur Saloon with the girl.

Well, she was not a girl, really. Not any longer.

Young, yes. And nicely shaped. But how long did a girl stay a girl at the Laredo prices? She was like McComas. Short on the calendar count, long on the lines at mouth and eye corners. If he had been there and back, she had made the trip ahead of him.

Pretty? Not actually. Yet that face would haunt a man. McComas knew the kind. He had seen them in every town. Sometimes going by in the young dusk on the arm of an overdressed swell— through a dusty train window at the depot—passing, perfume-close, in the darkened hall of a cheap hotel. Not pretty. No, not ever pretty. But always exciting, sensuous, female and available; yours for the night, if you could beat the other fellow to them.

Billie Blossom was that kind.

Her real name? McComas did not care. She accepted McComas, he did not argue Billie Blossom.

She came swinging up to him at the bar, out of the nowhere of blue cigar smoke which hid the poker tables and the dance floor and the doleful piano player with his two-fingered, tinkly, sad chorus of "Jeannie with the Light Brown Hair." She held his eyes a long slow moment, then smiled, "Hello, cowboy, you want to buy me a drink before you swim the river?" And he stared back at her an equal long slow moment, and said, "Lady, for a smile like that I might even get an honest job and go to work."

That was the start of it.

They got a bottle and glasses from the barman, moved off through the smoke, McComas following her. She had her own table, a good one, in a rear corner with no windows and facing the street doors. They sat down, McComas pouring. She put her fingers on his hand when he had gotten her glass no more than damp. And, again, there was that smile shaking him to his boottops.

"A short drink for a long road, cowboy," she said.

He glanced at her with quick suspicion, but she had meant nothing by it.

"Yes," he nodded, "I reckon that's right," and poured his own drink to match hers. "Here's to us," he said, lifting the glass. "Been everywhere but hell, and not wanting to rush that."

She smiled and they drank the whisky, neither of them reacting to its raw bite. They sat there, then, McComas looking at her.

She was an ash blonde with smoky gray eyes. She had high cheekbones, a wide mouth, wore entirely too much paint and powder. But always there was that half curve of a smile to soften everything. Everything except the cough. McComas knew that hollow sound. The girl had consumption, and badly. He could see where the sickness had cut the flesh from her, leaving its pale hollows where the lush curves had been. Yet, despite the pallor and the wasted form, she seemed lovely to McComas.

He did not think to touch her, nor to invite her to go upstairs, and she thanked him with her eyes. They were like a young boy and girl; he not seeing her, she not seeing him, but each seeing what used to be, or might have been, or, luck willing, still might be.

McComas would not have believed that it could happen. Not to him. But it did. To him and Billie Blossom in the Ben Hur Saloon in Laredo, Texas. They had the bottle and they had the sheltered corner and they were both weary of dodging and turning away and of not being able to look straight back at honest men and women nor to close their eyes and sleep nights when they lay down and tried to do so. No-name McComas and faded Billie Blossom. Outlawed killer, dancehall trollop. In love at first sight and trying desperately hard to find the words to tell each other so. Two hunted people locking tired eyes and trembling hands over a bareboard table and two unwashed whisky tumblers in a flyblown cantina at sundown of a hell's hot summer day, two miles and then minutes easy lope from freedom and safety and a second beckoning chance in Old Mexico, across the shallow Rio Grande.

Fools they were, and lost sheep.

But, oh! that stolen hour at sunset in that smoke-filled, evil-smelling room. What things they said, what vows they made, what wild sweet promises they swore!

It was not the whisky. After the first, small drink, the second went untasted. McComas and Billie Blossom talked on, not heeding the noise and coarseness about them, forgetting who they were, and where. Others, telling of their loves, might remember scented dark parlors. Or a gilding of moonlight on flowered verandas. Or the fragrance of new-mown hay by the riverside. Or the fireflies in the loamy stardust of the summer lane. For McComas and Billie Blossom it was the rank odor of charcoal whisky, the choke of stogie cigars, the reek of bathless men and perspiring, sacheted women.

McComas did not begrudge the lack. He had Billie's eyes for his starry lane, her smile for his summer night. He needed no dark parlors, no willow-shaded streams. He and Billie had each other. And they had their plans.

The piano played on. It was the same tune about Jeannie and her light brown hair. McComas feared for a moment that he might show a tear, or a tremble in his voice. The song was that beautiful, and that close, to what he and Billie were feeling, that neither could speak, but only sit with their hands clasped across that old beer-stained table in the Ben Hur Saloon making their silence count more than any words. Then, McComas found his voice. As he talked, Billie nodded, yes, to everything he said, the tears glistening beneath the long black lashes which swept so low and thickly curled across her slanted cheekbones. She was crying because of her happiness, McComas knew, and his words rushed on, deeply, recklessly excited.

He did not remember all that he told her, only the salient, pressing features of it: that they would meet beyond the river when darkness fell; that they would go down into Nueva Leon, to a place McComas knew, where the grass grew long and the water ran sweet and a man could raise the finest cattle in all Mexico; that there they would find their journeys' end, rearing a family of honest, God-fearing children to give the ranch over to when McComas was too aged and saddlebent to run it himself, and when he and Billie Blossom had earned their wicker chairs and quiet hours in the cool shadows of the ranchhouse *galeria*, "somewhere down there in Nueva Leon."

It went like that, so swift and tumbling and stirring to the imagination, that McComas began to wonder if it were not all a dream. If he would not awaken on that uneasy bed upstairs in the Border Star Hotel. Awaken with the sound of the sheriff's step in the hallway outside. And his voice calling low and urgent through the door, "Open up, McComas; it's me, and I've come for you at last."

But it was no dream.

Billie proved that to McComas when she led him from the table and pulled him in under the shadows of the stairwell and gave him the longest, hardest kiss he had ever been given in his life. And when she whispered to him, "Hurry and get the horses, McComas; I will pack and meet you in the alley out back."

McComas pushed across the crowded room, the happiest he had been in his lifetime memory. But he did not allow the new feeling to narrow the sweep of his restless eyes. Nor slow his crouching, wolflike step. Nor let his right hand stray too far from the worn wooden grip of his .44. He still knew his name was McComas, and that he was worth $500, alive or dead, to the Encinal sheriff and his La Salle County posse. It was the price of staying alive in his profession, this unthinking wariness, this perpetual attitude of *qui vive*. Especially in a strange town at sundown. With the hanging tree waiting in the next county north. And a long life and new love beckoning from across the river, from two miles south, from ten minutes away.

He went out of the batwing saloon doors, glidingly, silently, as he always went out of strange doors, anywhere.

He saw Anson Starett a half instant before the latter saw him. He could have killed him then, and he ought to have. But men like McComas did not dry-gulch men like Anson Starett. Not even when they wear the pewter star and come up on your heels hungry and hard-eyed and far too swiftly for your mind to realize and to grasp and to believe that they have cut you off at last. You do not let them live because they are gallant and tough and full of cold nerve. You do it for a far simpler reason. And a deadlier one. You do it for blind, stupid pride. You do it because you will not have it said that McComas needed the edge on any man. And while you do not, ever, willingly, give that edge away, neither do you use it to blindside a brave man like Sheriff Anson Starett of Encinal.

What you do, instead, is to keep just enough of the edge to be safe. And to give just enough of it away to be legally and morally absolved of murder. It was a fine line, but very clear to McComas. It wasn't being noble. Just practical. Every man is his own jury when he wears a gun for money. No man wants to judge himself a coward. All that has been gone through when he put on the gun to begin with. Perhaps, it was even what made him put on the gun to begin with. What did it matter now? Little, oh, very, very little. Almost nothing at all.

"*Over here, Anse*," said McComas quietly, and the guns went off.

McComas was late. Only a little, but he was late. He knew and damned himself, even as he spun to the drive of Starett's bullet, back against the front wall of the Ben Hur, then sliding down it to the boardwalk at its base.

But he had gotten Starett. He knew that. The Encinal sheriff was still standing, swaying out there in the street, but McComas had gotten him. And, he told himself, he would get him again—now—just to make sure.

It took all his will to force himself up from the rough boards beneath him. He saw the great pool of blood, where he had fallen, but it did not frighten him. Blood and the terrible shock of gunshot wounds were a part of his trade. Somehow, it was different this time, though. This time he felt extremely light and queer in the head. It was a feeling he had never had before. It was as though he were watching himself. As though he were standing to one side saying, "Come on, McComas, get up; get up and put the rest of your shots into him before he falls; drive them into him while he is still anchored by the shock of that first hit. . . ."

But McComas knew that he had him. He knew, as he steadied himself and emptied the .44 into Starett, that he had him and that everything was still all right. But he would have to hurry. He could not stay there to wait for Starett to go down. He had to get out of there while there was yet time. Before the scared sheep in the saloon got their nerve back and came pouring out into the street. Before the sound of the gunfire brought the local law running up the street to help out the sheriff from Encinal.

He thought of Billie Blossom. . . . The good Lord knew he did. But she couldn't do anything for him now. . . . It was too late for Billie Blossom and gunfighter McComas. . . . They had waited and talked too long. . . . Now he must get out. . . . He must not let the girl see him hurt and bleeding. . . . She must not know. . . . He had to get to his horse at the hitching rail. . . . Had to find Coaly and swing up on him and give him his sleek black head and let him go away up the main street and out of Laredo. . . . Yes, he must find Coaly at the rail . . . find him and get up on him and run! run! run! for the river . . . just he and Coaly, all alone and through the gathering dusk. . . .

He could not find Coaly, then. When he turned to the hitching rail in front of the Ben Hur, his trim black racer was not there. He was not where he had left him, all saddled and loose-tied and ready to run. McComas was feeling light and queer again. Yet he knew he was not feeling that queer. Somebody had moved his horse. Somebody had untied him and taken him, while McComas was on the boardwalk from Starett's bullet. Somebody had stolen Coaly and McComas was trapped. Trapped and very badly hurt. And left all alone to fight or die on the streets of Laredo.

It was then that he heard the whisper. Then, that he whirled, whitefaced, and saw her standing at the corner of the saloon, in the alley leading to the back. Standing there with a black Mexican *reboza* drawn tightly over her ash blond hair, shadowing and hiding her hollow cheeks and great gray eyes. McComas could not distinctly see her face. Not under the twilight masking of that dark shawl. But he knew it was her. And he went running and stumbling toward her, her soft voice beckoning as though from some distant hill, yet clear as the still air of sundown—*"Here, McComas, here! Come to my arms, come to my heart, come with me—!"*

He lunged on. Stumbled once. Went down. Staggered back up and made it to her side before the first of the murmuring crowd surged out of the Ben Hur to halt and stare at the great stain of blood spreading from the front wall of the saloon. The moment her white, cool hands touched him, took hold of him and held him up, he felt the strength flow into him again. The strength flow in and the queer cold feeling disappear from his belly and the cottony mist dissolve from before his straining eyes. Now he was all right.

He remembered clearly, as she helped him along the side of the cantina, looking down at his shirtfront and seeing the pump of the blood jumping, with each pulse, from the big hole torn midway between breastbone and navel. He remembered thinking clearly, "Dear Lord, he got me dead center! How could it have missed the heart?" Yet, he remembered, even as he heard his thought-voice ask the question, that these crazy things did happen with gun wounds. A shot could miss a vital by half a hair-width, and do no more harm than a fleshy scrape. There was only the shock and the weakness of the first smash, and no real danger at all unless the bleeding did not stop. And McComas knew that it would stop. It was already slowing. All he had to worry about was staying with Billie Blossom until she could get him to a horse. Then he would be able to make it away. He could ride. He had ridden with worse holes through him. He would make it. He would get across the river and he and Billie would still meet on the far side.

She had a horse waiting for him. He ought to have known she would, a girl like that, old to the ways of Texas strays and their traffic through the border towns. He should even have known that it would be his own horse, saddled and rested and ready to run through the night and for the river.

Yes, she had slipped out of the Ben Hur before the others. She had seen how it was with McComas and Anson Starett. And she had untied Coaly and led him down the alley, to the back, where McComas could swing up on him, now, and sweep away to the river and over it to the life that waited beyond. To the life that he and Billie Blossom had planned and that Anson Starett had thought he could stop with one bullet from his swift gun. Ah, no! Anson Starett! Not today. Not this day. Not with one bullet. Not McComas.

There was no kiss at Coaly's side, and no time for one.

But McComas was all right again. Feeling strong as a yearling bull. Smiling, even laughing, as he leaned down from the saddle to take her pale hand and promise her that he would be waiting beyond the river.

Yet, strangely, when he said it, she was not made happy.

She shook her head quickly, looking white and frightened and talking hurriedly and low, as she pressed his hand and held it to her wasted cheek. And the tears which washed down over McComas' hand were not warm, they were cold as the lifeless clay, and McComas heard her speak with a sudden chill which went through him like an icy knife.

"No, McComas, no! Not the river! Not while there is yet daylight. You cannot cross the river until the night is down. Go back, McComas. Go back the other way. The way that you came in this afternoon, McComas. Do you remember? Back toward the cemetery on the hill. You will be safe there, McComas. No one will think to look for you there. Do you hear me, McComas? Wait there for me. High on the hill, where you saw the open grave. You can watch the Laredo road from there. You can see the river. You can see the sheriff and his posse ride out. You can see when they are gone and when it is safe for you to ride out. Then we can go, McComas. I will meet you there, on the hill, by that new grave. We will go over the river together, when it is dark and quiet and all is at peace and we know no fear. Do you understand, McComas? Oh, Dear God, do you hear and understand what I am telling you, my love—?"

McComas laughed again, trying to reassure her, and to reassure himself. Of course, he understood her, he said. And she was thinking smart. A sight smarter than McComas had been thinking since Starett's bullet had smashed him into that front wall and down onto the boardwalk. He got her calmed and quieted, he thought, before he spurred away. He was absolutely sure of it. And when he left her, turning in the saddle to look back as Coaly took him out and away from the filthy hovels of Laredo into the clean sweet smell of the mesquite and catclaw chapparal, he could still see her smiling and waving to him, slender and graceful as a willow wand moving against the long purple shadows of the sunset.

It was only a few minutes to the cemetery. McComas cut back into the main road and followed along it, unafraid. He was only a mile beyond the town but in some way he knew he would not be seen. And he was not. Two cowboys came along, loping toward Laredo, and did not give him a second glance. They did not even nod or touch their hat brims going by, and McComas smiled and told himself that it always paid to wear dark clothes and ride a black horse in his hard business—especially just at sundown in a strange town.

The rusted gates of the cemetery loomed ahead.

Just short of them, McComas decided he would take cover for a moment. There was no use abusing good luck.

Down the hill, from the new grave on the rise, were coming some familiar figures. They were the long-jawed preacher and square-built deputy sheriff he had passed earlier, on his way into Laredo. They might remember him, where two passing cowboys had shown no interest.

Up on the rise, itself, beyond the deputy and the parson's lurching buggy, McComas could see the two Mexican gravediggers putting in the last shovelfuls of flinty earth to fill the fresh hole where they had lowered the long black coffin from the flatbed wagon. And he could see, up there, standing alone and slightly apart, the weeping figure of the young girl in the black *reboza*.

McComas thought that was a kind, loyal thing for her to do. To stay to say goodbye to her lover. To wait until the preacher and the deputy and the gravediggers and the wagon driver had gone away, so that she might be alone with him. Just herself and God and the dead boy up there on that lonely, rocky rise.

Then, McComas shivered. It was the same shiver he had experienced on this same road, in this same place, earlier that afternoon. Angered, he forced himself to be calm. It was crazy to think that he knew this girl. That he had seen her before. He knew it was crazy. And, yet—

The deputy and the preacher were drawing near. McComas pulled Coaly deeper into the roadside brush, beyond the sagging gates. The deputy kneed his mount into a trot. He appeared nervous. Behind him, the preacher whipped up his bony plug. The rattle of the buggy wheels on the hard ruts of the road clattered past McComas, and were gone. The latter turned his eyes once more toward the hilltop and the head-bowed girl.

He did not want to disturb her in her grief, but she was standing by the very grave where Billie Blossom had told him to meet her. And it was growing dark and Billie had wanted him to be up there so that he could see her coming from town to be with him.

He left Coaly tied in the brush and went up the hill on foot. He went quietly and carefully, so as not to bother the girl, not to violate her faithful sorrow. Fortunately, he was able to succeed. There was another grave nearby. It had a rough boulder for a headstone, and a small square of sunbleached pickets around it. McComas got up to this other plot without being seen by the girl. He hid behind its rugged marker and tottering fence, watching to be sure the slender mourner had not marked his ascent.

Satisfied that she had not, he was about to turn and search the Laredo road for Billie Blossom, when he was again taken with the strange, unsettling chill of recognition for the girl in the black *reboza*. This time, the chill froze his glance. He could not remove his eyes from her. And, as he stared at her, she reached into a traveling bag which sat upon the ground beside her. The bag was packed, as though for a hurried journey, its contents disordered and piled in without consideration. From among them, as McComas continued to watch, fascinated, the girl drew out a heavy Colt .41 caliber derringer. Before McComas could move, or even cry out, she raised the weapon to her temple.

He leaped up, then, and ran toward her. But he was too late. The derringer discharged once, the blast of its orange flame searing the *reboza*. McComas knew, from the delayed, hesitating straightness with which she stood before she fell, that it had been a deathshot. When he got to her, she had slumped across the newly mounded grave, her white arms reaching out from beneath the shroud of the *reboza* in a futile effort to reach and embrace the plain pine headboard of the grave. McComas gave the headboard but a swift side glance. It was a weathered, knotty, poor piece of wood, whipsawed in careless haste. The barn paint used to dab the deceased's name upon it had not even set dry yet. McComas did not give it a second look.

He was down on the ground beside the fallen girl, holding her gently to his breast so that he might not harm her should life, by any glad chance, be in her still.

But it was not.

McComas felt that in the limp, soft way that she lay in his arms. Then, even in the moment of touching her, the chill was in him again. He *did* know this girl. He knew her well. And more. He knew for whom she mourned; and he knew whose name was on that headboard.

It was then he shifted her slim form and slowly pulled the black *reboza* away from the wasted oval face. The gray eyes were closed, thick lashes downswept. The ash blond hair lay in a soft wave over the bruised hole in the pale temple. It was she. Billie Blossom. The girl from the streets of Laredo.

McComas came to his feet. He did not want to look at that weathered headboard. But he had to.

There was only a single word upon it. No first name. No birth date. No line of love or sad farewell.

Just the one word:

"McComas"

He went down the hill, stumbling in his haste. He took Coaly out of the brush and swung up on him and sent him outward through the night and toward the river. It was a quiet night, with an infinite field of gleaming stars and a sweet warm rush of prairie wind to still his nameless fears. He had never known Coaly to fly with such a fleet, sure gait. Yet, swiftly as he went, and clearly as the starlight revealed the silvered current of the river ahead, they did not draw up to the crossing. He frowned and spoke to Coaly, and the black whickered softly in reply and sprang forward silently and with coursing, endless speed through the summer night.

That was the way that McComas remembered it.

The blackness and the silence and the stars and the rush of the warm, sweetly scented wind over the darkened prairie.

He forgot if they ever came to the river.

Portrait of a Gunfighter

by Hal G. Evarts

Hal G. Evarts, son of a writing father, is a resident of La Jolla, California, and has served as a Director and Vice President of WWA. He has appeared many times in the *Saturday Evening Post* and has published a couple of juveniles and a shelfful of novels. The story in hand is a first-run job, never before having appeared in print.

❦ ❦ ❦

THE PAINTING HANGS BEHIND the bar in my saloon. Strangers who know about such things tell me it shows real promise, and I've turned down cash offers more than once. I'll never sell that picture, not for any price. It's still too close.

Back in those days nearly every man packed a gun on his hip. The good ones, the real gunslingers, only carried one—never two. Like this fellow in this picture. Nothing fancy, a single action .45 with a black grip swinging free and easy. Holster whanged down to his thigh like part of his body. That's how the fast ones wore their guns, and this gent was deadly fast. I know, because I saw him draw one night to kill.

It started the morning young Dave Chandler came into my place —the One Strike, same as now—only then my customers were mostly cowmen off the range. Dave didn't drink nor pack a gun. A tall gangly kid with blue eyes and a shock of yellow hair, he looked younger than his eighteen years—like he still belonged in school. The quiet kind, colt-shy, he ducked his head and turned pink when I asked if he wanted sarsaparilla or lemon soda.

"Thanks, Jake," he gave me that sheepish smile. "But not today. I—I'm drumming up trade."

"Trade?" I put down a glass and stared. Across the bar he smelled of turpentine and his bib overalls were speckled with paint. "What kind of trade?"

"Your sign out front. It's peeled pretty bad. I'll paint you a new one for three dollars."

I ran the only saloon in fifty miles. I didn't need a sign. But I liked Dave Chandler, and his old man too. "You in the sign painting business now?"

He nodded. "I paint anything. Barns, houses, chicken coops—you name it. Been working out in the country. Now I'm starting in town."

Ever since he was a button Dave had been dabbling with crayons or pencils, drawing pictures the way a kid will. Whenever you dropped by the Chandler house there'd be young Dave with his nose in a sketchbook. Polite, well mannered, but lost from this world. You'd never find him helling around with other boys his age. "So you picked me first?"

Dave grinned. "Figure you need me most."

Well, he had me there. The One Strike was a weather-beat old false front I'd never bothered to fix up. It could stand a coat of paint, inside and out. But right then—I'll admit it—I got curious. "Fixing to stay in this business permanent?"

"Till the customers run out."

That wouldn't take long. Big Butte had five other stores, maybe two dozen houses. Trouble is, this desert wind can scour the paint off a building in one good blow. "Then what?"

He blushed. "I got some plans."

"What's your Dad think about this?"

"I don't care what he thinks," Dave said. He said it nice, but firm too, telling me to mind my own business. "All right, Dave," I said. "You got yourself a job."

He pumped my hand and hurried out, saying he'd be back soon as he rounded up his gear. "One more thing," I called after him. "Tell your Dad I got some news for him. Might be important."

He kept right on up the walk, like maybe he hadn't heard. My news would keep. But I wondered, because he didn't catty-corner across the street toward the jail and the house behind where he lived with his father and brother.

Dave was hardly out of sight when Walt Chandler—Sheriff Chandler, that is—stepped out of his office. Right behind Walt stepped Dud, his older boy and deputy. They looked alike, those two, big solid men with twin stars pinned to their vests. From my front window I watched them tramp across the street. They walked like soldiers. And right then I got a feeling—hunch. That trouble was on the way.

They clomped inside, old Walt first and Dud a pace behind. That time of day the place was empty except for me. "What'd he want?" Walt demanded.

"Yeah, what'd he want?" Dud echoed.

"You mean Dave?"

Walt Chandler scowled and gave his shell belt a hitch. "I mean Dave."

Dud Chandler hitched his belt too and said, "Yeah, he means Dave."

Walt had been sheriff for so long he was sort of a fixture around town, like that wooden Injun in front of the mercantile. Most of his life he'd packed a gun and a law badge, back in the rough frontier days. He could chill you with his eyes. But today he looked like a grizzled old badger with a big paunch. Dave didn't favor him much, took after his mother more. She'd died years ago and Walt had raised both boys himself. That can age a man too.

"He's going to paint my sign," I told Walt.

"Don't give him the job, Jake."

"But I already promised the boy."

"As a favor to me," Walt said.

"Yeah, as a favor—" Dud began, but Walt cut him short. "Keep outa this, Dud." Like he'd shush up a four-year-old.

For a fact Dud wasn't much older in his mind than four, though he stood six feet and could bend a horseshoe straight with bare hands. Some claim he'd been injured at birth. Dud was slow and easy-going, just not very bright. But nobody deviled him—he was Walt Chandler's son.

"Now look," I told Walt, "I gave my word and I can't back down. Not without you give me some reason."

"I got one," he growled. "Good one, too."

He was like that, close-mouthed, proud and quick to bristle. But at heart I took him to be a kindly man. "Walt," I said, "this is between me an' Dave. Seems like he's big enough to make up his own mind."

Walt grunted and slacked his bulk into a chair. So I poured him a shot and broke out a bottle of strawberry pop for Dud. That's one way Dud never copied the old man. Walt wouldn't let either of his boys touch the hard stuff. Then I remembered my piece of news. "I hear a lot of gossip over this bar," I said. "One of the Bar-J riders was in here early. He ran into Chalk Kirby over at Pyramid yesterday."

Walt stared from under his shaggy brows. "So?"

"So you sent Kirby to the pen five years ago. He got out last week. Might be he'll turn up here."

"Chalk Kirby ain't got the guts to come back."

I wasn't so sure, but you didn't argue with Walt. I went on polishing glasses while Walt and Dud watched the street through my window. Maybe thirty minutes went by before Dave pulled up out front in his rickety wagon behind one swayback mare. They both got up as he pushed through the doors. Dave hesitated, then said in a real low voice, "Morning, Pop. Morning Dud."

Walt's eyes softened a bit, then he stiffened when he saw the paint can and brush in Dave's hand. He said, "Get back over to the house, Dave."

Dave's smile died. His mouth set.

"You quit this foolishness," Walt said, "and we'll forget the rest."

"We talked it out last night," Dave said. "I'm not moving back."

Walt's face turned red. "You'll move back today, or you're never movin' back. That clear?"

"Pop, please—"

"A—a damn paint dauber!"

"Pop, will you listen—"

But Walt stormed past him through the doors, Dud trailing like a shadow.

There was a hurt look in Dave's eyes but he squared his shoulders and walked out to the wagon. After he'd mixed his colors he climbed up to the sign. He didn't look back across the street toward the sheriff's office. But I could see Walt peering out the window at him over there, face pressed against the pane. It might have been funny except that Walt was the stubbornest man in six counties.

During the day customers drifted in and out, most of them joshing Dave on his ladder. But he never let on and I didn't interfere. About suppertime he finished and I stepped out to inspect my sign. He'd done an A-one job, spruced up the whole saloon front. When I paid him off he thanked me and said, "How 'bout painting the inside tomorrow? Make you a good price."

"I don't reckon—"

"Jake, I need the money. Need it bad. And that back bar looks terrible."

It did. The One Strike's original owner must of purely loved gilt paint. He'd had gold slapped all over the back wall—cupids and angels and such. Artistic, if you got that turn of mind. Only now it looked downright scabby, the gilt had flaked off so. But mainly I was thinking of Walt Chandler.

"Pop won't make any more trouble," Dave said. "Not for you. I promise, Jake. How about it?"

"Well—" I hedged. He was a hard one to turn down. Stubborn like his Dad. "I'll sleep on it. See me in the morning."

He stowed his gear back in the wagon and drove off out of town.

Soon as his dust settled I walked over to the sheriff's office. Walt was slumped in his cowhide chair, staring at the floor, Dud beside him, glum as a statue. "That Dave—" Walt began.

"Didn't come here to talk about Dave," I said. "You know your job, Walt. But Chalk Kirby's on the prod for sure."

Walt frowned, like he'd forgotten the name. "Chalk Kirby?"

"Three-four people saw him in Pyramid yesterday. Heard him brag. He's got it in for you."

Walt snorted.

"Walt," I said. Chalk Kirby had been a killer in his day, a professional gunhand, and five years behind bars is a big chunk of any man's life. But I might of been talking to a stump, for all the heed Walt paid. "Anyway, I warned you."

I turned back to the door. Walt said, "What's got into that kid, Jake?"

"Somebody's got to paint signs," I told him. "There's worse ways to earn a living."

"I ain't talking about signs. He wants to paint pictures. Kind you hang on a wall." Walt slammed a fist on his desk. "Dabs on a wall!"

"What's wrong with that?"

He gave me a pitying look. "Dave has it in his head to go East to some art school. Study for two years. That's why he's savin' every dime." Walt shook his head. "We had a row last night. Lost our tempers. He moved his stuff out. Camped down by the creek."

"Yeah," Dud said, "down by the creek."

Walt fished a nickel from his pocket and his voice turned gentle. "Step over to the mercantile, will you, Dud?" he said. "Buy yourself a bag of gumdrops."

Dud's eyes lit up. After he'd gone Walt leaned back and sighed. "I can't help Dud much. Keep him out of harm. Dud's the way the good Lord made him. But Dave—Dave could be anything. Only why in hell can't he be a man!"

There was genuine bafflement in Walt's voice and I knew how strong he felt, to be talking so free.

"I always figured he'd grow up and take my place here. I'm not getting any younger. This is where Dave belongs."

Walt's fingers, not quite steady, touched the badge on his vest. I realized then how old and tired and sick looking he was. It was a shock to see him with his guard down because for years he'd been the giant of our town, respected and feared, strong as a mountain. "Maybe Dave don't want to be sheriff," I said.

"Even that I wouldn't mind so much. If he'd take a job punching cows, or in the stamp mill. A man's job. But this—"

I put a hand on his shoulder. I felt sorry for Walt, but kind of put out, too. He was so bull-headed blind. "We been friends a long time," I said. "But a man's got to follow the way his stick floats. Or he's nothin'. You know that. You done it all your life. Dave's not a kid any longer. Why not give him his chance?"

"No, by Judas!" Walt's fist slammed the desk again. "No boy of mine's goin' to make a fool of himself, and me too!"

"How'll you stop him? Tell me that."

"I dunno yet," Walt said bleakly. "But I will."

Next morning when I opened up, Dave was waiting. I gave him the job. I admired his grit. He set up his paint cans on a bench behind the bar and went to work on those cupids. You couldn't smell the whisky for the turpentine. Every now and then I peeked out at the sheriff's office, knowing Walt wouldn't back down. He never had in fifty years.

During the morning I picked up another piece of gossip about Chalk Kirby from the mail rider. According to him Kirby had left Pyramid, fifty miles down the line, and disappeared. I didn't know whether to be worried or relieved. But at dinnertime, when Dave cleaned off his brushes and came back from the wagon with a sandwich, I passed on the word. Dave looked over at Walt's office. "You want *me* to tell him?" he asked.

I nodded.

"He can look after himself."

"Maybe," I said. "But how long since he's had to tame a man like Kirby? A few payday drunks is about all Walt's bucked up against lately."

"He won't listen to me," Dave said bitterly. "He'd just get mad and chew my ears off."

I let it go. After a bit I noticed Dave hunched over one of my tables with a sketchpad and pencil, sandwich in one hand, drawing with the other. He was so absorbed he forgot to eat. I come up behind and peered over his shoulder. Gave me quite a turn. He'd done a picture of me wiping the bar. Real as life—mustache and apron, sleeve garters and all. So doggone real I give out a grunt and Dave looked up, embarrassed.

"You just did that? Just setting there?"

He tore off the sheet and handed it to me. "Compliments of the artist," he said and laughed.

I'd never seen any of his pictures. Never bothered to look, I guess. "You got any more?"

"Whole trunk full." He shrugged. "Mostly chicken tracks like this."

I reached for his sketchpad. Dave turned pink, like Walt had caught him chawing out behind the barn, but let me have it. The first picture was a stud game in my place, five faces around a table, and every one a regular I could name by sight. There was a picture of old Felix, the sheepherder, with his goatskin wine bag, another of the professor at the piano. Mostly folks around Big Butte, they were—a couple of cowpokes, the blacksmith, a drummer in his derby. One of Walt Chandler too, big and bushy-haired, head like a lion.

They all had a feel that made your skin prickle. With those little squiggles on a piece of paper Dave had caught us all. Not prettyfied—the way we really looked. I kept staring at those drawings until, grumbling, he reached for the pad. "They're not very good."

"Dave," I said, "no man who can draw like that needs to go to any school. There's nothing they can learn you."

He gave a funny little smile. "Pop's right. I'm just a dauber. Got to get away from here."

"I'm sure no critic but these look good to me."

He told me what was wrong—perspective, technique, anatomy—a lot of words I didn't rightly savvy. But one thing I knew: He was hellbent to leave Big Butte and go back East to New York, maybe even to Paris, France, which he said was the capital of the art world. Study the old masters and paint in oil. A five-hundred-dollar stake would get him started. He talked like a starved man at a feast and I let him ramble, watching that glow building up in his eyes.

Our schoolteacher had loaned him all her art books and borrowed more. He'd took some courses by mail—learn to draw in ten easy lessons. All the while Walt was hammering him to quit and take a steady job. Not that Dave was lazy. To earn his keep he hauled wood and dug wells, even loaded freight. But every spare minute, to hear him tell, he'd kept at his drawing until he'd drove old Walt half crazy.

When he finally ran down I said, "No hurry, Dave, you've got years to spare. Walt ain't go so many left. Couldn't you maybe put this off a bit?"

The glow faded. "He's got Dud," Dave said.

"Not the same," I told him. "Dud's the cross he has to bear. In his way Walt's proud of you."

"Of me?" Dave shook his head. "The only thing he's proud of is that office across the street, the badge he wears." His voice shook. "He's ashamed of me, Jake. It's why he wants me to quit."

I thought he was wrong, wrong as an eighteen-year-old can be, but I didn't say so. Because just then Walt himself walked in with Dud at his heels. Walt glanced at the half-finished cherubs behind my bar and sniffed. "Still trimmin' up the One Strike, I see," he said to Dave.

"Yes, sir."

"Got your license?"

"What license?"

"Had a meeting," Walt said, "with John Throop this morning." Throop was the only lawyer in Big Butte and doubled as county prosecutor whenever we had a trial. "Seems there's a statute on the books says any itinerant's got to have a license. That means peddlers."

"I'm no peddler."

"You got any fixed place of business? Then accordin' to the law you're a peddler."

Dave said weakly, "How much does a license cost?"

"Fifty dollars."

I stared at Walt, not believing he'd job his own son like that. "If you're short of cash," he went on, "you might borrow on your outfit, or sell that wagon."

"But I'd be out of business!"

Walt stood there like a fence post. "That's the law," he said, and Dud echoed, "Yeah, that's the law."

I walked over to my cash box, scooped out a handful of silver and slapped it down on the bar. "There's your money," I told Walt. "But damned if I'll count it for you."

Dave got up from the table and it looked like all the blood had drained out of him. "Thanks, Jake," he said. "But I'm not buying any license. I'll work somewhere else."

They stood there, Walt and Dave, squared off like two fighters. Walt's chin was trembling and I think he might of relented some then if Dave had given him any encouragement. But Dave was a chip off the old block—a block of solid granite.

Finally Walt said, "Not till you pay that fifty dollars."

"Don't do this to me, Pop."

"Hold on," I broke in. "Dave's got to finish up my bar. Can't walk out and leave it like this."

Walt gave me a bare half-inch nod. "I got some papers to serve out on South Fork but I'll be back by suppertime. If you're still here, Dave, I'm going to impound your horse and wagon."

Maybe he expected Dave to slack off, offer some compromise, but Dave didn't budge, just kept staring. So Walt motioned Dud and they went out. For a minute it was so still you could hear the wall clock ticking. Then Dave ripped his sketchpad in half, tossed it in the stove and without a word went back to work.

After a long while he said, "Pop raised us strict, Dud and me. He was always fair, up till now. Never gave us a licking unless we deserved it. But I won't take this."

A lot of thoughts ran through my head, but mostly how obstinate two proud men can be. Maybe you'd call it principle. But it seemed a crime to me. Because somebody was bound to get hurt. And Walt Chandler most of all.

That turned out to be the longest afternoon I ever spent. About four o'clock a couple of ranchers wandered in and began ragging

Dave to paint some dimples on a cupid's behind. Dave joshed them back while I drew two beers. When I turned around I almost dropped the glasses. A third man was leaning again the bar. Slipped in so quiet we hadn't heard a board squeak.

"Howdy, Jake," he said, like he'd seen me only yesterday.

I swallowed. "Howdy, Chalk."

Chalk Kirby always had been yeasty-faced and jail hadn't improved his color. He looked a little older, gaunter, but I'd 've known those eyes any place or time. Gray and cold as river pebbles, and with no more feeling. He stared around the saloon and said, "Gettin' mighty fancy."

"Passing through?" I said.

"Depends."

That's when I got a good look at his gun—a single-action .45 with a black butt, shoved down in a worn holster tied to his thigh. Before he'd gone away there used to be talk about how fast he was, how many men he'd shot. Maybe most of it was true. Personally I could swear to only one man he'd killed for sure. But I wished I had a sawed-off handy under the bar-top.

He slid into a chair easy and quiet as a snake. "What'll it be, Chalk?" I said. "On the house."

He shook his head. "Maybe later." His gaze fastened on Dave who was still busy up behind the bar. "What's your name, sonny?"

Dave turned slowly and wiped his hands on a rag. He'd been a kid when Walt wounded Kirby and brought him down from the hills on a murder charge. At the trial Kirby claimed that Walt had sneaked up in the dark and shot him from behind. Nobody who knew Walt believed it, including the jury. No kid could forget a thing like that about his father, but I don't think Dave had quite tagged Kirby yet. "Chandler," he said in a puzzled voice. "Dave Chandler."

Kirby sized him up. "You must be Walt's younger boy. Not the dummy."

Dave frowned. "You looking for him, mister?"

"I tried his office but it's locked. So I come over here."

"He'll be back directly."

"I know he will, sonny." Kirby picked up a deck of cards and laid out a game, his back to the street but with his eyes straying frequent to the mirror. He was cool, I'll give him that, the way he ran those cards like a black queen was the only worry on his mind. Maybe, I prayed, he won't brace Walt. But instinct told me different.

The two cowmen drunk up fast and left. I had to get Dave out of there, or anyway try. "Dave, you might as well finish up tomorrow. Light in here is fadin' fast."

Dave looked over at Kirby, a tight squint around his eyes. "I can see well enough," he said.

Hardly any time passed before two new customers sidled in. The first pair had spread the word. Times like that I wonder about all humankind. Man gets a whiff of somebody else's trouble, it draws him like a cat to liver. Before long we had a dozen or so, Walt Chandler's friends and neighbors, itching to see what Walt would do. Nobody howdied Kirby or slapped him on the back. Behind that poker face of his he must of been despising us all.

What Dave was thinking I can't guess. Expect he knew by now who and what Kirby was, but he wasn't ducking out. He went on gilding those damnfool cherubs. Then I spotted a dust across the flats south of town.

I sneaked back into the washroom and out the rear door into the alley. It was three blocks to the livery but I ran all the way. Walt and Dud rode under the arch as I came panting up. Walt swung down and stepped back, staring at Dave's horse and wagon hitched in front of the One Strike. "Still there," Walt said. "By grab, I meant what I said."

"Never mind that," I snapped. "Chalk Kirby's in there! With a *gun!*"

Walt hauled out his watch. "Five o'clock. Go pick up his outfit, Dud."

"Walt!" I yelled. "Don't walk in there! He's waiting for you—Kirby!"

He didn't pay me no mind, not the thinking part of him. My sense didn't get through. He shook his head and there was sadness in his eyes. "He's a good boy, Jake. Always minded. But he's gettin' too big for his britches."

"Walt, for God's sake—"

He walked up the street with that heavy stride, Dud close beside him.

And that's how we came back to the One Strike, pushing through the batwings three abreast. Walt took a step or two, gaze seeking out Dave, and froze. Chalk Kirby slapped down his cards and stood up. Every other man in that room went silent, holding his breath. Kirby, showing the faintest smile, said, "Been a long time, Walt."

Walt blinked. Until that moment he hadn't wanted to believe. He'd shut his mind up tight like you shut a door to keep out the dark. Now Kirby was here, grim and deadly and determined, with a gun on his hip. A nerve jumped in Walt's cheek. "How are you, Kirby?"

Kirby waited, neither moving nor speaking, his eyes fixed on Walt and his mouth still pinched in that hard half-smile. Finally Walt wet his lips. "So you came back after all?"

"I came back."

"For good?"

"I don't think so," Kirby said. "I never liked your town much, Walt. It hasn't changed. Neither've you."

A stain spread up from Walt's collar. Gruffly he said, "Your privilege."

"Haven't changed a bit, Walt. Still the same big empty blow-hard you was five years ago. That's what I came back for—to tell you to your face."

A shudder ran over Walt's frame but Kirby spoke on, like he had to get the words out before they choked him. "Look at you! Old and fat and soft as blubber. I could shoot you twice before you touched your gun. You're not sheriff. You're nothin' but a has-been hidin' behind a rep. You and that booby of a kid you call your dep'ty."

Dud looked from Walt to Kirby and let out a little whimpering noise. Sweat glistened on Walt's forehead. His hands were knotted at his sides. He wasn't afraid—not for himself. But he saw the truth now. Knew he was a tired, burnt-out old man. No match for Chalk Kirby. All of us saw it. If he tried for his gun he was dead.

Slow bitter thoughts moved across his face. Maybe he thought of Dud, who needed him so much. Or maybe of Dave, who didn't need him at all. I never felt sorrier for a man in my life, nor admired one more. Then his shoulders sagged.

Kirby had won. In seconds he'd cut Walt Chandler down, smashed him. But he couldn't leave it there, not Chalk Kirby. He had to rub Walt's nose in it. "Whyn't you quit this job while you're still alive?"

Walt stared.

Kirby took two quick strides, reached out and ripped the badge off Walt's vest, flinging it on the floor. "There's your pride, Walt."

"Kirby!"

Kirby spun. I'd forgotten Dave. But Dave was coming around the end of the bar, paint brush in hand, moving slow and quiet. Moving like Walt used to move, straight and sure of himself, eyes like blue ice. He looked as big as Walt ever had—man size.

"Kirby," he said, "pick that up off the floor."

Kirby laughed. "Get away from me, sonny."

The crowd squeezed back to let Dave through and he came up by Kirby's table. Walt growled in his throat, started forward. I caught his arm. "Kirby," Dave said, "pick up that badge."

Kirby measured him, tiny puzzle lines webbed around his eyes; and laughed again. He stepped on the badge and ground it under his boot.

The rest happened so quick it's hard to tell. Dave slapped his paint brush in Kirby's face. Turpentine splashed. Kirby screamed, jabbed a hand at his eyes and drew with the other. His gun came out. His arm was just a blur but he shot blind and wild, the slug smashing my front window. Then Dave had his wrist, twisting the gun free, clubbing him with the barrel. Kirby dropped without a sound.

The gunshot was still roaring in my ears, but I heard Dave's deep wracking gasp. He was shaking when he turned to Dud. "Dud," he said, "take him over to the jail."

Dud's face brightened, like the sun sliding out from under clouds. "Yeah!" he said. "Yeah, I'll take him to jail." He got Kirby over one shoulder and carried him out.

Not a one of us moved while Dave picked up the badge. He

straightened and slipped his arm through Walt's. "Come on, Pop," he said, in the gentlest voice I ever heard. "Let's go home."

Dave Chandler never left the Big Butte country. Never studied art back East or saw the museums in Paris, France. Stayed right here at home. Still draws and paints in his spare time a little. That's one picture he did, up behind the bar. The gunfighter. Chalk Kirby. The other one is Walt, back in his prime, the way I like to remember him.

Dave is packing the tin for us, now. Youngest sheriff we ever elected. And Dud's still packing the deputy's star.

The Tomato Can Kid

by William O. Turner

After several years in promotion, Western-born Bill Turner got into the writing of fiction. His grandfather operated the first stage line between Virginia City, Montana, and Salt Lake City, Utah. Still unmarried, Bill resides at Hendersonville, North Carolina, in charge of WWA's library promotion program. "The Tomato Can Kid" was written especially for this anthology.

SAM RILEY TOPPED a low ridge and saw the ranch below him, its neglected buildings clustered in as pretty a little valley as a man would come across in a sight of Sundays. A woman and a boy were in the yard. Sam rode a bit closer, then reined up and hallooed—as Sheriff Art Harkie had warned him to do.

The woman was young, redheaded, and was doing a washing in a tub set on a bench. She straightened. The morning sun glistened on her wet arms as she shielded her eyes. She dipped into a clothes-basket at her feet and came up cocking a shotgun.

The boy had been splitting stovewood beside the lopsided,

weather-grayed house. He was seven or eight and as redheaded as the woman. He moved to her side now with a double-bitted ax in his hands. Sam took a deep breath and rode into the yard.

"Stay on your horse," the woman said. "You get down, I'll evaporate you down to a grease spot."

Sam decided not to get down. He took in her slender figure and flame-blue eyes. The eyes flicked his badge and there was a change in them. Suddenly self-conscious, the woman looked cross-eyed at a dangling wisp of red-gold hair and tried to blow it into place.

"You Mrs. Peggy Bronson?" Sam said.

"Who wants to know?"

"Why, I do, ma'am—Deputy Sheriff Riley. Also the sheriff and the school board and County Judge A. J. Pucker."

"They ought to know me well enough, I guess. I've run most of them off the place one time and another. But how do I know you're a deputy? I never saw you before, and anybody can pin on a badge."

"Why would I want to humbug about it, ma'am?"

"You might have a reason," she said. Her eyes swept the country behind him, and he saw she was afraid he might not be alone. "You might be a friend of—most anybody."

"I'm new." Sam couldn't keep a trace of pride out of his voice. "Rode into Basin two weeks ago and got put on as a deputy."

"They hired a stranger?"

"It was a mite unusual, I guess."

"If it happened."

"Ma'am, when I arrived in town, three fellers were pistol-shooting at tomato cans out back of the stable. I always had a knack for that sort of foolishness and I invited myself in. Put five shots into a can at thirty feet—slip-shooting. The sheriff stepped up and said I was the new deputy. Got the highest grade in the civil service examination, you might say."

Peggy Bronson snorted, but he could see she wasn't really afraid of him any longer. Her eyes seemed a deeper blue now, and there was something like sassiness in them.

"You came to tell me I've got to put Bobby back in school," she said. "I'll give you the same answer I gave the sheriff and the school board and—"

"I didn't come to tell you anything," Sam said. "I've got a subpoena here, and I've got to serve it."

"I'm teaching Bobby myself. Isn't that good enough?"

"I wouldn't know, ma'am. Why you so set against school?"

She lowered her eyes as if she was afraid he might see beyond the sassiness. It was Bobby who answered the question.

"She got a letter from my father," Bobby said. "He found out where we are."

She lowered the shotgun and pulled the boy against her. "Bobby! I thought we agreed—"

"Mom, we got to have help." He looked up at Sam with a plea in his face. "Half the time she don't even go to bed at night! She sits and watches the door with that old shotgun in her lap."

"Ma'am, if it's as bad as that, why don't you move into town?" Sam said. "Neighbors are about the best protection there is."

"Neighbors have long blue noses and idle tongues. You might as well give me that subpoena and let me get my washing done—but I haven't admitted to being Peggy Bronson. Remember that."

Sam handed over the subpoena. It commanded Mrs. Peggy Bronson to appear before Judge Pucker and show cause why her son should not attend school. She read it and tore it up.

"That's no way to do," Sam said.

"You make me sick!" She tilted her chin at him defiantly. It made her look right pretty, but it seemed kind of an empty gesture now that he knew how scared she was. "You and the sheriff and the whole bug-dusted clamjamfry of you! Haven't you anything to do besides add to folks' troubles?"

"No, ma'am," Sam said. She was close to tears, he guessed, and he was glad she had torn up the subpoena. If she hadn't, he might be tempted to take it back and report that he hadn't found her at home. He tipped his hat and wheeled his horse around. When he glanced back, she had gone back to her washing.

He got back to Basin around noon. Sheriff Art Harkie lounged in the doorway of his office, consulting his watch.

"You stop to fish Rock Crick?" he demanded sarcastically.

Sam dismounted stiffly. He wrapped a rein around the hitch rail and bit back an equally sarcastic reply. The sheriff was a critical, short-tempered man. It was hard to hold your tongue sometimes— till you remembered how much you wanted to hold your job. You remembered those other tomato-can shooters, too, and you reminded yourself that Art's short temper had been a lucky thing for you. Annoyed and then infuriated by the eagerness of the local boys, the sheriff had taken a malicious pleasure in awarding the badge to a stranger. From a political point of view, of course, this choice hardly seemed wise. And there were signs that Art Harkie was beginning to regret it.

Sam wanted to keep the job—Lord, how he wanted to. He had drifted through cattle country from Texas to eastern Washington, drifted through it since he was orphaned at thirteen. He'd worked for more brands than a man could remember, sticking a month or a season or a year, bumming meals at cookhouses in between jobs, never saving enough for a start on his own. Now, at thirty-two, he'd fallen into this deputy job in this remote little county seat in Montana Territory. It wasn't much of a town by some lights, but folks were friendly and a law officer had a certain standing. He'd already been asked to a church social and an Odd Fellows picnic. And the pay was sixty a month—twice what a brushpopper made. If he lived careful, he might save half. In three years that would tot up to a thousand dollars, enough for forty-fifty head of cattle. . . .

"You serve the subpoena?" Art demanded.

"I did. She tore it up."

"Damn snippety little flip-tail widow."

"Widow?" Sam said. "I gather she's got a husband somewhere. She's scared he'll take the boy away from her."

This was plainly news to Art. "She tell you that?"

"The boy let it out."

"Damn snippety little grass widow."

"I take it she ain't lived in the county long," Sam said.

Art squinched up his face in an effort to recollect. "Not more'n a year or two. Her uncle owned that little place she's on, and she come to keep house for him. Old man died last fall. Left her the ranch and a few head of stock. She'd sold off most of it a cow at a time."

"Pretty little fixin'," Sam said.

Art gave him a sharp look. "Wonder you ain't full of buck-shot."

They went into the office. Sam grabbed the broom and started to sweep out, but Art complained of the dust. After a few minutes, Art went home to dinner, and Sam did the sweeping then.

Art got back around two. At two-thirty Lee Freemont, who kept the general store, dropped in with news of a stranger in town. He had bought a sack of food at Lee's store and was now at the black-smith's.

Normally, Art would have paid little heed, but this was the thirtieth of the month with the payroll for the Lucky Cut mine due on the afternoon stage. On the thirtieth, he was interested in strangers. He challenged Lee to a game of checkers and sent Sam to investigate.

Sam found the man at the smithy—a big black-bearded man who looked like a bear and moved like a cat. He was just riding through, he said, and had stopped to have a loose shoe fixed. He was on his way to a ranch down on the Yellowstone, where he had a job break-ing horses.

At three-thirty, the stage rolled in. Sam and Art saw the payroll stowed into the express office safe. The agent would lock himself into the office tonight and sleep on the floor with a shotgun beside him. In the morning, the mine manager would arrive with a guard and take the money up to the mine.

The stage also brought a telegram for the sheriff, sent over from Roundup, the nearest telegraph town. Art whistled when he read it, then shoved it into a pocket. It wasn't till they were back at the office that he soberly handed it to Sam.

It was from the sheriff of Wheatland County, northwest of here. It said tersely that Will Barnett had shot his way through a posse and might be headed toward Basin. As everybody in the territory knew, Will Barnett had broken out of the pen at Deer Lodge two months before and had led lawmen a bloody chase clear into Idaho and back. They had lost him. Until now, there had been no recent news of him.

Art pulled a circular out of a drawer and slid it across the desk.

It carried a description of Barnett and an inky picture of a bearded man. Sam remembered the man he had talked to at the black-smith's.

"Could that be the man?" Art asked.

Sam grunted. "It could be. It could also be Ulysses S. Grant."

"This is no time to be funny," Art said. "We'd best see if he's still in town. The both of us."

"What's this?" Sam was reading the smaller print. " 'Alias Bill Barber, alias William Bronson.' Hey, that widow's name is Bronson."

Art squinched up his face while he digested that, then he reacted cautiously. "Probably a coincidence. Let's don't take to chasing white horses in the fog."

The bearded stranger was not at the blacksmith's—or the saloon or the livery stable or Chung Wing's restaurant. At last they found a small boy who had seen the stranger come out of the express office. He was carrying a black bag and had ridden out of town in a hurry, headed north.

They reached the express office at a run. The clerk was uncon-scious, dying maybe, having been half-scalped by a gun barrel. The safe was open. The black satchel that held the payroll was gone.

Art rang the fire bell and announced that he wanted three men for a posse. The three tomato-can shooters whom Sam had beaten were the first to volunteer, and they were the ones Art swore in. He commandeered five good horses at the livery, and in ten minutes he, Sam and the temporary deputies left town at a lope.

Sam felt a growing sense of catastrophe. There wasn't much doubt now that it was Will Barnett they were after. A good lawman would have recognized him at the smithy, Sam thought; at least, he would have been suspicious enough to keep a sharp eye on the man.

I bobbled it, he thought. *Art hasn't faulted me yet, but he will if we don't bring this* hombre *in.*

Barnett's trail was plain enough, leading straight north along the stage road. The center of the road had been churned to powder by the stage horses, but Barnett had ridden mostly to one side, where his horse had left clear tracks in the smooth baked soil. It seemed an obliging thing to do.

Rock Creek, a mile out of town, was low-banked, shallow and bridgeless. Here, Sam thought, the outlaw might have made an effort to hide his trail; but this seemed a bad guess. The tracks led straight into the water and straight out—still a little to one side of the road. Art Harkie grunted his satisfaction and waved the posse forward.

From time to time now Barnett's tracks veered into the road and were lost for a spell in its hoofbeaten confusion; then they would appear again outside the ruts for a spell, easy enough for any half-way skillful tracker to identify. Suddenly Sam jumped his horse ahead of the others and held up his hand for them to halt.

"Art, there's something wrong with this sign," he said. "The horse we're following has a loose shoe. Off hind foot."

Art bent in his saddle to study the tracks. "So he has. So much the better. We ought to catch him inside an hour or so."

"Wait!" Sam persisted. "He had a shoe fixed in town, remember? Off hind foot."

"So it come loose again," one of the possemen said. "That blacksmith ain't reliable after lunch."

The sheriff nodded grimly. "Bull starts nipping early in the afternoon sometimes. Well, he done us a favor."

His horse plunged forward and they moved off in a swirl of dust. Sam overtook Art and made him pull up again.

"You sure got the slows," Art said. There was a glint of anger in his eyes now.

"Remember that Bronson alias?" Sam said. "Barnett could be that woman's husband."

"What in the black damnation has that got to do with a lame horse?"

"He could've turned up the crick to her ranch. She was scared half to death—"

Art snorted.

"Now you hold on a minute," Sam said. "It ain't easy to explain about the tracks, but I fig—"

"You maybe getting scared we'll *catch up* to our man?" Art barked, letting his temper go. "You wouldn't be the first of the kind I've seen—a right artistic shot at a tomato can but all jumps and jelly when it comes to facing a killer. Even when you ain't alone."

The other possemen had swung their horses close. Sam's eyes sought one man after another in an appeal for support, but he found only ridicule in their faces.

"Men," Art said, "the trail is plain as the decorations on a birthday cake. But the Tomato Can Kid here wants to go scouting up Rock Crick!"

The men laughed. One of them muttered appreciatively, "The Tomato Can Kid!"

Sam said, "Art, I'm going to do it. I'd appreciate to have a man with me."

Art leaned forward in his saddle, looked Sam squarely in the eye and spoke in a snow-soft voice that Sam had never heard him use before. "You jelly-gutted drifter. How'd you like to give me that badge back?"

It was like the sky fell in. But Sam held the sheriff's eyes and kept his own voice under control. There was more at stake now than a job, or even a man's pride.

"Glad to," he drawled. "After you get back from a goose chase. You can apologize then or I'll shove it down your throat."

He pulled his horse around and headed back toward the creek. Behind him there were jeers and profanity and the sudden thunder of hoofs as the posse drove on. He was pretty sure about the tracks and he supposed he should have had the patience to make the others understand. But Art didn't give a man a chance.

They would see those tracks beside the road from time to time all the way to Prospect Pass—maybe clear into Wheatland County. Will Barnett had ridden into Basin from that direction. He had ridden in the road—between the ruts. Every so often, he had turned and ridden back a short distance, veering off the road to leave clean sign that wouldn't be obliterated by the stage. Then he had ridden into the road and turned around toward Basin again. Traveling south, he had laid down a trail pointing north.

After the robbery, he had left a plain trail to the creek. He had turned up it, riding in the shallow water and counting on his pursuers to follow the false trail on the other side. The one tiny flaw in his plan was the loose shoe. And even if the marks of that were noticed, who would figure that it was loose before he got to Basin and not after he left?

I figured it, Sam thought. *And I figured myself right out of a job, it looks like. I'm too damn smart for my own good. But maybe this Barnett is, too. Maybe he plans just a little too elaborate-like.*

Reaching the creek, he turned up it without hesitation. If Barnett's only purpose were to circle and head south, he might as well have gone downstream as up. But that Bronson alias left little doubt in Sam's mind. Peggy Bronson's place was upstream.

It took him the better part of an hour to get there. He approached the weathered buildings circuitously, keeping the barn between himself and the house. He dismounted beside the neglected bunkhouse. There was one horse in the pasture, he noticed, a heavy harness animal. This morning there had been two.

Peggy Bronson's washing hung dry on the clothesline. He used it for cover till he was almost to the house. He listened warily at the door, then pushed it open and stepped into the kitchen. A sound like a muffled sob came from another part of the house. Colt in hand, he moved toward it.

He found Peggy in the bedroom, bound and gagged and nearly out of her mind with pain. The mattress had been dumped off the bed and her wrists and ankles bound to the springs with wet rawhide. The thongs had already dried enough so that circulation was pretty well cut off. Her hands and feet were milky white. She jabbered half-coherently as Sam cut her loose.

"Will. Took Bobby. Said I was a cinch to lose my hands and feet. Laughed about it while he was tying me. Said how could I be a good mother to Bobby without hands or feet?"

"Hell of a thing," Sam said. "But you'll be all right. Lucky I came by."

"Yes," she said gravely. "But Bobby's gone."

"I mean to bring him back to you," Sam said, a little surprised at his own confidence. "Why does Will Barnett hate you so much?"

"I married him nine years ago. He used to beat me, and Bobby, too. Once he started for Bobby with an ax handle. I put a bullet into him. When I saw he wasn't going to die, I went to the law and told his real name. He was sentenced to Deer Lodge for life. Couple months ago he broke out. He wrote me he was coming for Bobby."

"You should have told the sheriff."

"Art Harkie? What protection could he give me? No, I meant to kill Will, to finish it once and for all. I would have done it, too, but he grabbed Bobby and I didn't dare shoot."

Sam helped her to her feet. She limped to a chair and sank into it, rubbing her hands. Sam knelt and rubbed her bare feet and ankles.

"Any idea which way he went?" Sam asked.

Peggy shook her head. "Don't go after him alone. He'll ambush you."

"I don't know. He's used to dodging posses. Alone, I just might be able to get close."

"He's cunning," Peggy said. "And he's a madman. He'll kill Bobby to save his own life, Mr. Riley."

"I'll be careful," Sam said. "Soon as you feel up to it, hitch up your wagon and start for town. The sheriff won't be there, so go to Lee Freemont at the store. Tell him to ring the fire bell and send some good men after me. I'll try to leave a clear trail."

On his way through the kitchen, Sam opened the bread box and helped himself to a handful of cold biscuits, which he wrapped in a bandanna. As he began a circle of the buldings, Peggy limped out of the house to the pasture gate. He paused to see if she was going to need help in catching the horse, but the animal was sugar-trained and trotted up to her. She didn't fool with any buggy; she swung herself up on the animal's back and headed for town—bareback and with only a hackamore.

Sam cut Barnett's sign without trouble. His tracks were joined now by another set—those of the horse missing from the pasture. Bobby would be riding him. Barnett would be slowed down some, Sam figured.

The trail led straight south. Just at sunset, it ended at a shallow stream. After a few minutes search, Sam discovered shoemarks on a sand bar. They pointed upstream. But he knew his man now and he judged this an attempt to mislead. He reined downstream and eventually found the trail on the far bank.

With twilight thickening fast, he reached a hilltop sparsely bearded with pine. Below him lay a deep gulch, maybe a mile long. A line of thick brush indicated a creek at its bottom. On the far slope, two horses were picketed.

Sam ate two of Peggy's biscuits and washed them down with a long drink from his canteen. When it was good and dark, he slid his Winchester from its boot and began the descent on foot. After a few yards, he stopped to study a rosy flicker up the gulch to his left. Will Barnett felt completely safe, it looked like. He had built a fire.

The bottom of the gulch was a jungle of brush and boulders and confusing shadows. It was impossible to move silently, and Sam trusted to the chatter of the creek to cover the small sounds he made. It had been a dry spring, and the creek filled only a small channel in a wide bed that lay between ten-foot banks. Barnett had built his fire in the shelter of the near bank.

A few yards below the blaze, Sam went down on hands and knees, hoping that the altitude was too high for rattlers. Creeping close to a clump of brush at the edge of the bank, he peered over. There was nobody near the fire, no gear scattered around. The blaze was a decoy, another of Will Barnett's tricks.

Sam rose to his knees, knowing he had discovered the trap too late. It had already closed on him. He felt scared and sick even before the harsh voice cut the night.

"Don't move."

He froze. The man behind him chuckled.

"Lay your rifle on the ground. One-handed now. . . . Now raise up your hands and stand up."

Sam obeyed, turning slowly as he stood. He squinted into the darkness at a big man five yards away. A rifle glistened darkly in the man's hands.

"I spotted you ridin' up that last slope," Will Barnett said. "I was up in the pine. You're the deputy spoke to me in town, ain't you?"

"I am," Sam said, wondering how many seconds he had to live. He was trapped on the brink of the bank, silhouetted against the glow of the fire a few yards up the creek bed.

"How come you're alone, Deputy?"

"Where's Bobby?" Sam demanded.

"My boy? What's that to you?"

"What do you want with him, Barnett?"

"I'll teach him things a man ought to know. To take care of himself, to live like an Injun." Barnett chuckled again. "I'll teach him to shoot deputies on sight. Now answer my question. How come you're alone?"

"You fooled the rest. They went north. I reckon they're over the pass by now."

"You was the smart one, is that it? The smart one and the one who is going to die."

"You made one mistake," Sam said. He inched backward toward the edge of the bank as he spoke. He couldn't have got away with it in daylight. But the darkness, the brush and the fact that he was a flat silhouette against the firelight made the slight motion unnoticeable. Sam kept talking. "You got that loose shoe fixed in town. That gave me the answer. And another thing—"

Sam took a long step backward and went over the brink—a split second before the rifle barked. He hit the rocky creek bed painfully, rolled, whipped his Colt from its holster. Barnett loomed above him, aiming the rifle, looking about twenty feet tall in the soft firelight.

Sam fired and kept firing, holding the trigger back and slipping the hammer with his flattened left hand. He barely managed to roll out of the way as Barnett pitched over the bank. Sam rolled him over on his back. Barnett gave him one last astonished, suffocating look and died.

Sam walked toward the place where he had seen the horses. He stopped every few yards to call Bobby's name and listen. At last he heard a thrashing sound and found the boy in a clump of brush, bound hand and foot and gagged with a bandanna.

"Your father's dead," Sam said as he untied him.

Bobby nodded somberly. "He was sick in his mind. Mom explained that to me."

"I killed him, son. I hope you won't tally that against me."

"I heard the shooting," Bobby said. "I hoped he was the one that got killed. Is Mom all right?"

They cooked food they found in Barnett's pack and ate and slept and started back at the first stab of dawn. An hour later they met the men Peggy had sent from town, hunting the trail they had lost in darkness the night before. The whole party reached the Bronson ranch before mid-morning.

There were four horses in the yard. As Sam and the others dismounted, Art Harkie appeared in the doorway of the house. He called something over his shoulder and strode out to meet them. Others streamed out of the house behind him—the other possemen and Peggy.

Art plainly had been riding all night. His face was grimy and haggard. His bloodshot eyes took in Will Barnett's body, Bobby, the black satchel tied to Sam's saddle. Sam got the satchel and handed it to him, tersely giving an account of what had happened. Then, while all eyes were on him, he couldn't resist a vindictive gesture. He unpinned his badge and extended it.

"I promised you this," he said.

Art shook his head. He spoke very solemnly. "You said you were going to jam it down my throat. I guess you could do it, too. I was a pighead, Sam, and I apologize. Now put that thing back on."

Sam saw what the words cost him and felt a glow of respect for him. He returned the badge to his shirt. One of the possemen clapped him on the shoulder.

"You crazy, Sheriff?" the posseman said. "Sam should stick to a deputy's pay with the reward money he's got comin'? There's a thousand ridin' on Barnett, way I heard it."

"Wouldn't surprise me the express company adds a mite to that," Art said.

Peggy Bronson was on her knees, alternately hugging Bobby and holding him off at arm's length to look at him. She rose now, giving the body of Will Barnett a look and a frown that quickly faded. She met Sam's eyes and came to him, soberly, then smiling. It was the first time he had seen her smile, even slightly, and there was a whole new meaning to the world.

"Thank you, Sam Riley," she said.

Just that—no gush or fancy phrases. Just that and the smile.

Sam couldn't find the words to say what he wanted. His head was in a whirl. He looked beyond her at the run-down ranch buildings, the verdant crease of the creek at the foot of the slope, the good yellow grass of the surrounding hills. Never was there a land to claim a man's heart as this Montana claimed it—never in twenty years of drifting through cow country from Texas to eastern Washington.

The others were swinging into their saddles. Sam turned toward his own horse. Peggy's fingers found his arm.

"Stay and have some breakfast, Sam Riley. You've been riding a long time."

He met the blue eyes again. There was just a trace of sassiness in them now.

"Yes ma'am," he said. "I have. A long, long time."

Smart

by *Wayne D. Overholser*

Wayne Overholser needs no introduction to Western buffs. One of the founding fathers of WWA, he has twice served as Director, has sired a whole herd of tophand books, and two years in succession, 1953 and 1954, won the coveted Spur for Best Western Novel.

☙ ☙ ☙

WE CAME DOWN OFF Big Mesa early Monday morning, Barney Nolan, Babe Dode, and I—Jimmy Ryan. Our object—to rob the bank at Three Forks.

Barney was the leader, so he rode in front where the leader should. Babe was in the middle, I brought up the tail. I couldn't help looking at Barney's back; he was the kind you just naturally looked at. I guess he'd have been a leader no matter where he was or what he was doing. He was big and tough and mean, and he was smart—real smart, the way he looked ahead and planned everything out and all that.

He rode his saddle as if he were made for it. He had a .30-.30 in the boot and he packed two guns on his hips. I'd heard of men who carried two guns, but he was the only one I had ever seen who actually did it. Any way you looked at him, he was quite a man, Barney was.

Babe was different. He was just a big, fat nothing. The only thing he was good for was to do what Barney told him and I'll admit he was good for that. He never questioned an order. If Barney had told him to go stand on his head in the marshal's parlor at midnight, Friday the thirteenth, Babe would have done it. But Barney wouldn't have given a foolish order like that. Like I said, he was smart. That was the whole thing about Barney. I guess he was about the smartest gent I ever ran into.

The plan was to hit Three Forks just at noon when the marshal always stepped into Dolan's Bar for a drink before he went home to dinner. Barney picked Monday to do the job because Monday was usually a quiet day, the chances being good that we wouldn't run into cowhands from the ranches that were strung up and down Three Forks Valley.

Barney had stayed in town most of the weeks we'd been holed up in that cave on Big Mesa. That is, Babe and I holed up while Barney had himself a time. It didn't bother Babe, being Barney's Number One yes man the way he was, but it bothered the hell out of me, especially since I was the leading candidate for getting my hide perforated with lead.

At twenty minutes to twelve, we pulled up at the edge of town and stepped down. We watered our horses and Barney took a good, long look at his gun. I didn't know why because the only one likely to be using a gun was me, good old Jimmy Ryan, nineteen my last birthday, and too young to die. In my opinion, that is—not Barney's. Somewhere along the line I got the notion that the only reason he had picked me up when they rode through Meeker was to have a man handy to throw to the wolves.

Barney got back on his horse and had Babe check his watch to be sure they were together. Then he asked, "You're sure you know what to do?"

"Sure," Babe said. "We wait fifteen minutes. If you ain't showed up by then, we'll know there ain't no cowhands around and we'll come on in. Jimmy stops at Dolan's Bar and I go on to the bank where you'll be."

"That's it," Barney said.

He'd have ridden off then if I hadn't said, "Barney."

He looked down at me, kind of as if he figured I was a fool to have got into this deal in the first place and a bigger one for staying. I was and knew it, but I'd give my word and wasn't about to crawl out now and let Barney think I was yellow.

"Well?" Barney asked.

He looked exactly the way I had always pictured Blackbeard the Pirate, face covered by a heavy black beard like it was. He wore a flat-topped black Stetson that he kept pulled down. His brown eyes were squinted half shut because the sunlight was sharp. He gave his hat a yank to settle it tighter. I could see he was impatient, but he needed me and he wasn't giving me any excuse to get off the hook.

"Suppose I get into trouble when I jump the marshal?" I asked. "Just supposing?"

"I've told you a dozen times and now I'll tell you for the last time," Barney said. "You won't get into no trouble. None of us will have trouble unless there's some cowboys on hand. If there is, we ride out, quick and peaceful. This thing will go slicker'n goose grease 'cause there ain't a fighting man in this burg—and that's counting the marshal."

He rode off, fast because I'd used up a couple of minutes when he should have been riding. I sat down and put my back against a cottonwood and rolled a smoke. He hadn't answered my question.

That's another way he was smart. He never had answered the question. That was why I asked it the thirteenth time. If I got into trouble, Barney and Babe wouldn't be coming back for me. That was plain. But I still wasn't backing out. If I got into trouble, I'd handle it.

I suppose any smart man looks ahead. Same with a woman, I expect. It sure was the trouble with Annie Peck. She'd been way too good at looking ahead. That was how I got hooked up with Barney Logan and Babe Dode.

I'd been going with Annie for a couple of years, figuring on marrying her all that time. I thought she'd been figuring the same with me. We had an understanding that seemed plain enough. I had a steady job riding for the Box A and I'd been saving all I could so we'd start married life with a little spread of our own. I had about two hundred dollars in the bank, and I'd done without a lot of things to put it there. But it wasn't enough to suit Annie. The night before I left Meeker she told me she wouldn't marry a man who hadn't at least one thousand dollars. Then she gave me my walking papers.

"Two hundred dollars in two years," she said scornfully as if it were two cents. "Jimmy Ryan, if you think I'm going to wait ten years for you, you're crazier than I thought."

"I figured we were in love," I said. "I thought . . ."

"Then you can just quit thinking!" she snapped. "Takes more than love to live on if you're married to a cowboy making thirty bucks a month."

I couldn't see anything to do but walk out, which was what I did.

A new man had come from Denver to work in the bank and he'd been shining up to Annie. It didn't take any brains to figure out she didn't want to discourage him by having me clutter up her parlor when he came calling. So I guess Annie was smart the same way Barney Logan was. In looking ahead, I mean.

I finished my cigarette and tossed the stub into the creek. Babe Dode looked at his watch. "He ain't showed," Babe said, "so I guess it's time to ride."

I got into the saddle and we moseyed down the road that became Three Forks' Main Street, just taking it easy so we wouldn't attract any attention, but I sure didn't have my mind on my business. Thinking of Annie, I couldn't think about anything else. She was little and cute—a decided blonde, and the way she kissed made a feller think tomorrow was Fourth of July with fireworks and everything.

After she tied the can to my tail I swore I'd dig up the thousand dollars she claimed a man had to have to marry her. I was just about drunk enough to tackle a bank myself when Barney and

Babe showed up, riding south from Wyoming. They bent an ear to my troubles, agreed about women and said I was a chowder-headed chump to stick around Meeker with Annie sticking her nose in the air every time she walked past me.

"Better ride along with us," Barney said. "There's plenty of big deals that three men can handle but two can't."

This was the big deal he had in mind, I guess. I was to jump the marshal and work him into a fight. Call him a few names— anything to attract a crowd while Barney and Babe knocked the bank over.

Barney hadn't seen me pull a gun, but it was plain enough he didn't care whether I was fast or not. It amounted to the same thing whichever way it worked out. Any kind of excitement that would create a diversion was all Barney wanted.

Barney had been around town enough to size everything up. He said the marshal was a young buck not much older than I was. Had a wife and a baby, and the only reason he carried the star was because no one else wanted it, this being a gone-to-seed town not paying enough to keep a good man. According to Barney, the marshal was just a bluff, the kind who wore a great, sweeping mustache to make him look older and fiercer than he was.

"A gent of his caliber likes to play big," Barney said. "I know the kind. He struts around town wearing a shiny star. He's got a deep voice that sounds like God talking. Every noon he stops at Dolan's Bar, has one drink and talks a few minutes before he goes home. That's when you'll brace him."

By the time we got to Dolan's Bar, I pretty well had Annie out of my mind and this show-off marshal in. I stopped and got off my horse in the middle of the street while Babe Dode rode on toward the bank. Barney was already there, leaning against the wall with a cigar in his mouth.

I waited until I saw Babe step out of his saddle. I was looking up and down the street as if I was trying to see someone, which I was. The marshal must have got here ahead of me. I pulled my gun and banged away at the sign in front of the saloon, putting a hole right in the middle of the o in Dolan.

A man was going into the saloon when I fired. He fell flat on his belly in front of the batwings just as two men ran outside to see what the shooting was about. They walked right down his back. As soon as they got off him, he crawled inside. The two who had come out took a look at me as if they weren't sure whether they liked what they saw or not.

"Is the marshal inside?" I asked.

All the one guy could do was swallow. The other one wet his lips and finally managed to nod.

"Send him out," I ordered. "I got something to say to him, something that'll burn his ears all the way down to his heels."

Town men on the street began working toward me. They wanted to see what was going on but they didn't want to get close enough to have any part in the trouble. Barney was right about that bunch. Some came barging out of the saloon and walked away fast until they figured they were out of danger, then twisted around to watch. There wasn't a fighting man in the bunch.

I waited two, three minutes, standing so I could see the front of the bank. By that time a dozen or more jaspers were in the street watching me. I still had my gun in my hand. Waving it at the batwings I yelled, "Where'n hell is that marshal?"

He came out then, blinking as the sunlight hit him. He was exactly the way Barney had described him, a kid pretending he was plumb growed up. Takes more than a mustache, gun, star, wife and baby to make a real man. He stood there in front of the saloon looking at me and not knowing what to say or do. Anybody could see that he was having a hard time keeping his feet where they were.

"You wanted to see me?"

All I wanted was to use up time. If I pushed him too hard, he might go for his gun. Then I'd have to kill him and I didn't want that. I said, "Yeah, I wanted to see you. Look up there at that sign. I put that hole there. What are you going to do about it?"

The marshal stepped off a piece and squinted up at the sign. Then he looked at me, grinning as if he thought it was a kid antic. He said, "Well, that's fair shooting, sonny, but what makes you think I'm going to do anything about it?"

Calling me sonny made me sore. "Your job, ain't it?" I said, throwing the words at him fast.

He shook his head. "You're a drifter, I figure. Keep on drifting and we'll all be happy."

I said, "You're just a wet-nosed kid packin' a piece of tin. I don't like star packers. I don't like you in particular."

"I'm sorry about that," the marshal said. "I was in hopes you'd like me."

Somebody snickered. I turned part way around and threw a shot that kicked up some dust in front of the gent who had done the snickering. "This kid with the tin star ain't funny," I said. "Now if you think he is, start laughing, big and loud."

The fellow was wearing a green eyeshade and cut-off black stockings up to his elbows. His face turned almost as green as his eyeshade. He backed up some, spluttering, "I didn't think he was funny. He's not a bit funny."

I turned back to the marshal. He didn't look half as scared as I had been thinking. He didn't look scared at all. I waved my gun some more, feeling like a fool, and said, "Go roll your hoop."

I had been figuring on holstering my gun and inviting him to make his play, but that didn't look so good to me now. Barney had this huckleberry sized up wrong. He'd go for his gun if he had a fair chance, and one of us would be toted off on a shutter, which was exactly what Barney wanted.

So I made a spiel about lawmen being crawling things which ought to stay under rocks instead of getting out into the sunlight and I kept waving my gun. Then Barney and Babe come out of the bank, Barney carrying a gunny sack that looked pretty heavy. They mounted and rode out of town, so slick nobody but me even noticed.

It was time for me to do likewise. A man can sit on a deal like this about so long, and then some fool is bound to get himself killed. I stepped into the saddle, still hanging onto my gun.

"I'll be sloping along, Marshal," I told him. "Just wanted to see if you had any guts and it looks like you have."

I cracked steel to my horse and took off at a run, not holstering my gun until I was past the last house. I looked around once and saw the whole bunch, including the marshal, standing in the street staring after me like I was loco.

I got to where we'd left the fresh horses ahead of Barney and Babe. They had farther to go than I had, having to cross the creek and circle back on the other side. I changed my saddle to my sorrel, the horse I'd ridden out of Meeker, and waited.

After a while they rode in, their horses all lathered up and mighty near dead. "Why didn't you plug that marshal?" Barney yelled as they swung down.

"Didn't need to," I yelled back. "Kept him busy, didn't I? You didn't have no trouble getting out of town."

Barney changed the saddle, so mad he was red clean around on the back of his neck. "You should have killed him. He got a posse together and he's on our tail. Better run those crowbaits across the creek."

Maybe he was sore because I was still alive, three-way split instead of a two-way. But I was sore, too. I'd done all I was supposed to and there was no sense getting his tail up. I hadn't heard any horses. I had a hunch he was lying about a posse being after us. But I ran the three horses we'd been riding across the creek and up the bank the way Barney had said, then I followed him and Babe, keeping in the water the way we had agreed.

Any posse on our tail would probably lose some time following the tracks of the horses we'd run across the creek, then they'd have to come back and work up and down it until they found where we came out. That would take time. Meanwhile we'd be back on Big Mesa holed up in the cave. Or maybe keep on going if it got dark enough. I wasn't sure how we'd play it.

Funny thing, now that I thought about it. Barney hadn't ever said what we were going to do after we got the dinero. I grabbed onto the same notion I'd had before, only this time it was more than a notion. Barney'd figured I'd be kicking my life out on Three Forks' Main Street. Now they had me on their hands.

By the time we got to the cave, I knew what I was going to do. I said, "Divvy up. I'm riding one way and you can take another. I don't want to see either one of you again."

"Suits me," Barney said.

He glanced over at Babe and I could see they figured I was dead sure enough. When we went into the cave, Barney said: "Take all you want of the grub, Jimmy. I'll split the dinero and we'll ride. We ain't got much time."

If I had gone on past Barney to the pile of grub like they figured me to, I'd have been plugged in the back. I took three steps, then turned fast, pulling my gun as I came around. Caught him right in the act. He was looking at me, gun half out of leather.

If I'd waited another second, he'd have got me cold turkey. Way it was, I got him. He tried to hurry his draw when I started to turn, but I was too fast, nailing him in the mouth, the slug angling up into his brain. He never got off a shot. Neither did Babe Dode who made a try for me when he saw what had happened, but he was way too slow. He caught two slugs in the brisket, and that tied everything up neat and pretty.

I picked up the gunny sack and looked inside. Some loose greenbacks, gold, and silver, and half a dozen buckskin sacks that were filled and heavy enough to contain lead. I tied the gunny sack and started toward my horse, thinking I'd high-tail off the mesa and keep on going. Wasn't even going to be a two split now. It was all mine.

It hit me just as I was tying the sack behind the cantle. There was Barney Nolan, smart as all hell, figuring things out so careful like, a piece of dead meat. That was where being smart had got him.

If he hadn't been so smart, picking me up in Meeker and tolling me into Three Forks to get killed, he wouldn't be where he was right now. What kind of a sucker would *I* be, taking off on the owl-hoot! I wasn't in trouble yet, but I sure would be if I took this bank money.

I headed back to town. When I got to the place where we'd changed horses I found the posse, six men including the marshal. They was floundering around, not knowing up from down, going round in circles.

I had my gun in one hand and the gunny sack in the other. I said, "The gents you want are back there in a cave." I jerked my thumb in the general direction. "Except I've got what you're huntin' right here. Leastwise I found it on them."

The marshal looked me over kind of puzzled. "That looks like the stuff we lost from the bank."

"I figured so," I said, "them bags being marked." I knew I couldn't let on to knowing anything about the robbery. I said, "I was camped in this cave when two gents rode up. Guess they figured I'd blab. Anyhow they tried to kill me." I waggled the gunny sack in front of the marshal. "How much reward is there for bringing them in?"

"About five hundred," the marshal said. "Hand it over."

"Look—" I said. "I could have gone over the hill with it but I didn't. Now I sure don't aim to lose the reward."

"All right," he said. "I'll ride into town with you. The rest of you boys go look in that cave. Fetch me back whatever you find."

He nodded at me. "Put your iron up. We'll get along fine if you keep a civil tongue in your head. When we get to town, you can turn the dinero in and pick up the reward. Fortunately them fellers in the bank were knocked out. There's no killing to answer for."

We started back down the creek. I put my gun in the holster and took a good look at this kid with the star. "Wouldn't have bothered me none if there had been a killing," I said.

He grinned under that big, sweeping mustache of his. "Think not?" he said. "After that hoorawing you gave me in town?"

He had it figured out, I guessed. I was kind of uneasy even though I knew he couldn't prove anything.

"From the description the bank fellows gave me," this tinbadge went on, "the two robbers are worth two-fifty apiece. I'm guessing the big one to be Barney Nolan. Other's probably Babe Dode. He used to ride with Nolan. Nolan's been hanging around some. I been watching him, but I sure wasn't watching him at the right time." He looked me over. "You made yourself a quick thousand bucks. I'm gonna let you collect it and git outa town. I got nothing against you except them names, but I'll tell you one thing: Keep your nose clean from now on."

"I aim to," I said. "What's your handle, Marshal?"

He said with a chuckle, "Brazos Sam Jones."

I'd have flopped right out of my saddle if I hadn't grabbed onto the horn. No wonder Barney didn't expect me to show up alive. Brazos Sam Jones was just about the best marshal in Colorado. The main thing was he had the fastest draw in the country. If it had come to a showdown between him and me I'd be as dead as Barney Nolan and Babe Dode.

I had to stay in Three Forks a while to get my money. I didn't get over the shakes all the time I was there. I rode back to Meeker with the thousand dollars in my pocket and bought that spread up on White River that I wanted. It wasn't a big outfit and I was into it up to my ears, but I figured with any luck I'd make out.

Somewhere along the line that day I heard that the bank fellow who had been shining up to Annie Peck had quit town. Seemed a wife and three kids had showed. After making eyes the way he had at Annie, I guess he figured he'd better light a shuck out of there.

News gets around pretty fast in a town like Meeker. Annie must have heard about me buying the ranch. When I came out of the courthouse, the deal all wrapped up, she was waiting.

She hugged and kissed me without me doing a thing but just standing there. I didn't even put my arms around her. Kind of funny the way it was. That hugging and kissing wasn't like it used to be. The earth didn't shake. I didn't hear any bells ringing. I didn't even see any fireworks.

All I could think was that here was a woman smart as Barney Nolan, looking ahead, figuring everything out. Smart. Both of them. Well, I walked right past her and got on my horse and rode up the river. I aimed to spend the night on my new ranch. It was a right-down good feeling to be a land owner—even if I wasn't smart.

A Pinch of Dust

by S. E. Whitman

This previously unpublished story is Whitman's first appearance in a WWA anthology. Most of six-foot Sid's writings have had a cavalry background. His father commanded such troops in many places and Sid's own younger days were spent on and around the posts. A bear for research, he is author of half a dozen novels and not a few short stories. He resides at Walpole, Massachusetts.

❧ ❧ ❧

THE BONE-BREAKING ROAD FROM Salt Lake City made a final swing and without warning became the main street of the booming Montana gold camp. From the box of the lead wagon long-jawed Ethan Lowe pointed and said, "There she is, Miss Jennie, Miller's Gulch, the home of four thousand gold-crazed gophers."

He watched her dismayed glances with quiet amusement as the heavily laden wagons lurched along the pitted street, a street which also seemed to serve as community garbage heap and dump. It did not bother Ethan, he was happy to have made it in before impending winter sealed the pass. As for the mess in the street, snow would soon cover it and kill the stink.

But it bothered Jennie Orren. She was appalled at the astonishing collection of disreputable cabins, cockeyed tents, brush wickiups and the few bare buildings of whipsawn lumber. Everywhere there were horses, wagons, and miners; especially miners—rough men plastered with mud and running to wild, shaggy whiskers. The Gulch was noisy, dirty, smelly and, compared to her own trim village of Hampton Falls, Vermont, a municipal nightmare.

"Good Lord, Ethan," she exclaimed, "it's a junk heap—how can people live in such a place!"

"Gold," Ethan answered. "Life here is just a tight circle—dig, drink and fight; fight, drink and dig."

Jennie felt suddenly the first premonition of disaster. She looked around her. She sought to reassure herself by thinking of the things that rode behind her in the wagon. The big cherrywood bed and dresser, the table and chairs. Also the fat roll of new Brussels carpet, the trunk of new clothes. Somehow they failed, and she hurriedly brought up the mental picture of Ira Payne, the boy from back home who, somewhere in this bawdy, dirty place, was waiting to marry her.

She turned to the big, friendly freighter. "Do I look all right?"

He gravely inspected the scant five feet of her, no longer in traveling clothes, but filling a stylish, plum-colored jacket and skirt set off by a ruffled white blouse and tricky little hat. With some regret for his past youth he grew keenly aware of the small piquant face under dark hair; a face notable for very direct gray eyes and a snub nose across which lay a light band of freckles—freckles which diverted attention from a very firm chin.

"You'll paralyse the town," he grinned.

"I do want to hold my own with the other ladies."

Ethan said, "Hah!," and spat between the two sweating wheelers. "Miss Jennie there's mebbe thirty respectable women here—and a hull sight more who ain't."

She glanced along the street. "I don't see any."

"Them that's respectable is home, workin'; them that ain't . . . wal, you can tell 'em by the feathers when you see 'em."

Jennie said, "Oh," and involuntarily touched her little hat with its two small and perky feathers. Ethan chuckled. "Not them kind of feathers—big frilly ones." He called greetings to a couple of friends, then asked, "Where was you to meet your feller?"

Jennie's chin firmed primly. "The place he mentioned in his letter was the Whoop Up saloon. It surely doesn't sound like much of an address."

"Shucks, that's Dean Ringer's gilded slaughterhouse of local morality but, being right in th' center of things, it's something like your town hall back home."

"I doubt that," she told him firmly.

They drew up before a long planked structure which gave out a profane uproar above the tinkly background of hurdy-gurdy music. The boardwalk was cluttered with whiskery men, well smeared with the chocolate-colored mud of the district.

"See your feller?" asked Ethan.

"Perhaps he doesn't know we're here."

"The hull town knows. Them riders who camped with us a couple days back took the word."

Ethan was right, for a great slump-shouldered man with blazing eyes and the whiskers of a Russian grand duke stepped to the front wheel and peered up at her.

"Be you Miss Jennie Orren?"

Hesitating a moment she bobbed her head and said, "Yes."

He jerked off his dirty hat, bowed, then replaced it. "I'm Holy George Van Gaskin, ma'am, a firm believer in the Lord, also a carpenter. I bring a message."

Jennie said, "Thank you," and waited while Holy George clawed through his disreputable clothing until he found an envelope. It was well marked with smudgy fingerprints and garnished with a dash of tobacco juice.

"A message, ma'am, to which I add—only God is love."

The words seemed to sap his strength and he staggered back into the saloon like a man sighting an oasis. Jennie glanced at the envelope. "It's Ira's writing," she said eagerly, tearing it open. A moment later she leaned forward, arms on her knees, conscious of the horde of men staring like calves in a stock pen. Ethan turned his head and asked, "Gone?"

"Yes."

"Gold, mebbe?"

"Yes. He doesn't have enough to make marriage possible and he's gone to the Sawtooth Mountains. He's been generous, though, left me a cabin on what he calls a 'played-out' claim."

Ethan rubbed his long jaw. "Don't hardly seem th' right way to act for a man who's asked his intended to come way out here."

There was no reply and for a moment he studied the distrait girl beside him.

"He did ask you, didn't he?"

"No," Jennie admitted reluctantly, "I told him I was coming."

It brought back to her that evening two years earlier when Ira had announced he was giving up the plow handles on a rocky Vermont farm and heading West. She had neither argued nor wept on his string tie. Instead, being Jennie with a mind of her own, she had run a quick inventory of the eligible males of Hampton Falls, found them wanting and, walking with him as he was about to leave, placed her straight back against the door and said, "I think you have something to say to me, Ira."

The surprised Ira, who had been by no means that certain, finally said it and, under her guidance, repeated it to her parents. Thus she had fixed that and now, arriving in Miller's Gulch, found she had fixed something else—herself.

Ethan Lowe did not pry, he simply got the big wagon rolling and remarked, "Gold purely makes some people notional."

Sitting beside him, dry-eyed and erect, Jennie pulled up her chin. "It won't do that to me."

It was not only a good cabin, it was a superior cabin, the sort of thing a Vermonter would build. Two rooms, well chinked, with a plank floor, a fireplace at one end and, rarest of all, a cookstove. Ethan brought in and placed her furniture, finally unrolling part of the Brussels carpet and running it from the cherrywood bed out into the living-room. He would not walk on it, only stood gazing at its pattern of red and blue flowers set in circles against a tawny background.

"Th' first danged carpet in this here part of Montana, Miss Jennie. It and your toney furniture makes you th' finest lady in th' Gulch."

She looked at him unhappily. "You mean the finest jilted lady."

Ethan picked up his hat. "I'll just mosey down to Garsey's store and tote you back some grub."

To the growing conviction that she had placed herself in an impossible situation was added the sight of her sole remaining resources; eight ten-dollar bills. She shook her head and folded them away. Ethan returned, put down his load and gave her a slow smile. "Along with th' grub, Miss Jennie, I brung a list of twenty-seven men wanting to be introduced—object matrimony."

Jennie stared aghast. "You mean this whole place knows I've been jilted?"

"They knowed it before you arrived."

"How will I ever be able to show myself?"

"Shucks, Miss Jennie, you've already showed yourself—that's why these here fellers are in such a rush to get introduced. A girl what's spoke for is one thing but a unattached girl is better'n a rich strike."

In some desperation she picked up the list of names and read them with a growing look of dismay. "Oh, no!" she exclaimed in a stricken voice, "Shacknasty Bill Blivens, Peanut Johnny Green, Sweet Oil Bob Kemp, Nosey Ford Getty!"

Ethan dismissed them with the flip of one hand. "Them's th' willow-wickiup boys. You can do better."

Jennie passed a hand over her face, her expression one of sudden worry. "If things are like this, how can I ever be safe here?"

"Why, when you walk out, you'll see nothin' but doffed hats and hopeful smiles," the freighter assured her, "th' boys are strong for the social amen-tities."

The depths of the cherrywood bed brought Jennie scant comfort that night. Paying Ethan for a week's groceries had taken more than half her greenbacks. The prices were shocking and, upon questioning him, she had learned, "This here's gold country—Lincoln-skins are at consider'ble discount."

It meant that she had but one more week to find some sort of work, or face the unpalatable prospect of marrying some mud-daubed miner with a name like Shacknasty Bill. It began to appear that the business of becoming a lady in Montana Territory would take some doing. Outside, a quartet of boozy miners dawdled past her cabin singing "Lorena," only to have the ravaged song abruptly change to a loud splash and laughing curses as one of the group fell into the creek. She turned over and wept in frightened loneliness.

In the morning Jennie nerved herself to the ordeal of running the gantlet of public curiosity and set off into town to make her entry as the community's jilted bride. The perky hat topped her dark hair and a wrist-loop kept the hem of her skirt clear of dust. Nothing could prevent the chocolaty stuff from dulling her shoes, though.

She soon had other things to think about, and found herself busy returning the briefest of nods to the never ending procession of grimy men who snatched off hats in passing. She also had her first glimpse of the "feathers," discovering a pair of the "girls" approaching. One was a chubby brunette, the other a slender redhead. They met Jennie's estimating glance with compound interest. Jennie had the unpleasant feeling they were sizing her up as possible future competition and she did not like it.

As she passed the Whoop Up saloon Holy George Van Gaskin pushed himself free of the wall and swept off his hat. "Good morning, Miss Orren, the Lord delivereth—have faith in the Lord."

He clawed at his whiskers as Jennie nodded and hurried her step, more than a little fearful of just what the Lord might deliver in a place like Miller's Gulch. She entered the several stores to make skimpy purchases while estimating the possibilities of securing future work. She listened to and carefully observed the ebb and flow of local business, astonished at the utterly fantastic prices. Forty-five dollars for a pick or shovel; forty dollars for a pair of gum boots and sixty for a sack of flour. From open pokes, merchants would take a casual pinch of dust for a half-dozen dried-up cigars, and two or three pinches for other items. She watched the larger sales where dust was weighed up in jeweler's scales, and always where the sun's rays hit, flecks of scattered gold dust glinted from counters and floors. The careless scattering of the precious metal reminded her bitterly that the Gulch was immensely rich and everyone but she had wealth to fling away. On the return walk to her cabin she became aware, for the first time, that the presence of so much gold was doing something that was not quite comfortable to her.

As she approached her cabin she came upon a group of excited men standing around someone on the ground and one of them, seeing her, exclaimed, "Here's a lady—mebbe she kin help." The circle opened and Jennie found herself staring down at one of the "feathers"; the redheaded one she had seen earlier. Beside her knelt her companion looking like a startled heifer.

"What's the matter?" Jennie asked of a huge red-shirted miner.

"One of Madam Dooley's girls," the man replied in some embarrassment, "wid her leg broke." He jabbed a blunt finger at a cowhand holding a horse by one rein. "This cow-chaser run her down."

The cowboy was indignant. "I wouldn't do no woman a meanness. My horse just never seen the likes of her—he cut up and that'un got kicked."

"Th' thing is, Miss," explained the big miner, "we was debatin' what to do wid Callie, here. Th' Gym don't seem much of a place for a girl wid a broken leg."

Jennie did not smile. Even in one day she had heard of that local institution known as Madam Dooley's Gymnasium and Recreation Emporium and it was not a subject over which a lady could reveal amusement. It was her effort to avoid a touchy subject that unexpectedly caused her to make the obvious, if not the wisest, decision.

"Take her to my cabin." She pointed out the place.

In the abrupt silence that followed the big miner strode to the nearest shack, tore off the door and brought it back. "Now, here's a real lady. Jest heave Callie up and put her on this."

The injured girl possessed a cold courage. With the rough handling she was in torturing pain but only her wet eyes revealed it. The willing miners muscled the door and its burden into Jennie's cabin and slid Callie into the depths of the cherrywood bed, then stood around staring like lost sheep until the big man pushed them outdoors with orders to fetch a bottle of whisky—and the doctor. Only Jennie and the other "feather" were left by the bedside.

"What's her name?" Jennie asked.

"Callie Beeman," the chubby girl answered resentfully.

"And yours?"

"Rosy Lee Estill, if it's any of your put-in."

"I'm making it my put-in," Jennie told her bluntly. "Now just trot back to your Madam Dooley, tell her what's happened, and say that Callie's being cared for."

Satisfied that she made nearly two of little Jennie, Rosy Lee said, "Callie needs me—I'm staying."

Like a striking cat Jennie slapped her. "She needs a doctor—not you. Now, scat!"

The startled Rosy bolted, just missing collision with a man about to enter. He was a solid specimen, about thirty, with a square clean-shaven face and friendly eyes. He placed his hat and black bag on the table and said, "I'm Buford Cross, physician and surgeon to this motley municipality, Miss Orren."

"I'm glad you could come so promptly, Doctor." Jennie led the way into the bedroom. Dr. Cross looked down at the patient and smiled.

"Well, Callie, looks like you're starting a vacation."

The girl gave Jennie a glance of solid resentment. "Get me outta here, Doc."

Jennie turned and left the room but heard the doctor answer, "Nope."

The next half hour brought snatches of Dr. Cross's orders and comments embroidered by bursts of talented profanity from Callie. When he finally came out he placed the bottle of whisky on the table and said to Jennie, "Give her a stiff shot a bit later but don't let her get the rest of it all at one time."

"Anything else?"

"That's as may be." He studied her frankly. "Did you suggest bringing her here?"

"It's better than the, ah, Gym, isn't it?"

Buford Cross gave her a crooked but engaging grin. "Eminently, for her, but hardly for you. This generous gesture will finish you with the ladies of this grubby place, you should know that."

Jennie rubbed a cheek absently. "Callie stays."

He touched her arm with a friendly grip. "I like you, Miss Orren, even if you are a mite crazy. I'll see Callie tomorow."

Jennie cooked supper for the two of them, placed a board across Callie's lap for the dishes and rationed her half a glass of whisky. There was little wrong with the girl's appetite but she remained suspiciously uncommunicative. Jennie did not push her and, when she was ready for the night—herself as well, Callie finally demanded, "You gonna sleep here?"

"It's my bed. Where did you think I was going to sleep?"

With unexpected meekness Callie replied, "Sure, dearie."

The next day brought visitors. Toward noon there was a solid banging on the door and Jennie found herself confronted by a ponderous woman, black Irish, with a fine trimming of lip whiskers and a truculent air. "I'm Mrs. Dooley. Where's Callie?"

There being little else to say, Jennie replied, "Come in. I'm Jennie Orren."

Mrs. Dooley's jaw stood out. "I know ye are." She pulled a bottle of whisky from her bag, adding, "Callie needs her nip."

Jennie deftly hooked the bottle away. "She'll get it—from me— on doctor's orders." She pointed to the bedroom. "Callie's in there."

Obviously surprised at Jennie's firmness Mrs. Dooley entered, closing the door behind her, and remained for some time. When she emerged her truculence was gone.

"I've talked to Dr. Cross—and now, her. They seem to think you're all right. I'm surprised."

"So am I."

The Madam grunted. She looked Jennie up and down with hard eyes. A moment later she dug into her bag and tossed two fat rawhide pokes of gold dust on the table.

"For Callie's keep. You gonna tell me it's 'tainted' money?"

Jennie shook her head. "I couldn't afford to—I'm going to need it."

"Guessed at much," Mrs. Dooley sniffed. She went to the door, turning for a final word. "There'll be more where that come from."

With the slam of the door Jennie stood beside the table running a light finger over the shapes of the two pokes. A wry smile touched her lips. For a would-be lady in this new community she was making a real start being supported by the Gulch's leading Madam.

Another knock roused her from her reverie and she found Holy George Van Gaskin on the threshold.

"I bear a message for Callie," he announced.

Without thinking she indicated the bedroom and followed him as he walked in. He stood a moment pawing his whiskers and staring down at the girl somewhat severely. "The wages of sin," he pronounced harshly. "Thou shalt not commit—"

That was as far as he got before Callie grabbed up her whisky glass and hurled it at him. "Try committin' anything with a broken leg, you old booze-head! Now, get outta here!"

Holy George stalked out muttering Biblical imprecations and, with a touch of kindred feeling, Jennie reached down and touseled the girl's hair, then they both laughed. Callie pointed to some mud on the bright new carpet. "Lookit what that tin-horn saint done. It's a shame to have them dangfool men tromping over the likes of that."

"If they'd scatter gold dust around here," Jennie sighed, "like they do everywhere else, it might pay me to invite them."

From a wider experience Callie disagreed. "Wouldn't nothin' pay you to have 'em around."

But Jennie hardly heard her for suddenly she had uncovered a bright chain of thought. She sat on the edge of the bed and shook Callie's shoulder. "Look, there must be just thousands of dollars worth of gold dust scattered around this town by pure carelessness. I saw it in the stores, dust dribbled around like dirt."

Callie yawned. "Guess so—way they handle it in th' saloons you'd think it *was* dirt. Why fuss yourself about it?"

"How much is a pinch of dust worth?"

"Somethin' like two dollars."

"And it's taken in trade at sixteen dollars an ounce?"

"Yeah."

Jennie stared out the window towards the center of town. "Callie, what sort of men are the saloonkeepers?"

"Gawd, you wouldn't be fixin' to work for th' likes of them, would you?"

Jennie's eyes were suddenly bright. "No, no—just tell me about them; tell me about the saloons. There's a good chance, Callie, they might be working for me!"

When Buford Cross called to check on his patient he found Jennie deep in an experiment involving Mrs. Dooley's pokes of gold dust, a borrowed set of jeweler's scales and a piece of her new Brussels carpet. When the doctor had finished with Callie, Jennie hopefully explained her notion. His face reflected his astonishment as did hers when he patted her head and, picking up his hat, started for the door with a queer grin.

"You just set things up, Missey, while I drag Dean Ringer over here. The Whoop Up is the biggest place in town and if Dean doesn't love this I'll join the Chinks and take in washing!"

Dean Ringer turned out to be a quiet-spoken man in his forties with a hard chin and cold gray eyes. He expressed his pleasure at meeting Jennie, took a moment to say hello to Callie, then returned to study the cat-in-the-cream smile on Buford Cross's face.

"You turning tricky?" he asked.

"Hah, friend—just wait!"

Jennie seated the two men across the table from her, a table topped with the piece of her Brussels carpet on which sat the jeweler's scales and the two pokes of gold dust. To the saloon man she said,

"Consider this a section of your bar, Mr. Ringer, with you and the Doctor as bartenders and me as two customers. This is not a game. I expect to show you something which should benefit both of us."

She extended an open poke in each hand. "Start pinching dust from these just as it's done in your saloon and put it in the little boxes beside you. After twenty pinches, weigh out an ounce in the scales, then repeat until the pokes are empty."

The two men solemnly followed her instructions and, when the task was completed, Jennie leaned forward with her hands clasped. "Mr. Ringer, I weighed up those two pokes before you arrived. They held twenty-four ounces, or a total value of three hundred and eighty-four dollars. You have just accepted that dust over your bar. How much did you lose?"

Ringer looked puzzled. "Don't seem I lost anything. I got the gold, didn't I?"

"Let's see what you didn't get."

She turned over the piece of carpet and tapped it thoroughly. When she finished the table top was liberally sprinkled with gold dust. Brushing it up on a piece of paper she put it into one of the shallow pans of the scales and weighed it while Ringer watched.

"About an ounce," she announced, "do you agree?"

He sat back with an intent look. "I can think ahead. I'll save you some time. I employ twenty bartenders in two shifts and each man will take in about two pokes of dust—"

"Thank you, Mr. Ringer," she smiled. "Our experiment showed about an ounce of scattered dust. But let's be conservative. Would you accept the likelihood that each man mislays a half an ounce a day?"

"Seems low. I'll accept it."

"Very well. Let's say half an ounce a man, times twenty men, or ten ounces, which at the going rate means a hundred and sixty dollars a day. Isn't that quite a loss for any business?"

"No argument. I'll give you a thousand dollars for that carpet."

Jennie shook her head. "Mr. Ringer, you'll lease ten pieces of carpet at the rate of five dollars a day for each piece—payable weekly."

He gave her a cold smile. "No, Miss Orren. You've shown me a good trick and I'd like to see you get something for the idea but, if you won't sell, there's others will."

"Really?" she asked. "Who?"

Buford Cross burst out laughing and poked Ringer in the ribs. "She's got you caught in the door, Dean. Where are you going to get your carpet?"

Ringer's eyes narrowed. He said, "So that's the way it is, eh?"

"That's the way it is," Cross assured him. "This is the first carpet in town and nothing nearer than Salt Lake City. With the pass closed for the winter, that's five months away." He leaned back and gazed up at the roof beams. "Let's see—five months—a hundred and fifty days times a hundred and sixty dollars a day—"

Ringer growled, "Oh, Lord!" Then he rose and extending his hand to Jennie, said, "You have a deal, Miss Orren."

She looked up at him gravely. "I'm going after the other saloon men, Mr. Ringer."

"She sure will," Buford Cross remarked, his voice suggesting pride in Jennie.

"She should," Ringer agreed as he took his leave.

When they were alone Buford regarded Jennie with sly amusement. "All right, my prowling puma, or maybe its pumess, set 'em up again while I round up more of the ungodly."

She resented the allusion even from this friendly and, admittedly, increasingly interesting man. "And just what would *you* do?" she asked defiantly.

"Exactly the same. Get these fat cats over a barrel and whale the stuffing out of them."

Miller's Gulch richly supported twenty-two saloons whose proprietors soon richly supported Jennie. Buford made it his uninvited business to be present every Monday morning as the saloonkeepers arrived to settle, and watched as the mounting pokes of gold dust were later stacked under the cherrywood bed to the amount of some five thousand dollars a week.

In December he remarked, "This parade of the ungodly, bearing weekly tribute, isn't enhancing your standing as a lady."

"I've got to live," Jennie retorted with her old aggressiveness.

"My, yes, and I don't know a better prescription for your ailment."

In January, Callie returned to the Gym and Buford, on one collection day, peered solemnly under the cherrywood bed at the mass of gold pokes rising there.

"Are you beginning to bump on that stuff when you lie down?" he inquired. "As your doctor I wouldn't want anything to disturb your rest and peace of mind."

Jennie flushed. "What are you trying to do—make me feel like a robber?"

In February, and on the occasion of Buford's birthday, Jennie gave him a little party—just the two of them, with candles stuck in some of Dean Ringer's empty whisky bottles and snapping logs in the fireplace. She had seen to it that she looked her best. The cabin was cozy and inviting. But Buford again irked her by remarking,

"My, and she can cook, too."

"You've been utterly exasperating ever since I've known you!" she flared. "Just what do you expect of me, I'd like to know."

He dropped his taunting mien. "Isn't it rather, what do you expect of yourself?"

She stared back at him, suddenly unhappy. Only by a determined effort did she keep from bursting into tears.

By March, though snow still lay deep in the Gulch, it was plain it would not be there much longer. Soon Ethan Lowe would be lining out his freight teams for Salt Lake City. Jennie knew that her hour of decision had come and, regretfully, realized there was but one decision she could make. It was following another payday Monday that she told Dr. Cross:

"Buford, I'm going out when the road is open—back to Vermont."

He seemed to take the news calmly—much too calmly to suit her.

"Well," she continued with some defiance, "What else can I do? The ladies of this place will never accept me." And she quoted woman's most damning criticism, " 'You can be sure that Jennie Orren's no better than she should be.' "

"You mean," Buford said drily, "you're caught between the 'feathers' and the chicken pluckers."

She walked across the room, then returned to stare up at him angrily. "Sometimes I could shake you!"

He answered her quietly, the bantering gone. "You've had a chip on your shoulder since the day you arrived."

The words startled her but she was big enough to admit it. "I know, and it's not the way I want to live."

He put out a hand, briefly touching her cheek. "You're no longer the prowling pumess—you're a woman who wants to feel needed."

Instinctively she retreated. "What's wrong with that?"

"Nothing, Jennie, it's what I've been waiting for. The Gulch needs you. I need you."

It warmed her but, still cautious, she inquired, "How?"

"I've talked of it before, the mass of accidents, the sickness and the shootings. Jennie, I want you to put up the price of a small hospital."

Suddenly resentful, for that was not what she had wanted to hear, she flared at him. "Are you insinuating that the way to become respectable here is to buy it?"

"Not entirely."

"You're pushful, Buford."

He nodded. "So are you," and watched a flush mount in her cheeks. Then he asked, "Doesn't the Jennie Orren Hospital sound good to you?"

Jennie was Jennie. She made up her mind to settle things with that exasperating man for good and all.

"Once I told a man he had something to say to me. It didn't work out. Maybe if I told a man I had something to say to *him*, things would be different."

"No harm trying."

"You're a big help!"

Buford grinned engagingly. "You don't need help."

Her chin came up. "I never thought I'd see the day! Very well," she said grimly, "I *like* the sound of the Jennie Cross Hospital."

His grin turned into a soft-quirking smile and he reached out both arms.

"Welcome home, Jennie."

The Marshal of Indian Rock

by Fred Grove

One-sixteenth Osage and one-sixteenth Sioux, with a B.A. in journalism from the University of Oklahoma, Fred Grove worked ten years on newspapers and another seven in public relations before trying his hand at fiction. Naturally enough most of his short stories and three of his novels have had Indians as an integral part of the action. Fred lives in Oklahoma.

❦ ❦ ❦

A SMOKY DUST WAS still hanging in the dry air when Buck Dancy stepped down from the Indian Rock stage. A high man, slack-shouldered and long of arm, he turned to watch the other passengers gather up their belongings.

Afterward he claimed his own leather grip and moved up the street, feeling a familiar depression already settling. He moved toward the row of high-faced frame buildings, his attention at once on the fair-skinned man waiting in the shade of Hoffman's Saddle Shop. The usual reception, Buck decided, as the man stepped forward, eyes sharpening.

"I guess you're Dancy," he said, staring.

Buck, nodding, took the outstretched hand, soft as a woman's and quickly withdrawn.

"I'm Arthur Crowder." The tone was direct and Buck remembered the urgent letter. "I got in touch with you for the Citizens' Committee." Crowder's voice bordered on impatience with a tinge of self-importance that Buck did not miss. "There was considerable hurry because we're short a town marshal. Old Mike Haney's in Pawnee with three bullets in him. Peace officers don't last long here." Crowder raised his square-on glance again.

Unimpressed, Buck felt himself scowling as he met the long look, aware of his rising annoyance at being set apart and gawked at. He forced it back wearily, through controlled habit.

"What did you expect?" he said with thin amusement. "Some wild man with four Colts and a Bowie knife to cut notches?"

Color climbed into Crowder's face. "I guess," he said, giving a hasty, pushed-out laugh, "it's because you don't look like a notori— I mean a famous peace officer. I was expecting a hardcase, and older."

"I know," Buck shrugged, and the ancient fatigue came on him and a resentment of Crowder's slip. Because *notorious* was what he'd meant. You soon acquired a reputation, if you survived this solitary game, and you were expected to look the awesome part. You took the stares, always more curious than friendly, though you never got used to them.

Slowly, Buck let his temper die and he eyed Crowder, appraising him. He was a tall man, somehow out of place here on the frontier where the new land rolled up to the broad river, an almost handsome blond man with fine features the savage prairie sun would always burn. A man whose moody face showed the pull of unbounded ambition, a kind of rashness.

The man, with a trace of restlessness, said, "This evening you'll meet with the committee. There'll be questions." Buck felt himself measured and sized up again. Then Crowder, half turning in his walk, added, "I picked you for the job," and Buck thought dryly, *You've put your money on a horse you figure's fast enough to win.* Crowder's stare hung on, bright, asking for reassurance.

Contempt rose in Buck and he ignored the man to read the sign in this Territory town, methodically filing the details away. The low-roofed sandstone jail, the gray-weathered string of buildings. The beaten street, the single pulsebeat. Deceptively quiet in daylight, as now with the clump of horses tail-switching flies in front of the Boomer Saloon.

Buck thought of an awakening old renegade, stirring to smoke and noise in the night. If Indian Rock was no Abilene, Oglala or Caldwell, where Charlie Stewart had died doing his job, it was a bad place to have your gun stick.

Below the town he could see the shallow Arkansas, the river sand bleached and shimmering. Timber stood in thick files on the far, green bank, with beyond it the knuckled hills. They raked up a quick hunger, something distant and waiting, a phantom still mocking him through all these years. Always in his mind had been the desire to take up land. He guessed it went back to the rich Missouri soil which he had known before striking out for fabled Texas. Yet he had held off at the thought of trying it alone. In his quieter moments, he knew it was because of the loneliness, the uncertainty. Even as a peace officer you had people around you, friendly or not, and forever drawing you on was the challenge of another wild trail town.

Crowder lifted a hand, long-fingered and white. "That's the Osage country over there across the river. Kent Beeler's country. You'll hear about him soon enough."

They moved up the street and as it flattened out, Buck saw the black lettering on a fly-smeared office window: *Arthur B. Crowder, Attorney at Law*. Next door, at the Pawnee Hotel, Crowder stopped and said in apology, spreading his soft hands, "Not much, but the food's good."

A dark-haired young woman stood at the door, pieces of dress material over her arm. Her eyes, watching Crowder, held a pleased expression. "Ma Price," she said with mock dismay, "wants a rose pattern. I would be out of that."

"Whatever you have, it will take plenty of it," laughed Crowder, possessively taking her arm. "Hetty, this is Buck Dancy. Miss Ahrens has the distinction of being Indian Rock's only dressmaker."

Buck held his hat and said, "Miss Ahrens, I'm mighty glad to meet you." She wore a bright blue dress and he noticed the ivory shading of her neck against the ruffles. She had a full, striking face and rather high cheekbones. She regarded him, the gray eyes frank and smiling, until Crowder spoke significantly. "This is Dancy—*Buck Dancy*—going to be the new marshal."

Her glance slid about in sudden understanding. When she looked at Buck again, curiously, he had the feeling that she was displeased.

"Without the horns," he said, but she didn't smile.

"I've heard of you," Her voice was polite and complete rejection. In that moment, Buck saw himself. A big-boned man trimmed down too hard and the mark of his chancy trade stamped on him.

He was staring after her, watching her go with a flutter of long skirts into a shop close by, when Crowder's voice brought him around. "I'm going to marry that girl."

"You're a lucky man." Buck stepped inside. He signed the register while the clerk looked on. Crowder followed upstairs.

"There's something you should know," he said. "Solomon Wight, who owns the Boomer, figures this town should suit the saloon trade. He's thick with Beeler!"

Buck took this in, feeling surprise without showing it. "I'll remember that."

"Eight o'clock, remember, over Tarpley's store."

For some while Buck thought of the tall, cool girl and of Arthur Crowder, whose wildness lay printed in pale tracks across his high-strung face. Coming out of the dining room after supper he saw a heavy-bodied woman behind the desk.

"Never thought I'd have the real Buck Dancy in *my* place," she greeted him, brassy and friendly. "I'm Ma Price. Welcome to Injun Rock. You've seen worse and you'll see better." She studied him, judging him, approving him. "No secret why *you're* here."

"Business." He canted his head at the still street, listening.

"Quiet now," she told him. "Wolves don't howl till the church folks, what few there are, go to bed. If there's ever a mass hangin' we'll have to send to Kansas City for rope."

Her laugh rolled out and he smiled and went outside, suddenly sober. Checking himself, testing the street's current down which early riders drifted in, he could feel wind lifting off the prairie, grass-

sweet and cool. He drew the fragrance in deeply before his restlessness, coming on, drove him forward. He ended his swing on the far
side in front of Tarpley's Mercantile, short of the blazing Boomer
Saloon. There were other whisky mills, but the Boomer was king.
He heard a woman's tired voice, and the off-key thump of an ancient
piano.

He watched and smoked, the cigar dull and flat. At eight he
climbed the stairs over the store. Four men sat around a table with
Arthur Crowder, and Buck sensed they had been there a good while.
It was Crowder who rose and spoke their names. Buck shook hands
with Solomon Wight and Adam Tarpley, with Hap Spann, who ran
the Pioneer Livery, and Mack Rains. Buck read Rains at a glance,
a surly, thick-chested watchdog at Wight's elbow. His light-colored
eyes showed sly interest while he chewed on a match stem.

Still standing, Buck regarded them with a feeling that brushed
indifference. Years ago he'd have jumped at the chance to take on a
new town for five hundred dollars a month. Now he said flatly,
"There are certain matters about this job I want made clear," and
saw Wight's head come up. "A peace officer can't keep order playing
a skimmed-milk game. He can't keep it with blood in his eye.
Neither can he work with interference, aimed at improving business
for one side of the street."

Wight stared at the tip of his black cigar. "Indian Rock," he
said, "is no ordinary town, Mr. Dancy. We all know Kent Beeler's
boys are wild. Most of them have records in the States. But a part
of our trade comes from across the river, whether we like it or not.
We get only a fair play on this side from the ranchers and settlers.
Lean too far either way and we lose. Mike Haney played it too
rough. No understanding of business problems. I say let the boys
have their fun."

Buck gave Wight a closer attention. Not a big man, he looked
big. His shoulders were solid bulges of muscle, his neck a short,
powerful column. Shrewd, speculative black eyes looked out on a
cynical world in which little escaped him or, Buck guessed, foxed
him.

"That's about it," agreed Spann, an easy-going smooth-face.

All at once, Tarpley shoved back from the table and stood up.

"I will put it stronger than that for the other side," he declared and looked Wight in the eyes. "This Osage bunch is driving decent people away. More cowmen are leasing the Pawnee and Oto grasslands. We could get more homesteaders. They will be here long after Beeler's buried and forgotten." He swiveled his stubborn gaze around. "I want Dancy to crack down. Give us a clean town." He had a Yankee's blunt frankness, an uncompromising distrust for soft-handed methods.

There was a run of silence as Tarpley sat down. They waited on Crowder now. Buck watched his lips pinch together, saw caution. "Dancy's the man to handle it," Crowder said, yet, saying it, sounded evasive. "He will be fair."

"I will try to be," Buck said, "but it will have to be done my way. Without interference." He heard his voice forming the usual words, conscious of a weighted weariness. "I've seen some good officers—Wild Bill, Tilghman, the Earps and Charlie Stewart."

"Stewart's dead," Wight said promptly. "Saw it in Caldwell."

"That's right," Buck nodded, holding his voice down. "Shot in the back trying to break up a hanging. He happened to be my best friend." Wight's eyes were unreadable. Buck's voice drove into him. "Troublemakers will get first call. Beeler's crew included. That understood?"

Tarpley's head jerked agreement, but the others, undecided, eyed Wight and waited. He was silent for half a minute, stiff-faced. "All right. But don't ruin this town. Takes more than a Spanish bit to break a wild horse. Remember that."

Wight was the key. The meeting adjourned. Wight let the townsmen flow past him. Buck met his stare. "This is a town with the hair on," Wight said.

"So I hear." For once Buck let his bitterness spill over. "Haney get it in the back, too?"

Wight's face never changed. "Come to think of it, he did. Haney had his enemies." His mouth spread into an easy grin. "Marshals drink on the house at the Boomer," he said and walked out. Rains threw Buck a narrowed look and followed.

When Buck came down to the street, the woman with the seamy voice was singing again, while the race-horse piano player ran the keys. Riders came yowling from the darkness of the river ford. They swung in at the Boomer, swirling up dust that gritted between Buck's teeth. Sallow light slanting from saloon row made a greasy shine on horseflesh rowed along the hitch racks. A bleak feeling touched him as he observed the flow of traffic into this outlaw town. Beginning his usual slow stroll, he observed a mechanical watchfulness and, threading the planks crowded with booted men, he was alone again, following a familiar path.

For three days he paced the street and there was an uneasy calm in Indian Rock.

"The longest peace we've ever had," Adam Tarpley informed him. "I believe your reputation has put the fear into these wild men. It is good to see."

Buck shook his head. "They're not afraid of me. We haven't had the right mixture yet. It will come when a Beeler rider and some cowboy get enough tanglefoot at the same time."

Each twilight Buck stood alone in front of the hotel, waiting, showing a patience he didn't really have for the violence that always came. The fourth night he had stationed himself in the early shadows when a horse pounded in off the Pawnee trail. The rider swung down and hurried inside. Presently, Hetty Ahrens came along the walk. He could almost time her arrival in the cool of the evening to visit Ma Price. She entered the hotel, nodding, and he lifted his hat. Seeing her again, he realized he looked forward to this break in the lonely routine, to their few brief words before she started home.

Thought slid away on the sound of loud talk. Simultaneously, two riders trotted in from the west—ranch hands. As Buck watched them dismount by the Boomer's rack Hetty Ahrens left the hotel suddenly.

Over his shoulder, Buck said, "Might be a good idea to get inside. Never know what a drunk will do with a gun." It occurred to him then her visit had been short. Feeling her eyes upon him he swung around, vaguely disturbed. She seemed taller in the half-light from the door, shadow-eyed.

"What is it?" Her voice was low, almost detached.

"Party's gettin' bigger over there." He turned away, hearing the voices again, flat and sharp. He saw her take a step, and hesitate.

"I guess you can feel it. That's why they hired you. We know your story. You started driving cattle. The gun fever got you. You learned to tame towns, became a professional with a name. Men have tried to kill you—somebody will. What can you hope to find in this?" Her words, so close to the truth, spun him back. He had a queer feeling then.

"Why," he said, momentarily startled, "I'll quit some day."

"You'll wait too long."

"Indian Rock will cool down. Once the wildness wears off, I'll go somewhere else. There's new land west of here. One of these days—" He broke off, knowing he was clumsy before this cool woman.

"They why do you wait?" She moved, her shape slim, her large eyes solemn and frank. "There's a man from Pawnee . . . Mike Haney died today."

He started to speak and it caught up with him, shaking him. Why had she deliberately withheld word of Haney's death until the last? Voices ground out hard by Wight's saloon. A single shot, chased racket along the street. Buck took her arm. "Get inside," he said.

He saw the knot of men and, as he stepped toward them, somebody rushed past, yelling. "Tip Steves shot Johnny Garr!"

Buck halted along the rim of scattered light, taking in the groaning cowboy flattened close to the Boomer's doors. His partner stood rigid before a young-faced man who teetered on boot heels, waving a pistol. A big-hatted rider made a move toward the horses. "Tip!" he called. "Come on!"

"No saddlebum's crowdin' me!" Tip answered.

Buck drew breath to the bottom of his lungs, slipped out his pistol and stepped behind the horses. When he cut in, he saw Steves, swaying, half-faced away from him. Buck said, "Put it up," and closed in.

Steves wheeled, gun lifting. This was the game that Buck knew well. He swung his gun. He felt the barrel connect, the impact jarring along his arm muscles. Steves, groaning, crashed backward against the saloon wall. Frantic, the man strained to drag up his weapon. Buck sledged him savagely, heard Steves cry out. The fellow grabbed his smashed wrist. His six-shooter clattered on the planks.

It was over. Buck's eyes went to the wounded man, swept across the ranked circle of watchers. "Get a doctor," he ordered wearily.

At last, a man detached himself and went running across the street. There was a pushing out from inside the saloon. Buck, anxious to avoid the crowd, shoved his prisoner into motion. He forced Steves down the street at a rapid walk to the darkened jail. Buck lit a coal-oil lantern while Steves cursed out his pain, his wild, young, shamed pride. Some of his fight returned as Buck jammed him inside the gamey-smelling cell.

"I won't be here long!" Steves shouted, furious.

Buck said, "You better hope that cowboy pulls through."

He was aware of a mixed relief and dread. He found himself thinking of Hetty Ahrens and discovered her beside Ma Price observing the milling crowd. He walked over and said, "I will see you home."

The older woman said, "Who is it this time?"

"Tip Steves shot a cowboy named Garr."

"Steves," Ma said knowingly, "is a Beeler man."

"Sounds about right," Buck nodded. He held his arm out to Hetty. They walked toward the river. There was a silence between them but he didn't mind this. He could feel the damp coolness rising off the water as they paused before a house that stood silent and dark at the street's edge.

He spoke a low "Good night," and started to turn.

"So there will always be another town," she said, quietly condemning him, yet troubled for him in a way he had never noticed before in a woman.

"A man can't stop in the middle of the current," he said, "nor can he go back to where he began. I don't believe in mooning over what might have been."

She stood quite close, almost touching him. The nearness of her, faint and clean and sweet, drove a feeling around through the sap rising in him. She hadn't moved when his arms came up, reaching for her. Yet there was a holding back in him. She watched him, and he let his hands fall. He said, "Good night," and left her.

He was filled with a terrible loneliness. He had thought for the briefest moment there had been a wanting in her, and then he'd remembered this was Crowder's woman. She was not for Buck Dancy stained with violence and blood.

He had his place in this town, and went back to it—the hard-bright world of saloon row, where rolled out its ugly sound of unsatisfied lusts. All along the slattern stretch these night noises placed their wild, insistent demand upon him and drew him on.

He put his shoulder to the Boomer's doors. Over by the poker tables Solomon Wight stood watching the play with Mack Rains at his side. Crowder was at the main table, gray-cheeked, morosely pondering his cards. Seeing Buck, Wight eased over. "Come on back," he said, waving Rains away, and Buck followed him into the office.

Wight said curtly, taking a bottle from the roll-topped desk, "First crack out of the box you pistol-whip Kent Beeler's lieutenant. Haney's style." He poured two glasses. Buck let his stand.

"Haney's dead," Buck said.

"I heard."

"Well?" said Buck.

"Beeler will come brawlin' in here. You're too rough, Dancy."

Fire was leaping inside Buck. He said, carefully, "Steves shot Johnny Garr."

"Garr will live. But Beeler will tear this town up by the roots. Let Steves go."

"To start something else?"

"Let 'em work off their cussedness."

"I can't see wild gunplay."

Beeler's eyes narrowed. "It's a short life and the gravy's thin. Could be something here for you each week."

The man was blunt enough certainly. From the start Buck had known it would work around to this. "Wight," he said softly, "is that the best you can do?"

"I can break you!"

"I won't be caught like Charlie Stewart."

They stood there, glaring. Wight's furious stare broke first and Buck, tight-mouthed, wheeled out of the room. His rashness growing, he elbowed over to the table where Crowder sat mired in his loser's dejection. The man was bent forward, in strain and frustration. He said angrily, "Damn the luck!"

Suddenly he reared out of his kicked-back chair. The house sharper, mouth curling, said: "Sol is particular about his I.O.U.'s."

"He'll get his money!" Crowder flared. Jerking away, he noticed Buck and a surge of relief splashed across his face.

Buck nodded at the door. "Cooler out there."

Crowder, preceding him, attempted a swagger. Outside, Buck said, "You can't beat Wight at his own game, Crowder."

"Wight's crooked!" Crowder snarled. "The whole town knows it!"

"Why play sucker, then?"

"Something ought to be done about him," Crowder said in a more thoughtful tone. He stood silent and reflective, as though feeling his way through something important. "Maybe you could—" He hesitated, peering at Buck.

"Could what?"

"Handle him—break him! Listen, I can—"

Buck understood, for this also followed a familiar pattern. "Get off the street," he said in disgust.

Crowder, shifting his boots, turned hurriedly away.

Watching the retreating shape, Buck worked this whole business over in his mind. Crowder was wild. He was weak. He owed Wight money for his gambling debts. He would like for Buck to stop Wight with a bullet.

A man, Adam Tarpley, stepped into the light.

"You put a fast halter on Steves," he said. "Now what do you propose to do with him? There is no court here."

"If Garr doesn't pull through, I will take Steves to Pawnee for trial. But the doc thinks Garr will live. So Steves is the honey that draws Kent Beeler."

Tarpley said, "I was never one to horn in, Dancy. But Beeler's got twenty men. If you want help—?"

Buck sighed. "Much obliged, Adam, only this ain't your worry." He left the man then, going on with his rounds.

The solitary feeling was like a shadow at his shoulder. Much later, in the straining light of early morning, he watched the deadfalls disgorge their trade singly and in bunches. When the final whoop swelled and died and the Boomer's lights went dead, he tramped to the hotel.

He was taking his last look from the doorway, relishing this quiet, when a horse started up from the Pioneer barn. Wight's chunky shape bulked in the saddle. The man did not see Buck as he jogged toward the river. Another piece of Indian Rock's puzzle slipped into place for Buck.

This thinking was still with Buck, heavy and dark and cold-running, when he looked out from the lobby the following afternoon and saw Crowder going into the Boomer. Buck, watching him come out, read nervousness into the man's drawn face. Crowder headed directly across to Hetty Ahrens' shop. Almost on the man's heels Mack Rains shouldered out of the Boomer, drilling a glance at the shop before going down the street.

Buck found Wight at the Boomer's deserted bar, counting greenbacks into a black tin box. He did not look up.

Buck said, "You ride a fast horse."

"Don't you ever go to bed?" Wight demanded.

"I've seen it before." Buck told him tiredly. "Both ends against the middle. You and Beeler agree on how to break Steves loose?"

"I told him the straight of it."

"Your side. Where does Crowder figure in this?"

"Young Mister Crowder," Wight said savagely, "is in debt right up to his goddamn ears. Three thousand dollars! He can't play here again until he pays up. But I can't have him running out on me. As for you"—Wight's hard piggish eyes came around, "you've gone too far. Beeler's riled. I won't be responsible."

"Still," Buck insisted, "it's you that's pulling him in." The cynical eyes told him nothing. "I'll be here. Steves stays in the jug."

Wight's black glance was button bright. He slapped the box shut and went into his office, slamming the door.

Wight was pretty sure of himself. Buck stepped back on the street. Beeler would come with darkness. Buck could sense the swift pull of events. He could die in this place. In this powdery street. In gun stink and blackness. Hetty Ahrens deepened his doubts. She was too much in his mind—why he'd held back. In this game a man had no business thinking of women.

The stale depression clawed at him and he walked grimly to the shop. Crowder had gone. Buck sensed excitement in the girl.

"What does that feller really mean to you?" he said.

"He . . . well . . ." She seemed uncertain and then her chin tilted up. "He just asked me to marry him."

"A sensible man."

"He wants us to leave immediately. Oh, he's talked about leaving before this. There's nothing here for him. Perhaps in a new town. . . ."

"Sure," Buck nodded. *I wonder if he told her how much he owes Wight.* "You goin' with him?"

She tossed her head. Anger colored her cheeks. "We've got to go. He's being watched. I know he likes cards, but he'll make good what he owes. He promised me . . . Can't you see? He's got no chance in this place. . . ."

She was loyal, Buck thought, loyal to a man who, expecting everything, gave nothing; and yet Buck wouldn't have changed her. "There's a way," he said, stringing out the thought. "After dark I'll have two saddled horses behind the hotel. Ma Price can tell Crowder."

Her mouth parted. Her face changed and what he saw there he could not place, but he was stirred. She seemed unsure and he hesitated to say more. When he did find words she was looking away and the moment, whatever it might have held, was gone.

"Thank you," she said.

He went out and walked to the Pioneer. He told Hap Spann, "Saddle two horses," and felt a cold shock when Mack Rains came from the stall shadows, staring suspiciously when Spann led the geldings out.

"One rider," Rains grunted. "Two horses."

Buck swung up.

Rains was a slow-thinking man. Yet, looking down, Buck could feel the backed-up surliness. Rains said, "Marshals ain't so tough."

"What do you know about marshals?"

"They all get it in time!"

"Ever been in Caldwell?"

"Go to hell," Rains said.

Buck turned the geldings and rode off.

Striking west, he thought of Charlie Stewart and Mike Haney, who had died the same way. Of Mack Rains and his killer's pride in his irons. Rains would be waiting somewhere in the shadows.

After an hour, Buck cut around to the southeast. Darkness lay across the rounded hills when he came to the shed in the alley. He got down, tied, and moved through the thick, warm blackness between the hotel and Crowder's office.

Pulled back in the gloom he watched riders fill the town, watched it emerge from its daytime shell for another headlong night. At the corner of his store Adam Tarpley stood with his silent dislike. In the corn-yellow light Solomon Wight, a chunkier shape, came through the winged lattices of the Boomer, stepping out to the walk's edge to drive his impatient look toward the ford. He jerked Tarpley a curt nod and strode back inside. Buck interpreted this byplay to mean Beeler was late.

All Buck's instincts came alive as he took in the wide-bodied man ranging up from the stables. Rains walked into the light and continued to search the street, up and down. Still looking, he drifted into a black wedge of shadow. At that, Tarpley wheeled and entered his store.

Silence ran on into the drag of minutes and Buck heard the hotel's front door slap gently. Heavy steps made the planks creak. Ma Price stopped in front of him. "Hetty's waitin' out back." She stared at the street.

"Where's Crowder?"

"Holed up in his office. Buck, I don't like this. I don't like *him*. He's running—"

"Hetty's problem. She wants to go."

Ma Price had scarcely moved her heavy body past him when a growing scuffle of horses came up from the river. The sound cut into him and riders showed in a black, bobbing wedge. They drummed up a swelling racket that bucketed hard along the street. They came at a gallop and pulled up in a tangle of dust before Wight's place. The man came out at once.

One of the riders called, "Where's that marshal?"

At that moment Crowder stepped out of his office. Sight of the horsemen seemed to freeze him. Buck's low call, "Over here," put him in motion, too obviously fleeing, his boots jarring racket from the boards. "There he goes!" Rains shouted.

Crowder loomed suddenly near, breath coming in ragged gusts. "Back here!" Buck ordered, feeling the frantic fear in the man. Buck saw Hetty's blurred figure by the horses.

Only then did he know that all along he'd had the unreasoning hope she wouldn't go. Disappointment unleashed a recklessness in him. He wheeled and faced the street.

Directly toward him charged Rains, pistol lifting. Flame touched its tip and lead slapped the wall at Buck's shoulder. Cool, Buck raised his arm and fired twice. He saw Rains stumble. Rains' hand strained upward, fell away. He made a small crying sound and dropped on his face.

"It's Dancy!"

Wight's furious voice lashed Beeler into action. As the outlaw reined his horse, Buck heard a drum-fire of hoofs break out in the alley. He shifted position while he watched Beeler twist his head to stab a look through the darkness, watched Wight, abruptly bold, center his gun.

"Come out, Dancy!" Wight waggled the pistol. It was Beeler's signal to throw down, but he sat his horse like stone.

Buck stepped out. "Like when Rains shot Charlie Stewart in the back?" he called. "Like Mike Haney?" Horses stomped, leather squeaked. He saw a man come out of Tarpley's store and stop on the porch.

In a flutter of movement Kent Beeler dropped his shoulder, bringing up his gun. Buck's pistol barked. Beeler's scream sheared through the reports. As Buck whirled toward Wight, knowing he was late, one loud blast overrode all sound. The gun fell from Wight's fist as he sagged.

Buck held his fire.

Heeling back on Beeler, he saw the outlaw with hands clapped across his chest. Shuddering, Beeler rolled out of the saddle.

Buck's glance raked across Beeler's muttering riders. They were beginning to press forward when a voice ripped their flanks: "Clear out! Clear out!" Adam Tarpley ran from his porch with a shotgun. He swung the double barrels in a sweeping arc until they gave ground, until they began a retreat toward the dark river ford.

Afterward, Tarpley walked over to Wight's form. He tipped his head at Buck, who came across. "Meaning no disrespect for the dead," Tarpley said. "But Solomon Wight was too rough for this town."

Men gathered around, talking in subdued tones. Buck was filled with a powerful revulsion, with a solid weariness. Turning, he noticed Ma Price.

"Buck."

He kept gazing past her, watching Hetty Ahrens coming out of the shadows. Light touched her face, drawn tight, big-eyed. He started toward her.

"Arthur's gone. I sent him on."

She seemed to wait for him to speak, as she had that afternoon; and he knew that nothing in his life, before or after, could equal this moment. As he turned her away from the street, something in that motion told him that here, tonight, was his real beginning and Indian Rock his last town.

Way of the Law in Calico

by John Prescott

Journey by the River won for John Prescott the Spur awarded for Best Western Historical of 1954. Many times a contributor to the *Saturday Evening Post* Prescott, who lives in Phoenix, Arizona, has authored half a dozen published novels.

❧   ❧   ❧

EVERY SPRING WHEN SCHOOL let out in Calico and I could help my mother and sister run our boardinghouse, my father went into the mountains to dig in our mine. It was required that he do so much assessment work each year to keep the claim. Sometimes he would be away a week and other times a month, or more; and the year that Mr. Dean arrived in Calico, Father was gone for seven weeks. The reason for this variation was not related to the quantity of gold he was removing, but to the quality of fishing when the assessment work was finished.

As a matter of fact, through all the years we held our claim, my father found no gold whatever, though he often worried that he might. Since we had come to Arizona for his health, he felt that he could handle only certain kinds of labor, and he developed a fear of finding a paying vein. He came to believe that a real bonanza might so interfere with fishing that his recovery would be threatened.

So, while he was away my mother would collect the money and do the cooking, Elaine would do the cleaning and the beds, and I would be the outside man.

It was on a day that I was being this outside man that Mr. Dean appeared. I was sweeping the gallery clean of dirt from muddy boots when I heard someone speak.

"Such ardent labors are worthy of that other Hercules in the famed Augean stables."

I looked, and there he was. First I saw the bright yellow shoes, then his flowered waistcoat, then way above all that his high, gray beaver. He was young and willow tall, and his smile and dress were those of a drummer.

I told him my name was Sammy, that this was Bayley's Boarding-house.

His name was Dean. "A fair place," he then said of our boarding-house. "Aye, it brings to mind the palace of Fontainebleau."

He seemed surprised that I should ask him what that was. Setting down his carpetbag he crossed his arms and examined me.

"You know not," he asked, "the seat of the Frankish kings?"

It was not the usual thing to hear a question of that kind in Calico. I shook my head. I'd never seen the seat of any king.

"What, then, do you know of that noble Roman, Caesar?"

But I could only shake my head at Caesar, too.

"Can we converse upon Ulysses, friend?"

I felt really bad.

"Have you knowledge of Galileo?" When I said I hadn't he clicked his tongue. "What of James Watt, then? What of Dante? What of Burke?"

There were more and they were all, I guess, the ringing names of emperors and dragon slayers, or the chemical names of scientists, the papery names of poets and philosophers. His voice rose and fell, his arms moved in the air, but I didn't know any of them.

Mr. Dean laughed gently and made another gesture.

"Their greatness lay in their aspirations, Samuel. They were of high heart, children of wonder."

He fixed his hand in a fist and beat upon his own high heart. He smiled again and raised a finger.

"Mayhap I should be your mentor, Samuel. Together, we might give pursuit to the wonders they wrought. Aye, and many another marvel, too. In time you could be educated."

I began to say that school in Calico was educating me for nearly six months every year, but at that moment my mother and sister came out of the door.

"Ah," said Mr. Dean, sweeping off his beaver and bending like a reed, "the fair Penelope; and lo, a vestal virgin in attendance."

This made my sister turn the color of sunset, but my mother had been in the boarding business quite a while. All she did was primp a little at her hair.

"What are you selling?" she said to Mr. Dean. "I'll hear you out, but I give no promise to buy."

"Good madam, I come not peddling trifles to your annoyance," Mr. Dean said, his thumbs now in the armholes of his waistcoat. "My traffic is all of replevins, torts, briefs and letters testamentary. Permit me, if you will"—and he bowed again—"the name is Dean, Edwin Corinthian, barrister, solicitor, counselor at law. I seek in this salubrious clime a haven from my wanderings. I seek lodgings at your hands."

When he finished, my mother looked at him for some time. In Calico, where people did their litigating with their fists or with an ax handle sometimes, lawyers were unknown. Elaine looked at him, too, and I remembered a doe I had startled in the hills one time when I was hunting with father.

"It's a lawyer you are, I gather," Mother said in a moment. "And you want a room."

"Precisely," said Mr. Dean with still another bow.

My mother regarded him again.

"Very well; I have a room if you wish to see it," she said. "It's small, though, and at the back."

"Lead on," Mr. Dean replied. "Let us see to the appointments of the suite."

Although that song about the first man up being the best man dressed is stretching the rope, a boardinghouse is still an interesting kind of place. While individuals like my father often had their little gopher pockets, Calico depended on the Copper Princess for its bread and butter, and the men who lodged with us were hunkies at the Princess. They were men with complicated names, who dug and drilled all week, and then, on Saturday nights, engaged in terrible recreation in the honky-tonks. On these nights of payday revels they would drink, swear, prance and fight. Often mother locked them out, and other times the marshal, Mr. Bolt, would lock them up. Sometimes it was necessary for Mr. Bolt to damage them, and there was none among them he hadn't beaten up at least once; he liked his authority understood. Other evenings they sat wearily on the gallery, each beside his cuspidor, where they could see the roasters fill the night with flame and hear the stamp mills pounding out the gold and silver and copper.

Besides the lodgers there were some who only boarded with us, men like Mr. Bolt who came to take his supper at evening. My father used to say that we would all be better off, Elaine especially, if Mr. Bolt spent more of his time at the jail. It was a curious thing how other men became discouraged when Mr. Bolt came calling.

Now it might be thought a man like Mr. Dean would feel himself a stranger in such an atmosphere, but the odd thing of it was that he got on well with everyone—leastways for quite a while.

I expect this was because he had a way of making people laugh. On those evenings when the men were sitting by their cuspidors, he told them stories. Sometimes they were animal tales which had been written long ago by Mr. Aesop. They always laughed to hear about the fox and grapes, and the dog that dropped the meat on seeing his own reflection in the river. There were quite a few like that, and yet, when thought of later, some of them had parts that didn't seem so funny as they had at first.

Maybe it was just the way he told them that was funny, waving his arms about and making his hands go high and low.

Once, when he was doing a part in an old-time play he called Hamlet, the men went black in the face with laughing.

Then there were the things he'd say. One time when Elaine went riding in a rig with Mr. Bolt, the horse was so slow in starting that Mr. Bolt was forced to smack it with a club. It was after they'd gone on that Mr. Dean remarked there would come a time when a rig would run without a horse. Another occasion, when they were speculating on the blind side of the moon, he said a man would one day go and look at it!

You can see how anyone who talked in that way would be appreciated in our boardinghouse. Some of the lodgers even bragged him up to those of other houses not so lucky as to have a Mr. Dean to entertain them. In a couple of weeks, when he began to play the Game with them, they came even to look upon him as a kind of regular.

As the test of skill, the Game was played to see which man could stream a cheekful of Old Puma Pelt the farthest into the yard, with the loser going down to the Apex for a bucket of beer. In a while he got so good at this that on occasion he bested even Mr. Bolt, a master. The only time he wouldn't play was when Elaine was on the gallery. When that was understood by Mr. Bolt he made his greatest efforts in those moments.

But it wasn't all sitting on the gallery with Mr. Dean. In those early days when mandamuses and habeases were slow in coming, I sometimes tramped the countryside in his company; and there would often come a moment high on some hill when he would waft me off to other lands.

"Samuel, let us sail the ocean blue," he'd say. "What do you see below us there?"

"Grass," I said, for I did not see any ocean blue. "It looks white and shining in the sun."

"Aye, the burnished look; the glint the westering mariner sees upon the face of the sea."

I looked very hard, but couldn't tell if he was right or not, until he launched a ship.

"Let us consider that we sail upon that vessel there," he said. "It is very small, a caravel, not like the ironclads we know today. And

the men who sail with us are frightened, for they go upon an unknown water in whose deeps may lurk great serpents, and which
ends in a timeless void at the lip of the world."

I closed my eyes, and when I opened them again, it was as he
said. The ship was frail and made of wood. The scuppers ran with
smelly water, and little bugs crept out upon the planks. The eyes
of the men showed white and wide, and they scratched themselves.
It was strange how I could feel the pitching decks and hear the
storm winds howling in the yards, and the flapping of the sails when
we lay panting in a calm. Sometimes the men bent over the rails in
agony, other times they cursed the captain. But the captain simply
stood above us, resolute and tall, and it was hard to tell if he, too,
feared the serpents. Mr. Dean said the captain's name was Columbus.

Another time, he pointed off at faraway mountains.

"How tall would you say they were?" he asked.

"Close to a mile, my father told me."

"Then, imagine them at twice that elevation. Nay, make it two
and a half times, close to thrice."

I did, and they lifted until they filled the sky. The rocky flanks
soared sheer beyond the timber line, the peaks remote and icy with
eternal winter.

"Now, let us look for elephants," he said.

It took some doing to see elephants in Arizona, but when I
found them we weren't in Arizona any more. We'd gone to the middle of Europe and were in the Alps. It was very cold, and the wind
shrieked through the mountain passes. In certain places there were
chasms, and when an elephant would slip and fall over, I'd hear
him trumpeting away on down to the bottom. The people, dark and
small, gathered up their cloaks for warmth. Some of them wore
leopard or lion skins, and their shields were made of bullock hide
and even the hide of crocodiles. A few of them slipped over, too,
with their burnooses streaming out behind. They carried spears and
swords, and at the head of them was Hannibal.

Mr. Dean made other pictures, too. It sometimes seemed to me
as though he opened up great doors and windows, and when looking
through them I was near to thoughts and meanings which would be
too big to know once they were closed again.

They weren't all in distant places. Once I took him up a canyon to an Indian ruin I knew about. There was nothing left but broken pottery, some old metates, a few adobe walls now nearly melted into the earth; but he was able to build these things into what they were in the beginning. He put people in them too; and for a while I saw them work and play, heard shouts and laughter in that place where there had been no sound for nearly a thousand years.

That was the time he found the pot. He pulled it out of one of the walls, and though there wasn't much to it, he gave it to Elaine when we returned that evening. He gave a little poem with it—"Ode on a Grecian Urn," he called it. All the while he talked Elaine held onto that dirty pot as if it was made of purest gold. When he finished, none of the hunkies knew if they should laugh or not. In some way it was different from other things he'd said.

Later, though, when Mr. Bolt was helping wipe the dishes with Elaine, and broke it on the floor, they did. It was always good for a laugh when Mr. Bolt was being useful.

A peculiar time had its beginning with that pot. Take the conversations Mr. Bolt began to have with Mr. Dean.

"Mr. Dean," he said to him one evening on the gallery, "there's things you don't seem to know about this country."

"How lamentably true that is," said Mr. Dean. "But then, are we not all of us slaves to ignorance in some fashion? I can but hope time brings familiarity."

"Calico ain't so big," said Mr. Bolt. "P'raps there ain't enough to it to make your stayin' on worth while."

"Oh, even the smallest of things have virtues and significance," said Mr. Dean.

Prying the nail of his thumb between his teeth, Mr. Bolt removed a shred of beef and flicked it over the railing.

"I been thinking, Mr. Dean," he said, "that a pettifogger's a surprising thing to find in Calico."

"The world is full of surprises, Mr. Bolt. They stand among the pleasures of life."

"That's as may be," said Mr. Bolt. "But it never seemed to me that Calico law was suitable for argufying."

"Mr. Bolt, I wonder if your thinking on that point is not disorganized?" said Mr. Dean. "I think it is clear the law in these United States is vested in the Constitution. Men have worn themselves down to an early grave through arguing about that document."

"Arguing the law in Calico has done the same for others, Mr. Dean," said Mr. Bolt.

That was the kind of talk Mr. Bolt began to make. On the face of it, it didn't look too much, and yet there was an undercurrent too; a kind of uncomfortable feeling. Whenever they talked that way, the men kept still by their cuspidors. Elaine would listen at the door, and even my mother, who never set foot on the gallery in the evening for fear they might be playing the Game, would bring her broom and sweep, no matter that I'd swept it all before.

Take the things my mother said to Mr. Dean one day when he came into the parlor to pay his weekly rent. After she'd put it in the book, she held him there for a moment of talk.

"Mr. Dean, as a man of culture, I expect you've seen far places in your travels."

"Indeed," said Mr. Dean, "I have been privileged to journey widely. It has been a passion with me."

"I wonder, Mr. Dean, if you've ever been to California? I've heard so many interesting things about it."

"No, unhappily not," said Mr. Dean. "I've never been into this Western part of our country before."

My mother smoothed her dress across her knees. "I should think a man of your interests would never rest until he'd seen it all. How I'd love to stand on the shores of the Pacific Ocean."

I'd never heard her speak before of California, and yet she made it sound as if a visit there might be a prime wish with her.

"Oh, I daresay California is a splendid place," said Mr. Dean, "but I have come to the point of thinking that travel is a search for something, and I feel my own particular search has ended. I would be pleased to spend the rest of my life right here."

"Oh," my mother said. "Oh, dear!"

Even Elaine was acting differently. She gave up joking and talking with Mr. Dean. He was just as nice to her as ever, but she was stiff and pale, hardly speaking at all, unless there was need. Once

I asked her why she'd turned so rude and she went to her room and cried an hour.

So maybe it was that pot that stood in back of it all. Maybe the pot was *chindi*, in the way that relics of the Old Ones are said to be among the Navahos. Maybe the pot was just a sign, the way an ore outcrop may show what lies below the surface. It was hard to put your finger on.

It took a burro to bring it into the open. It was one of those which Mr. Kee kept taking home with him. Mr. Kee was an old Chinaman who came each week to talk with Mr. Dean in what was called the Canton dialect. Mr. Kee knew only a little English because a mine cave-in had hurt his head and, until the coming of Mr. Dean in Calico, there'd been nobody he could talk to.

So, on Sundays, Mr. Kee would stand there pulling at his queue, and smile as if a warm light lay all over him while they talked of nobody could say what. Sometimes it seemed that there were tears in the eyes of Mr. Kee, but Mr. Bolt said that could not be, since Celestials had no feelings.

Sometimes Mr. Kee came with a black burro, sometimes with a gray one, other times with something else. Mr. Kee's own burro hadn't come out of the cave-in, yet he seemed to think that he would find it if he only looked enough. These that he took home did not belong to him, but after he'd had them for awhile, he'd come to see that for himself and take them back to their rightful owners. Nobody ever cared about it. Calico was full of burros.

Mr. Kee had brought a reddish one this time, and Mr. Dean was showing his admiration in the Canton dialect when Mr. Bolt came up. At first he made as if to walk up on the gallery where the hunkies all sat blinking in the sunlight of the morning after, but a couple of yards beyond the burro he turned around and looked at it. He studied it for some moments, and the hunkies all edged forward in their chairs.

"Say," said Mr. Bolt, "I seen that jack on a rope somewhere. Where'd you get him, Chink?"

Mr. Dean spoke to Mr. Kee; Mr. Kee pulled at his queue and spoke to Mr. Dean, and Mr. Dean then said, "It is a wanderer, Mr. Bolt. In his compassion, Mr. Kee has fed and watered it."

"Yair?" said Mr. Bolt. He backed off a ways from the burro while he squinted at it. "That thing come from Sig Czerney's place; I'd know it anywhere."

Mr. Dean didn't speak to Mr. Kee; instead, he spoke to Mr. Bolt. "If it has, it shall return," he said. "Mr. Kee has always found their proper homes. Everybody knows that."

"Yair?" said Mr. Bolt. "All I know is that he's got an animal as don't belong to him. That Chink's got a long record of stock theft in this town, and stock theft is a hanging crime."

It was strange to hear a burro elevated to the dignity of cows and horses, but nobody laughed. This began to look as if it might be going beyond the burro business now. In a way it seemed that Mr. Bolt was using the burro for something else. On the gallery men were leaving their chairs, coming down the steps as if they saw a treat in store. My mother and sister came to the door.

Mr. Dean considered Mr. Bolt a moment before he spoke to Mr. Kee. Then, when Mr. Kee, looking unhappy and confused, had wrung his hands and nodded, Mr. Dean said to Mr. Bolt, "I have been retained as counsel. In order to charge a theft the plaintiff must identify the evidence."

"I one time mentioned there was things you didn't seem to know about in Calico, Mr. Dean. Stand aside."

Mr. Bolt began to walk toward Mr. Kee, but Mr. Dean did not stand aside.

"You'll not take him into custody without due process, Mr. Bolt. You cannot jail or hang a man on allegations."

"Get out of the way," said Mr. Bolt.

"Under constitutional guarantee, Mr. Kee enjoys a freedom from unreasonable search and seizure." Mr. Dean raised up his finger. "You'll not infringe upon his rights of person."

No one had ever talked that way to Mr. Bolt before. Mr. Dean had a marvelous way with words, but as this hardly seemed to be the right time for them, I felt uneasy. This was a good deal different from yarning on the gallery or walking about in the hills.

"I'm takin' him, Mr. Dean," said Bolt.

But Mr. Dean stood firm in front of Mr. Kee. Mr. Bolt came up, and when his arm came over his fist caught Mr. Dean beside the jaw. Mr. Dean sat down in the road. His mouth began to bleed. Mr. Kee jumped all around him in agony and the hunkies yelled and shouted.

On the gallery Elaine began to cry. My mother pushed her through the door, then she brought her broom to the road and began to hit out right and left. Never had she done a thing like that in another fight, but they paid her no attention.

"Stop them!" she kept shouting the whiles she swung the broom, but no one listened. They just shouldered off her swats and swore. At last she cried, "Scum! Monsters!" and fumed back into the house.

By this time Mr. Dean was on his feet again. He held his arms before him and danced about in so elegant a manner that, for a moment, I forgot to be fearful for him. Mr. Bolt was fighting Calico style—arms low, face pushed ahead of him like a stump. It was the hunky style, but Mr. Dean's approach was new. The bunch of them laughed uproariously.

When Mr. Dean went down the third time he didn't get up so quickly. His nose was bleeding, he didn't dance around so much. Mr. Bolt had fists as large as melons. Whenever he caught Mr. Dean with one, Mr. Dean would sway as if a high wind was blowing. Except that he was tall and springy, Mr. Dean would long ago have been out. Mr. Bolt was widely known for his strength.

But Mr. Dean was wearing down. Each time he fell, he was slower rising; by now the whole of his face was bloody, he had given up his dancing but managed to stay in front of his client. If he had just stayed on the ground when he went down it would have ended. He seemed more intent on watching out for Mr. Kee than in watching out for himself.

That was when I remembered to be afraid for him. I knew certain things about him then that hadn't so clearly shown before. I was frightened for him, for Mr. Bolt was raging like a bull. As if one of the doors that Mr. Dean had shown me had swung open, I knew Mr. Dean would never quit. There was his high heart and his aspiration. Those had been fine words describing men of other times and places; but now I understood them to have expensive and dreadful meanings.

And I knew certain things about miners, too. I knew them to be callous, hard men of fleshly appetites and lusts. They enjoyed a fight above all things and could take a beating in stride. Mr. Bolt had beaten all of them, and so they didn't mind that Mr. Dean should be beaten, too.

When Mr. Dean went down again he stayed down; but it didn't end with that. Mr. Bolt, now backing off a few yards, made a run at him. But the badness in him threw him off stride, so that the kick he aimed at Mr. Dean went wide and the force so made him slew around he lost his balance and fell to the ground beside him. When, with such strength as he had left, Mr. Dean pinned down the legs of Mr. Bolt, Mr. Bolt went for his gun.

It seemed to me that time stopped then, and there was in the air a silence like none I'd ever heard. That gun kept coming up and out, and all the while no one moved or spoke. Then I heard a shout, and it was me. I started running—that, too, surprised me. I don't guess I thought to be afraid of what might happen; I was bent on stopping murder. Mr. Dean had been kind and good to me. He had opened up new thoughts and places, and now they would never be opened again.

So I ran toward Mr. Bolt, had almost reached his arm when one of the hunkies caught me by the middle and swung me back. At the same time, and with his other hand, he grabbed the barrel of Mr. Bolt's revolver, wrenching it out of his grasp to fling it far over the road. Then he bent to peer at Mr. Bolt.

"Nah, there, Mr. Bolt," he said, "you'll fight him fair. He's shown his mettle and the beating he's had at your hands has made him one of ourselves. So we'll no more stand for his killing than for that of another among us."

This was something strange to hear, and Mr. Bolt did not believe it until he'd pulled himself up and looked at each miner in turn. Then he did believe it, and there came over his face a terrible look. He stood for the whole of a minute while the knowledge of danger grew in him, and then he whirled and went quickly down the road. He didn't even stop for his gun.

Mr. Dean lay up in his room for seven days and, as Elaine was doing for him every minute of it, dust balls floated around like tumbleweeds, and everybody slept in rumpled sheets and blankets.

My mother set a penance on the miners, too. Every night that Mr. Dean was in bed she fed them cold potatoes. It made no difference how they pleaded; she held them to be full of beastly sin for being so slow in helping Mr. Dean, and all of the evenings of that week they sat glumly on the gallery with the cold potatoes inside them. Nobody played the Game. None of them went a-wallowing in the honky-tonks when Saturday came. Not till Mr. Dean was well enough to play the death of Romeo did any of them laugh again.

I guess I blubbered some when I was allowed to see him and he said I was a foolish but gallant boy. That was when I told him of the doors and windows, and how I'd been scared I'd never get to see through them again.

"Ah, the doors," he said in a smile that looked all out of shape on his battered face. "You were able to see. And they made you want to know? They made you curious?"

"Oh, yes!"

"Ah, blessed curiosity. It is the mark of the educated man."

It was on the day that Mr. Dean got out of bed and came down that my father returned from the assessment work and the fishing that inevitably followed. He was not a bookish man, but he had gained a deal of learning and, as he looked suspiciously at Mr. Dean, I sensed an encounter of powerful minds.

"Mr. Dean," my father said, when he was told of all that had happened, and had drawn conclusions from the way Elaine was taking care of the invalid, "I'm going to ask you one question."

As best he could with his injuries, Mr. Dean drew himself up and waited.

My father closed his eyes for a moment.

Then he said, "Given a sprightly day in May beside a tumbling mountain creek, what would the finding of a stone nymph suggest to you?"

Oh, it was a devilish question, and I feared again for Mr. Dean, but Mr. Dean was not afraid. For a moment, though, a vein stood out at his temple with the weight of his thinking.

"I would take the stone nymph," he began, "and I would put it on a small hook and cast it out."

"Ah," my father said, but then he sharpened again. "Down-stream?"

"Nay," said Mr. Dean. "Up. Against the current, and just below a rapids, where the trout feed best."

"Ah," my father said again, and this time he smiled benignly at Mr. Dean, and at Elaine, too. "What a pleasure it will be to have a man of wisdom in this family."

Some Learn Hard

by James Woodruff Smith

Jimmy Smith, a resident of Beverly Hills, California, has written at least three novels and several short stories appearing in national magazines. This original, done especially for this book, marks his first appearance in a WWA anthology.

❦ ❦ ❦

HE WAS TALL AND whipcord straight with powerful shoulders and the narrow hips of a man raised on the range. His face was guileless, clean and boyish.

The black stallion under him whickered, smelling the water and grain of the Square D ranch dead ahead. The rider pulled up this side of the sycamores and stepped down, holding a lead rope on the mustang behind. He knelt, found a small pebble which he wedged into the frog of the black's left front hoof.

Now he led the stud about in tight circles, watching the heavy limp with satisfaction. He stopped and patted the powerful silky neck, then swapped the gear, putting the black on the lead rope, mounting the mustang. As he went up into the leather he smoothed the sharpness from eyes and face. Coming out of the trees and bear-

ing down on the ranch yard he showed a youngster's open face, very
motherable, honest, eager.

It was quiet in the ranch house kitchen. Just the bubble of the
coffeepot, the splutter of chicken frying. Martha Drum, comfortably
full-bosomed, face pink with cooking and general good will, stood
with her back to the checkerboard waiting on the scrub-bleached
table.

Hugh Drum shot a glance at the back of her neck, silver thatch
bobbing over his red healthy face, big shoulders hunched, great
elbows anchored at either side of the board. One eye closed, the
other stealthily watching her, he moved a hand and with his fingers
edged a pawn over into the king's row. At that instant she lifted the
first piece of chicken to a platter and turned her head.

"I swear. Thirty-seven years and you still try to cheat whenever
my back's turned."

Hugh, flushing, put the man back.

"Just on little things, Mrs. Drum."

"Hmpf. You just can't stand to have anybody best you on anything."

She brought the platter to the table and he took up his napkin
and stuffed it under his chin. She was moving back to the stove
when they heard the whicker of a horse outside. Mrs. Drum was out
the door first. They stood on the top step as the youth with the
two horses came up to the house. He doffed his hat.

"Light down, son."

"Thank you kindly. You're Mr. Drum?"

"I am."

"Square D."

"It is."

"I'm Tom Dyce."

He got off.

"My wife," Hugh said.

"Pleasure, ma'am."

Martha Drum said, smiling, "We was just settin' down. Always
room for one more."

"You're mighty kind, ma'am."

He was all dogie now and she melted under the telepathy of his honest boyish need.

"Washbasin's back of the cookshack," she said.

"Thank you, ma'am. I'd just as lief eat with the hands."

"You'll eat with us," she said fiercely.

Dyce looked as if he'd lick her hand. Smiling, she hurried into the house. Hugh Drum walked toward the stable. Drum eyed the black.

"Lamed."

"Yes, sir. Couple miles back."

"Ain't permanent, likely. Few days rest."

"I—well, I got to go on."

Drum looked around but Dyce was watching a mare in the corral. Drum considered the black's leg, dragged a hand across his mustache and led the way into the stable.

They were finishing their last cup of coffee, Mrs. Drum busy at the sink, when Drum said through a cloud of pipesmoke:

"Mind a question, son?"

"No, sir."

"Said you had to go on. Sounded kinda urgent."

Dyce stared at his plate.

"Law?"

Tom Dyce, flushing, looked sheepish. Mrs. Drum swung fiercely. Dyce said, "Nothing like that. Got me a girl. California. Went out a year ago with her folks. I been working, saving. . . ."

Mrs. Drum's eyes brought the flush up again. Dyce looked uncomfortable and powerfully flustered.

"So now," Drum said, "your hoss pulls up lame and you got to ride the pack-animal."

"Yes, sir. Some pack hoss, isn't he? Not even a soda cracker."

Mrs. Drum swung about and bobbed her head at her husband. Dyce was apparently looking out into the yard.

"Son," Drum said, "that hoss needs rest."

"Yes, sir. But I've just *got* to go on."

"Suppose I was to buy the black off you? He'd be all right for breeding."

"But golly, sir—you're just doing that to—help me. I couldn't let you do that."

"Nonsense, son. It's a plain business deal."

"I appreciate it, sir, but—"

"Now don't go to bein' stubborn."

"Hmpf!" Mrs. Drum said.

"What's that, Mrs. Drum?"

"I said, 'Look who's talking.' Stubborn!"

Drum made a helpless gesture. Dyce smiled sympathetically as Mrs. Drum went back to her work.

Drum got down to business. "I mean it, son. I'll take him off your hands—you got papers on him?"

The boy appeared to give, a little.

"Of course. They're in my saddlebags. But, dang it, I just couldn't. Wouldn't seem right."

"Course it would."

"No, you'd figure I rode in just looking for sympathy."

"Not nohow."

"It's mighty white of you, sir, but . . ."

He got up resolutely and walked over to Mrs. Drum.

"Ma'am, I sure do thank you. That's the finest meal I ever tasted."

"You're mighty welcome, Tom," she said, patting his hands. "It's been wonderful good to have you stop by."

"Ma'am," he said, looking sober and serious, "I don't remember my mother. But do I ever get one by marriage, I sure hope she's exactly like you."

Bemused, Martha put her arm around him and started him toward the living room.

"You'll at least spend the night. You can use the spare room."

She looked back, grimacing, at her husband. He said, "Yeah—sure thing." Martha led young Dyce off down the hall.

"You ought to listen to my wife, son," Drum said after breakfast, going stableward with Dyce. "She give you good advice. Take our money and leave the black. That girl of yours ain't like to wait forever."

Tom Dyce, reluctantly, appeared to yield a bit.

"I'm scared you're right about that."

Drum went back to the old trader's device, fishing up some twenty-dollar gold pieces, he began to clink these from one palm to the other. Tom looked away as if fighting temptation.

He said, "I sure am anxious to get to her."

"Sixty dollars?"

Tom looked longingly at the flash of coins.

"Generally," Drum said, "a man can get a fine hunk of hossflesh for twenty dollars in these parts. But like I said, that black's some special."

"He *is* that."

Slowly, deliberately, Drum dropped an additional gold piece in among the others, watching the boy's eyes.

"Well, sir," Tom said reluctantly, "much as I hate to admit it, you've—I guess you've sold me."

They stepped into the stable to close the deal.

The ranch dogs barked it up that night and Hugh Drum opened the door and went out to see what was bothering them. The dark shape of horse and rider came out of the gloom. Two hands showed down near the bunkhouse, one of them holding a lamp over his head. Drum's glance took in the badge, the growth of beard and dark visage. Black eyes, black hat, dark shirt and pants.

"Howdy, friend," Drum said.

"John Timothy. Sheriff at Lincoln."

"Evening, Sheriff. Hugh Drum here. Light and have coffee."

"Thanks."

"Long ride?"

"And maybe longer. Any strangers pass through here?"

Drum, rubbing jaw against shoulder, held up one finger.

"Younker? Nineteen, mebbe?"

"About that."

"Tall?" Timothy said cynically. "Good shoulders? Riding a mustang?"

Drum, suddenly nervous, nodded.

"Did he happen—" the sheriff said softer but harder, "—just happen to have a black stallion?"

"That's right."

"You happen to *buy* that hoss?"

Drum, without enough spit to speak, nodded.

"Mmm. Bill of sale . . . ?"

"In the house."

"Damned shame."

"What's that?"

"Forgery, mister."

He drew out two papers. One was a dodger. It stated Tom Dyce was wanted on eleven counts of horse-stealing in three counties. Drum heard the door open as from a great distance.

"What is it, Hugh?" his wife said.

He looked up, stricken.

"Marthy, this is Sheriff John Timothy. From Lincoln County."

"Spend the night, Sheriff, you're beat. I'll go kill a chicken and feed you."

"Ma'am, I do thank you. I'll have coffee."

"You on a manhunt, Sheriff?"

"Yes, ma'am."

Hugh handed her the dodger and went to scanning the other paper. The man behind the badge eyed them with compassion, but somewhat cynically, then smoothed his face as Mrs. Drum held out the dodger, shocked.

"Why—why, this is young Tom. He was here this morning. Wanted? What *is* this?"

Hugh handed her the second sheet.

"The true bill of sale for that black."

"Hope you didn't pay too much," the lawman said.

"Eighty dollars."

The man with the badge spread his hands regretfully.

"I guess you know what I have to do?"

"I reckon." Drum thudded a fist into his palm, exasperated. "It ain't the money so much. It's being took. Like a greener. Pains me."

"He was such a clean boy," Mrs. Drum said sadly.

"Sure was," said the lawman. "Till he was fourteen, anyhow."

"Fourteen!"

"Five years now he's been riding pretty tall. Ma'am, that *boy* has killed three men."

He eyed Hugh Drum, who turned and trudged off toward the stable. Mrs. Drum said as the lawman put his foot in the stirrup and went up:

"Won't take an hour to supper you."

"Thank you, ma'am, but—no. You understand."

He had the black stallion on a lead rope when Mrs. Drum came from the house with a small sack of food. He leaned and took it gratefully.

"Cold beef chunks and biscuits," she said. "Tide you over."

"Mighty thankful, ma'am."

"Just can't figure that boy," Drum muttered.

The lawman said, "I've seen it before."

"You mean he does this kind of thing regular?"

"He does. Just like he did you."

"Just ask you one thing. Ride this way and lemme quirt him raw."

"Mr. Drum, you know the answer to that."

"It'd sure work off some spleen for me."

"Sorry about the money, sir."

"Ain't the money."

The sheriff tipped his hat and they called their "hastas." He rode off into the night.

They were breaking a horse the next morning and Hugh Drum sat in the old black leather buggy seat suspended from the top rails. Three hands were working the piebald at the snubbing post and Ted Holt, Drum's ramrod, sat on the top rail chewing a straw. He turned his head, made a sign to Hugh. Hugh moved in the seat to pick up the rider coming in.

Man on a big chestnut gelding. Buff hat, checked shirt, whipcord pants, tan silk at the neck. Shiny tin star. Rifle in the boot, pistol not far from his hand. They waved and he rode up and sat with both paws on the apple.

"Could be you're Drum?"

"I am."

"John Timothy. Sheriff, Lincoln County."

Drum's face changed. He spoke sidemouth to his ramrod. "Put a gun on this liar and run him off the place."

The foreman started but Timothy's hand didn't have so far to go. With his free hand he fished for papers and handed them to the foreman.

Ted Holt passed them gingerly to Drum. Drum scowled.

"Had us one Sheriff Timothy last night."

"That figures. His real name's Rudy Boaz."

Drum finished reading.

Timothy waited patiently.

"Rudy Boaz?" Drum said. "You mean he works with that younker, Tom Dyce?"

"That's right."

"Working this badger game?"

"Yep."

"You can put the hogleg away."

Timothy stowed the .45.

Drum appeared to be whipped.

"Mrs. Drum's nigh going to cut her heart open and pour salt in it."

"That's Tom's stock in trade. Playing the dogie."

"So straightforward he was. Both of 'em."

"Don't rawhide yourself, Mr. Drum. You're just one more in an awful long string."

"How long they been doing this?"

"All the way from Texas. Sold that black nineteen times. How far's the border?"

"Twelve miles."

"Expect they've crossed."

"Knowed you was on their heels?"

"Yep."

Drum said, "By God, I know that country."

He reached a sharp, final decision.

"Buck, go up and ask Mrs. Drum to fix a foodsack."

The puncher left.

"Mr. Drum," Timothy said, "you know I can't violate the border."

"I can."

"Mr. Drum—"

"When I was seven I learned I could escape chores if I could just get behind the stable. If Pap couldn't see me I couldn't hear him. You figure it's different with Uncle Sam?"

The sheriff looked undecided. Drum came over the rail and stood on the ground looking up at him.

"I hate sheep so bad," he said, "I'd die before I'd be a shepherd. But I don't mind herding men. I'll haze them two varmints back over the line to you."

Timothy spread his hands.

"Who really owns that black stud?" Drum asked.

"Bill Mudd. Van Horn's Wells, Texas."

"I swear, I hate to tell Mrs. Drum . . ."

When he waved to Mrs. Drum and the sheriff half an hour later, he wore his mackinaw, had rations and ammunition. Mrs. Drum's expression reflected worry.

"He'll take care of himself," Timothy said.

"Course he will. I wasn't worrying about him. I was thinking of them two varmints."

Her face softened. "Not really. Only that varmint, Rudy Boaz. And that poor boy he's dragged down with him."

Her eyes flashed.

"That Boaz! Back in Vermont they'll tell you, Never cheat a cheater."

The sheriff looked puzzled.

"My husband cheats at checkers."

Timothy looked a little shocked.

"That man!" She was waving now as Drum turned to look back

a final time. "Going clean over into Sonora just because he can't stand to have anybody best him. He just . . . can't . . . stand it!"

It wasn't much past noon when Drum rode down the baked slope into the single street of the little border town. On the north side a sign proclaimed this as Littlejohn, Arizona. Across the street another announced it as Juanito, Mexico. The buildings here were frame and weatherbeaten, there adobe cracked and rain-stained. A few sleepy men and donkeys lounged or moved lethargically. One saluted Hugh Drum as he rode slowly toward the ancient church with the cross on the steeple.

Before he could dismount, a young priest with solemn eyes came from the door. He was in the brown robe of a Franciscan, and his face showed recognition.

"Senor Dromm . . ."

"Buenas dias, Padre. Felicitas?"

"It is well."

Hugh Drum brought out a silver dollar.

"For the poor box, Padre."

"Gracias, gracias. God bless you."

"I have business with Pablo the Hablo."

"The Talker? I have not seen him this day."

"Last week? Yesterday?"

"He lives now with the eagles."

"Muerto?"

"No," with a smile, "he lives. High in the hills. In a skin tent."

He pointed out a promontory. Drum thanked him again and rode out.

Later he came riding down the side of the mountain with Pablo the Hablo astride a small Spanish donkey. They turned into a narrow trail.

It was half an hour to sundown when they came off this trail in a canyon far to the south. There was growth here. Clumps of willow. A small stream. The ranch house before them was small, of native mud, with a stable and corral nearby.

Pablo suddenly fearful, stopped on the trail and pointed. Drum handed him a silver dollar as he passed the Spanish donkey. Pablo bit it, smiled fleetingly and showing the fear again, whirled the donkey and heeled it back up the trail.

Drum tethered his horse in the willows, checked his pistol and, taking the rifle, moved to cover.

The only sounds from the house were those of Dyce cooking supper. Rudy Boaz lay on a bunk smoking, watching the boy through lidded eyes. The last of the sundown shone on the glass of the window and faded. Boaz raised up on an elbow.

"I asked you a question three minutes ago," he said.

Dyce didn't turn. Just lifted a shoulder and let it fall.

Boaz snarled, "You got cabin fever already?"

Dyce turned then.

"It isn't contagious." Dyce went back to the cooking.

"Eating you?" said the man who'd played sheriff.

"No."

"Spit it out. Do you good."

Dyce said nothing.

"Thinking of them people?"

"She was good to me."

"They all are."

"She was different."

"And the old man?"

"Him too."

"Like all the rest. Greedy."

"No. They were—"

The crack of a rifle cut that off. The bullet whanged into the wall. Dyce dived for the floor. Boaz rolled from the bunk. The shots came steadily, spaced, moving. When the racket quit they crawled to their guns in belts on the chairs.

The rifle started up again. Boaz edged up and stood flat to the wall near the door.

"When he reloads, cover me."

Dyce nodded. The firing stopped. Boaz got the door open fast and was out and running. Dyce fired through the window into brush.

Drum was reloading when he saw Boaz running crouched toward

the stable. The figure disappeared there and Drum got the rifle up for three quick shots. He sent one into the house. Boaz stepped out and snapped a shot from his pistol. Drum took it in his upper arm, reeled, let go of the rifle and fell against the brush.

Dyce came out of the shack as Boaz yelled. They ran to Drum. He rolled, trying for the rifle. Boaz threw down on him but missed, distracted by Dyce. He faced Dyce, didn't like what he saw and dropped his gun.

Drum came up, clutching his arm. Dyce motioned him into the house. He lurched toward it, Boaz close behind, Dyce covering both of them.

Presently Dyce, having bandaged Drum's arm, glanced over at Boaz who, disarmed, sat drinking coffee at the table. Boaz sneered.

"No need lettin' him bleed to death," Dyce grumbled.

"Dead men don't bleed."

Dyce stood silent.

"He's dead," Boaz said.

"Not in my book."

"Something different about this one?"

"You're not killing him."

Boaz said to Drum, "Old man, your string's run out."

"Hell with you," Drum said.

Dyce told the fake sheriff, "You had this figured. You *like* to kill. You always hope they'll follow."

Boaz stood slowly, eyes on the gun in Dyce's holster, then at his own holstered gun on the chair.

"If you didn't have me covered—"

Dyce made a curt gesture. Boaz eyed him, not believing it.

"Take it," Dyce said.

Boaz picked up his belt, clapped it around him and buckled it. Drum watched Dyce, wondering. He scarcely dared breathe.

Dyce watched Boaz unwinkingly.

Boaz lost his smile. His lips twisted. Dyce saw the intention take shape in his eyes. His own gun was out, flame raveling from its muzzle when Boaz cleared leather. Two neat holes appeared just beneath Boaz's shirt pocket. He plunged forward, straightened, staggered, crashed into the bunk and fell to the floor.

Dyce waited long seconds, then holstered his gun and helped Drum to his feet.

He was on the black stallion the next day just after breakfast, not manacled, sitting quietly by Sheriff Timothy, looking down at Mrs. Drum. Drum held her hand with his good one.

"No," the sheriff was saying, "I wouldn't think of putting cuffs on him."

"Shouldn't be too bad of a sentence, will it, Sheriff?" Drum's eyes pleaded.

Timothy regarded Tom Dyce with something close to affection.

"Law isn't all blue steel," he said. "There's flesh on it and blood in it. There's family in the law."

"You got a good chunk of the money back," Mrs. Drum said, nodding.

Timothy sighed.

"When you get out," Mrs. Drum said straight at Tom Dyce, "you're to come back here. You understand—"

Dyce started to nod.

"—Son?" she finished.

He smiled slowly, then broader, looking boyish again. They all smiled then. The sheriff lifted his reins and they rode out. At the sycamores, Tom turned, holding up a hand. His last view was of the two of them standing there together.

They went inside and he sat down at the table where the unfinished game was still laid out. She went to the stove for his coffee and, seeing a quick chance to invade her king's row, he moved a checker in and crowned it. He slanched a glance at her back. She was busy. He scowled, moved the checkers back the way they were and sat back with a great satisfaction.

She came with the coffeepot, glanced at the board, smiled broadly and tucked a napkin under his chin. Then she leaned and kissed the top of his head. He reached up with his good hand and found one of hers.

She said, "I guess he taught you something after all."

High-Carded

by *Lewis B. Patten*

Author of at least two dozen novels, Lew Patten—for the third time contributing to a WWA anthology—makes one of his rare appearances as a writer of short tales. A Coloradan, Patten is perhaps best known for the hard, tough, no-holds-barred yarn and some of the ruggedest heroes ever to climb a bronc.

☙ ☙ ☙

GEORGE SEXTON STOOD UP IMPATIENTLY. "Daggone it, Wesley, I don't need you to tell me what I have to do. If I resign you'll have to hoist your fat carcass onto that swaybacked mare an' go after him yourself."

He felt a stirring of disgust as he looked at Sheriff Wesley Terry, whose big body spread to fill the swivel chair like gelatin in a bowl. He took his gun belt down from a nail and strapped it on. He hesitated over the deputy's badge, then unpinned it and slipped it into his pocket. "Cade will know I'm after him without parading this. No use to rub it in."

As he rode down Main and out of town he kept ignoring the

gnawing at the back of his mind, as though by his refusal to recognize the fear he could eliminate it. But he could read the question in everyone's eyes as they furtively glanced at his set, bitter face: What if he won't come in? What if he says, "Go to hell, George. Come and get me."

George knew they'd be laying bets on that down in the Stock-men's & Farmers' Saloon. He wondered what the odds would be. He could almost hear the talk.

"Two to one he'll bring Cade in alive. Cade's too blamed used to losin' to George to put up much of a fight."

"Cade hates the air George breathes. He'll fight, but I reckon he won't have much chance agin' George."

George scowled. A man lived by a certain set of values and it gained him nothing to doubt them. Pa had always said, "Idea is to win—to come out on top. A winner is what folks respect in this world."

Suddenly George hated the townspeople. Pity for him in this predicament, or understanding, he saw in not one face—only the avid, waiting tenseness, their eyes dilated with expectancy.

They'd all wanted to form a posse and go along, but George had been firm about this. Too many accidents could happen when a bunch of townsmen went on a manhunt. He'd told the sheriff, "I'm hanged if I'll head up a posse. If you figure it's going to take more than one man, go get him yourself!" George well knew the sheriff had no intention of exposing himself either to the saddle or to hostile gunfire.

Wasn't much doubt where Cade would be. He'd been wounded and would have to head somewhere where he could rest up and heal. That would be the old Hollister homestead shack where as boys they'd gone on overnight pack trips whenever their father, old Luther Sexton, would let them off long enough from the ranch work in summer.

So George took the trail up Red Creek, staying high, out of the willow tangle in the bottom, but looking down at the tumbling, white water. He had fished with Cade in Red Creek when they were kids, before . . . well, a long time ago. Down there was a bend, a deep pool where he'd caught "Old Mossyhorns," the largest trout ever to come out of Red Creek.

Recalling that big fish set him to thinking. Cade had been awful sure that he, and not George, would get "Old Mossyhorns." Cade had hooked the monster three times, lost him all three. And Luther, hearing his two sons talking one day, offered the one that caught the fish a new Colt six-shooter. Pa was always doing that, George remembered. Pitting one against the other. Maybe that was most of the trouble—the trouble that came later. The spirit of competition was too strongly developed.

George's hand dropped unconsciously, caressing the worn grips of the Colt at his side. The same gun. He'd carried it all these years. Come to think of it, the thing must have been a constant source of irritation to Cade—a sort of symbol of failure. Because Cade had gotten an old one, one the foreman gave him, and somehow never quite came up to George's marksmanship with it.

It really went back further even than the fish. But the fish and the gun had been the beginning of the bitterness in Cade, and he had begun to blame George for his failures—George who couldn't lose at anything, who took each victory as though it was his due. George wondered why a realization as important as this one always came to a man too late.

George had been ten when he caught "Old Mossyhorns." Cade nine. Some way, old Luther Sexton thought continual striving would make better men of them both. Trouble was, George had always possessed just a little bit more persistence, a little more confidence, a tiny bit more ability—or possibly it was just his age. Too, George favored Luther, Cade his mother who had died bearing him, and maybe that accounted for the difference.

The small victories had been George's all along the line, but they had not seemed small at the time. And failure, continual, inevitable, had gradually begun to warp Cade's character.

The sun climbed in the sky and heat waves shimmered from the parched ground. "Funny," thought George, "how everything a man sees reminds him of somethin'."

There was the old corral, gray, weathered, mostly rotten and falling to the ground. It kind of marked the second important episode in the shaping of two lives.

Wild horses. That was the year the cavalry was calling for remounts. George was fifteen that year. Cattle were cheap. Luther figured if he could corral a couple of hundred wild horses, cull them and break the best of the lot, he could make some money selling remounts. Looking back at the incident, George's face suddenly felt hot and he was not very proud. He hadn't really meant it to turn out that way, and Pa's making such a to-do over it had just made it worse.

George let his horse have its head and, chin sunk to chest, his eyes turned blank and faraway.

Pa stationed George and Cade, one at the end of each corral wing, back far enough in the high brush to be hidden from sight, with instructions to ride in as soon as the wild horses ran into the corral and block the entrance until the rest of the crew could arrive and put up the poles.

Suspense tingled through George, waiting. Then horses, a hundred head or more, thundered down the valley, leaping washes, hammering through brush, beating it to the ground. Dust rose in acrid, choking clouds from their frantic hooves. Their sides gleamed with sweat.

Young George trembled with anticipation. "Go on in, you devils!" he whispered hoarsely as they slowed in front of the corral, went to milling. "Go on in!"

He glanced across the valley, looking for Cade, but his brother was invisible in the tall brush.

Half a mile away, Luther and the rest of the crew, knowing that the horses would now be very near the corral, released a volley of shots, a wild chorus of yells.

"Attaboy, Pop," said George softly, and watched the horses resume their slow forward movement into the corral. Half a dozen were still outside when he spurred his mount, thundered out of hiding and down toward the open gate. But Cade was ahead of him, riding like crazy, yelling like a Comanche.

George muttered, "You crazy fool! You'll put them all out, yelling like that. Take it easy!"

Cade reached the opening, leaped from his horse. He stood in the gate, waving his arms, yelling. George bawled, "Shut up, blame you! You'll scare them crazy an' they'll rush you!"

Bitter had been Cade's eyes, looking up, bitter his words. "Got to be first at everything, don't you, George? Can't stand to be beat."

Funny. George hadn't even been beat that time. He was still fifty feet away when a big sorrel stallion screamed, pawed, and rushed Cade, the whole bunch behind him.

Cade stood for a moment, whitening, his eyes wide and staring. Then his nerve broke and he abandoned his post, scrambling for the wing. George, who had thought his presence beside Cade might stop the stallion and who had already dismounted, found himself suddenly alone, thirty feet in front of the maddened beast.

Sheer terror overwhelmed him momentarily, froze him in his tracks. An awesome sight, that stallion thundering down on him. It would have been no disgrace for a boy to run, but George couldn't do it. Cade had run and George figured he was better than Cade. George pulled the Colt six-shooter and dropped the stallion, and the shot turned the rest of them back. Luther and the crew rode up just in time to see the whole thing.

Looking back on it now, George wondered why he hadn't told Cade and the rest of them how scared he was. It might have helped. It might have dulled the flame of hate that kindled in Cade's eyes. It might even have kept unsaid the puncher's comment, muttered, but heard by them both, "George's got twice the guts the young one has."

Water under the bridge. If any one of the episodes George could remember had been reversed, if Cade had ever won a really important victory over him, the whole course of their lives might have been changed.

He came to the place where the trail forked, took the right turn. Rising now, he could look back down the valley into hazy distance.

It was hard to believe, Cade Sexton wanted for attempted train robbery, the only survivor of the crew that made the abortive attempt. Cade Sexton, running, hiding, pursued by his own brother, the deputy sheriff, sworn to uphold the law. Cade, dark of hair, slim, laughing of eye in those early years, lately grown moody and sullen.

Down there, almost out of sight in the haze that lay over the valley, was the McCollums' place. George thought of Jenny Mc-Collum, and Jenny was another link in the chain of unfortunate events.

It made a man sick, looking back on it all like this. Of what good to him now was the fact he had always bested Cade? Why couldn't he have seen it as clearly, going along, as he did now? Things might have been so different.

Luther was ageing, failing, the year the McCollums moved into the valley. Most of the ranch work was falling on George, who seemed naturally to assume it, and he and Cade, formerly so close, were virtual strangers.

Jenny was a pretty, empty-headed little thing, her eyes perhaps a shade too calculating, her red mouth too likely to pout if she did not always get her own way.

But with women as scarce as they were, the punchers that hung around the McCollums' sod-roofed shack were not inclined to be too particular.

Cade went all out for Jenny. And Jenny, wise enough to weigh the size and richness of Luther Sexton's Square S outfit against the empty jeans of the drifting punchers, soon ran off everybody but Cade—and, of course, George.

The worst part of that deal, George reflected, was that he hadn't even wanted Jenny. Maybe he'd seen through her. Maybe he'd been too tired from overwork to react to her the way a healthy man should. His only visits to the McCollum place had been on busi-ness, and he'd had nothing whatever to do with what happened. But could Cade see that? Hell no! Not Cade with a chip on his shoulder.

George always suspected that what happened was Luther's last blundering act of building, stone upon stone, the wall that now stood between George and Cade. George figured Luther had gone that day and seen Jenny, maybe told her that George and not Cade would inherit the Square S. Luther must have known George was not interested in Jenny. He'd probably wanted to free Cade of her.

Telling Jenny that would have made a difference, all right, Jenny being what she was. And Cade was better off for being turned down by her. But even Jenny unwittingly added to Cade's bitterness when she said, "It's George I love, Cade, dear. I can't help myself. I worship the ground he walks on." Sure she did, thought George, as long as it was Square S ground.

Blunders, mistakes, things misunderstood. Well, Jenny was gone, the sod-roofed shack only a cattle shelter now. The fish, "Old Mossyhorns," had long ago been eaten. The remount horses were smooth-mouthed now and out on pasture—or dead. But all had marked Cade's character, and George's, and the marks remained. Now was left only the final act of indignity, for Cade to be captured or killed by his brother George.

The trail entered rimrock, wound back and forth half a dozen times, and came out on top of the butte. George rode unseeingly, engrossed in his memories of days gone by.

Luther had been gone five years when the panic struck, and blackleg hit Square S at the same time. George had been for tightening up, letting most of the hands go, trying to weather it. But Cade had advised in his belligerent way, "Hell, don't be a sissy, George! Go borrow some money, replace what we've lost and keep building. That's what the Old Man would have done."

And that's what George did, mostly because he didn't want to drive Cade any further away from him, because he was older now and beginning to see just how petty those small triumphs were. When it was finished they'd both gone broke and the Square S was divided up and sold to a score of newcomers to the country. But Cade's hate had been kindled anew, because George had been right, as usual.

"About a mile now," muttered George. "Another thirty minutes and it will all be over."

Autumn's early frost had colored the quakie leaves, had turned the long grass underfoot a dusty color. A deer bounded out of the trail, unnoticed. A breeze came whispering down off the heights, a cool breeze, full of the promise of winter.

How fast time went. It seemed only yesterday that George had accepted the deputy's job, but actually it had been almost a year. Cade had spent it hanging around the Stockmen's & Farmers' Saloon, cementing acquaintances formed through the years, acquaintances he could feel equal, even superior to. A year of working only when necessary, quitting as soon as he had a month's pay. For, quick as the Square S had gone out of their hands, Cade had dropped George like a bob-tailed flush, rejecting coldly all George's overtures.

George moved off the trail, down through the quakies toward the old Hollister homestead cabin. "I'll ride in openly," he told himself. "Cade wouldn't shoot without warnin'."

In his mind was a good picture of the shack, weeds and grass growing in profusion from its sod roof, half buried back in the side of the hill for warmth, its pole rafters extending in front to form a porch. "Bet it's gone to rot since I seen it last."

He would come out of the timber a hundred yards from the shack, the way he and Cade had come up on the place a hundred times together when they were kids.

In his memory the shack was a place of comradeship with Cade. A place of boyish dreams, a place where shrill yells echoed, where childish Indians and outlaws ran rampant. It was a place where charred steak and potatoes tasted better than anything they ever had at home, where rivalry and bitterness could be forgotten—at least in the beginning.

Impatiently he shook his head. A man took an oath and he was expected to live up to it. George rode into the clearing and there was Cade, a rifle in his hands.

George beat down the impulse to check his horse. He kept going, looking quietly at Cade, hoping desperately the kid wouldn't get panicked and do something foolish. Cade wasn't a kid any more. He was nearing thirty.

"I figured you'd be here," George said.

Cade's lip curled. "You're always figurin', an' you're always right, ain't you? Well, I won't be high-carded this time, George. If you take me back, I'll be dead when you do it!"

There was no use explaining to the hate in Cade's eyes that he'd taken an oath to uphold the law. There was no use explaining anything.

His hand and arm muscles tensed. This was an end to rivalry. Could old Luther have seen it years ago when he began to build up the thing between his sons? No. No man can see twenty-five years into the future. If he could he wouldn't make so many mistakes.

Cade's eyes narrowed, his knuckles showed white against the brown stock and blued barrel of the rifle. George waited.

Cade's nerve broke first. "Judge, jury and executioner!" he screamed. "God himself, ain't you? Funny as it sounds, you was always a God to me." The man was almost sobbing now. "I thought the sun rose and set on you when we was kids an' came up here. But you always had to be showin' Pa and the rest of the country that you was better than me. Now you come up here with that gun Pa gave you hangin' at your side to show everybody one last time. Well, get on with it! No use standin' here all day!" He moved the rifle muzzle ever so slightly.

For a moment, George made no move. Then, dumbly, he shook his head. His shoulders sagged. Slowly, his hand went to his vest pocket, withdrew the deputy's badge and tossed it at Cade's feet. "You got more to fight for than I have, Cade. I reckon I can't beat you this time."

Cade looked surprised. He had never seen weakness in George before. Then George saw something in his brother's face, too, he'd never seen there before.

Cade asked incredulously, "You mean you ain't going to try an' take me in?"

George shook his head. "Pa had you an' me workin' against each other all our lives, when he should have had us workin' together. We're through with that. Go where you want. I'll ride the other way."

Cade looked long and hard at George. "No," he said slowly, new strength and confidence in his voice. "No, I think I'll just go in an' give myself up." He turned abruptly to his tethered horse.

George watched him ride into the timber. George didn't know what to think hardly. Why did a man have to be thirty years old before he got any sense? If he'd done something like this years ago. . . . He yelled, "There's a place in Arizona called Tombstone —mining town. I'll be there, waitin'."

No answer came out of the timber, but he knew Cade had heard. And he guessed he knew Cade would come.

Double Barreled Jackpot

by Gordon C. Baldwin

Another first-timer, Gordon Baldwin has a Ph.D. in anthropology, was an archaeologist with the National Park Service for thirteen years, and taught classes at the University of Arizona and the University of Omaha. Since 1954 he has been a full-time writer with much scientific work to his credit, eight novels, and two nonfiction books now in the mill. Included here is his first short story.

❧ ❧ ❧

"HOWDY, NEIGHBOR. You working for George Warren?"

The sudden and wholly unexpected words coming from behind him startled Adam Baxter and he straightened from the half-dug posthole and wheeled around. The voice had already warned him that the speaker was a woman, but he hadn't expected to see a pretty girl smiling down at him from the saddle of a big black horse, and he stared speechlessly up at her.

She was worth more than a casual glance. She was not more than nineteen or twenty, a year or so younger than he himself, and a man's flannel shirt and blue jeans did nothing to conceal the rounded curves of her slim body. She was hatless, her auburn hair fluffed by the wind, and her smoothly tanned cheeks were flushed with healthy color. Her wide-set gray eyes showed a ready humor lying close to the surface. Her nose was snubby and her lips were a trifle full, but Adam thought she was the most beautiful girl he had ever seen.

As he continued to stand there, leaning on the long-handled shovel, staring up at her, the girl swung lightly to the ground and repeated her question.

"Where's George? I didn't know he'd hired anybody?"

Belatedly Adam remembered his manners and jerked off his hat and shook his sandy-haired head. "He hasn't, ma'am," he told her. "I bought this place from him yesterday. If it's him you're hunting I'm afraid I can't help you. He left on the stage right after we closed the deal."

His news didn't appear to surprise the girl. Nodding, she said, "I knew he was thinking of selling." She smiled again and extended her hand. "I'm Terry Crane. My father and I have the next place south. Welcome to Silver Bow Valley."

"Pleased to meet you," Adam said, taking the small brown hand. "I'm Adam Baxter." Her fingers were firm and warm in his and he released them reluctantly.

Terry Crane regarded her new neighbor with feminine curiosity. She saw a stockily built young man, open-faced, with China-blue eyes above a wide, humorous mouth and a stubborn jaw. His sun-blistered face was shiny with sweat, and his shirt clung damply to broad, hard-muscled shoulders.

Adam's cheeks burned under the girl's frank survey. Disturbed, he pulled his glance away. He turned to survey the broken section of fence. It looked as if someone had deliberately cut the wire. But why would anyone do that? It must have occurred late the previous afternoon, for it had been all right yesterday when he and Warren had inspected the one-hundred-and-sixty-acre homestead.

The girl followed his frowning gaze to the twisted tangle of barbed wire and broken posts and gave a short gasp. "Why," she cried, "that looks like some of Diamond O's work." She whirled on the young man at her side. "Have they been bothering you already?"

Bewilderedly Adam shook his head. "You're the first person I've seen since I got back from town last night. Came out this morning and found this. Been all day repairing it." He looked at her curiously. "What's Diamond O and why should they bother me?"

Terry, giving him a closer inspection, now noticed things she had missed at first glance. Adam Baxter's sun-reddened face and the newness of his bib overalls and square-toed cowhide boots stamped him as recently arrived from the East.

"Didn't you talk to anybody in town?" she asked him. "Didn't anyone tell you about this place?"

Again he shook his head. "It was just what I wanted," he said, smiling. "Good land, a house and barn, and a fine spring."

"Nobody said it wasn't good land. That's the trouble. It's too good, particularly the spring." She paused to brush back a straying lock of hair, adding, "I knew they were putting pressure on George, but I didn't think it had come to this."

Adam gave her a puzzled frown. "But this is Government land. Warren homesteaded it and I bought it from him. The deed's recorded. How can anyone take it away from me?"

Her glance was pitying. "That's true enough, but before George Warren homesteaded her it was open range and was used by Overton's Diamond O. Now, because of the drought, Diamond O wants it back. That's why they cut your fence." Noting Adam's still puzzled expression, she said, in explanation, "So his cows can get to the water."

Adam remembered now that the dozen or so cows he had chased back through the gap in the fence had been marked with a peculiar diamond-shaped symbol. Remembered, too, was Warren's attitude in town yesterday. The man had acted skittish as a colt until the deal had been concluded. Save for the two or three people necessary, he hadn't even introduced Adam to anyone. Adam understood now.

"So that's why Warren sold so cheap?"

"Of course."

"But how can Overton get away with it? Isn't there any law out here?"

She looked at him strangely. "This isn't the East," she finally said. "We have a sheriff—Henry Dobson. Henry's a good enough man, I guess, but Big Jim Overton runs this county and Henry generally goes along with whatever Overton wants." Her voice had grown increasingly bitter. Adam got the impression she didn't approve of Jim Overton. Then, with a girl's sudden changeableness, she smiled and said, "I could be wrong. Maybe you won't have any more trouble. Anyway, I'm glad you're here. Come over for supper tomorrow night. Dad, I know, will want to meet you."

The unexpectedness of the invitation came as a surprise to Adam. He had heard of Western hospitality, of the free and easy manners of this range country, but he hadn't really believed what he'd heard. The fragrance of the girl's hair oddly affected his thinking but he managed to nod. "Thanks. I'll be glad to come. Besides," he said, grinning a little, "I never did much care for my own cooking."

There was a trace of mischief in Terry's brown face. "You may not like mine." Before he could move forward to help her she had stepped easily up into the saddle. She looked down at him, smiling. "We'll expect you, then, about sundown. Our turnoff is a mile below yours."

With a wave of her hand she whirled the big black around and sent him flying across the flat bench. Adam stood there, watching her, envying the way she swayed surely and evenly to the horse's motion. Someday he'd be able to ride like that.

He continued to watch until she disappeared from sight beyond a gray ridge. His gaze swung to the squat cabin backed up against a high rock rim. It wasn't much, only two small rooms made of logs chinked with mud, but it was solidly built and plank-floored, and it and the big barn and pole corral were pleasantly shaded by towering cottonwoods. And it was all his, his to build up into a real farm.

Late afternoon shadows were long across the valley, and the smell of this Wyoming land was clean and crisp and wild, sweet with the scent of sage and grass, not at all like the moist, heavy-laden air of Ohio he'd left three short weeks before. This was a strange country, he thought, and yet already he felt at home and immediately caught himself wondering if the girl who had just ridden off had anything to do with that feeling. A vague excitement touched him. He knew now that he had found here the two things he wanted in life—a home and a girl. It was that simple.

Adam shook his head and turned back to his digging. There would be plenty of time to think about Terry when he had his place in shape. And while he was at it, he might as well add another room. Women liked plenty of space.

He was tamping the dirt around the base of the last post when, for the second time, he was startled by the sound of a voice. This voice was harshly masculine, authoritative, demanding.

"You there with the shovel. Turn around!"

Adam straightened slowly, turned and found himself facing four riders reined up in a semicircle twenty feet beyond the fence.

All four were strangers to Adam but, as the rider at the far end of the line reined his bay, Adam glimpsed on the horse's hip the same diamond-shaped marking he had earlier seen on the cows. This, then, was Diamond O and the big man slightly forward of the others, blocky and solid in the saddle, with a heavy jaw, tight-shut mouth and hard, dark eyes, could only be the Jim Overton the girl had spoken of. He had that air of importance about him—almost an arrogance, Adam thought. All four, he noted, wore holstered guns, and their appraisal of him was cold and calculating.

"Howdy," Adam said.

Big Jim Overton ignored the friendly greeting. "You the gent who Warren sold out to?"

"That's right," Adam nodded. "Baxter's my name—Adam Baxter."

He leaned the shovel against the post, had started to lift one of the wires, when Overton's harsh voice halted him.

"Hold it, Baxter. We'll come over there."

The words seemed casual enough, but for some reason Adam felt a definite unease. He took a long breath, eyes running around the half-circle of men. An ugly smile was stretching Overton's mouth, and there were matching grins on the faces of the others. Of a sudden it occurred to Adam that this was no neighborly call. These hard-featured, gun-toting men were here on business. As the thought came to him Jim Overton inclined his head to the man on his right.

"Tex, you and Hank make a gate—a nice wide gate."

The man called Tex, a rawboned, loose-lipped individual, laughed. "Sure thing, Jim."

Adam was totally unprepared for what happened next. Tex and a squat, heavy-bearded man at the opposite end of the line, shook out their ropes, dropped loops over two adjacent posts and sent their horses lunging off at an angle. Adam stared unbelievingly. The ropes drew taut, the barbed wire sang. The posts literally leaped out of the ground. A large section of the fence came down. He had to scramble frantically backward to avoid a snapping coil of wire.

Numbly he watched the four men ride through the wide gap and haul their horses up in front of him. There was something grim in their silence, in the cold, dispassionate way they considered him. Apprehension climbed Adam's spine.

He was opening his mouth to utter a protest when Overton said harshly, "That's just a warning, Baxter. There's no room for you here. Better shake dust inside of twenty-four hours or—"

"But this place is mine! I just bought it!"

Overton said impatiently, "I need this water."

Adam stared up at the cold-eyed rancher. He moistened suncracked lips, trying to fight off the tension in the pit of his stomach. This wasn't real. But it was happening. He was gripped by a sense of helplessness.

Overton looked back at him, seeming to speculate on the amount of defiance in Adam. Suddenly he glanced at the fourth member of his crew, a lanky, middle-aged man with graying hair and a stubby mustache, and said, "Hold your gun on him, Cass. All right, boys. Work him over."

Tex and the squat man dropped to the ground and began moving in. They were almost upon him before Adam realized their intention. Then he saw the clenched fists, caught the hunching of Tex's shoulder. He began to get the drift of this.

Something broke inside Adam, then. Normally he was a stolid young man, calm, peaceful. He'd had his share of boyish fights but had never hit a man in cold, hard anger. Now Overton's arrogance, this deliberate destruction—the unprovoked assault, were too much for Adam. He felt a growing panic, but if this was the way the cards were going to fall, he might as well get at it.

The rage in him exploded into sudden, savage movement. It took Tex by surprise, and Adam hit him with a solid right and left.

The first blow caught Tex low in the belly, driving the wind out of him. The second landed full on his jutting chin, slamming him flat on his back. For a moment Tex lay there, gasping for breath. Adam paused to look down at him, pleased at the ease with which he had accomplished this. But it was no time for daydreaming.

Too late, he remembered Tex's partner, Hank. He had a blurred impression of a shape hurtling at him. He tried to dodge aside, but the man was too quick. A fist clubbed him brutally over the ear. Adam staggered with the impact, but held his feet. He managed to twist around in time to block the next blow. He pounded the squat Hank with a jolting right, had the satisfaction of hearing a grunt of pain.

Then Tex was back on his feet. There were two of them now but for a minute Adam managed to hold his own, fighting with a savage ferocity. An angry shout came out of Jim Overton. Saddle leather skreaked and Adam guessed the Diamond O owner was about to mix into it.

He fought to break clear. A gun barrel cracked solidly against the back of his head, hammering him to his knees. For a moment he could not move, his head filled with a wild ringing. In that instant he felt his arms grabbed. He was rudely yanked to his feet.

"Hold him like that," Overton ordered, stomping around in front of Adam. The rancher put away his gun, grinning wickedly. "You going to leave tomorrow?"

Dazed, scarcely conscious, Adam tried to focus his eyes on the man. His head pounded. His mouth was dry. Scared and bewildered, he was still determined not to be driven off his land. He started to shake his head but the world slid into a sickening spin.

"No," he managed to mumble.

The word was barely out of his mouth when Overton hit him, splitting Adam's lower lip. The pain of that smashing fist cleared his head. He struggled violently to get free, but Overton's two punchers held him too tight to wriggle.

Deliberately, mercilessly, the rancher went to work on him, driving hard, sledging punches. Arms pinned, there was no way Adam could avoid the blows. All he could do was try to set his muscles against those belting fists.

He didn't lose consciousness. The man wanted him to feel every hurt he inflicted. The world became a shocking red haze as blood streamed from the cuts Overton's ring was opening. Adam was beginning to wonder how much of this slugging a man's head and ribs could stand when it stopped.

Adam sagged, knees buckling. Roughly the pair holding him jerked Adam upright. Dimly he caught Overton's taunting voice.

"You hear me, Baxter?"

Adam lifted his head. Through a pain-clouded haze he could see Big Jim Overton a few feet in front of him, hands on hips, a sardonic grin twisting his sweat-streaked face. There was blood in Adam's mouth. He tried to dredge up some words but couldn't.

"This is just a sample," Overton said, "of what you'll get if I find you around here after today. There's a stage out of Silver Bow tomorrow afternoon at three. You better be on it." Overton paused and laughed harshly. "If not, you better start packin' a gun."

Adam tried again to get out words, but his strength was gone. He saw Overton jerk his head at the two men holding him. He felt their hands leave his arms. He was starting to slump forward, relieved of their support, when he saw Overton's fist coming at him once more. He could do nothing to evade it. He felt its impact all the way down to his boot heels. His knees came unhinged and twisting, he fell face down in the dust, barely conscious.

Overton said, "All right, boys. Let's do a real job on that fence."

He heard the creak of saddle leather, a faint swish of ropes—more posts coming down. A few minutes later there was a drumming of hoofs, gradually fading.

Adam tried to get up. But the pain was too great and the strength was drained out of him. He seemed to be sliding down a dark spiral.

Consciousness came back very slowly and painfully. The ground felt damply cool beneath him, and he opened his eyes and the dark was all around. He guessed he had been unconscious for a considerable while. Fighting back a wave of dizziness he dragged himself to his knees.

His mouth was cotton dry. There was a hammer at the top of his skull. He felt the back of his head where the gun had clouted him and shuddered. He was sore and stiff; he ached all over from the beating he had taken. Slowly, laboriously, he pushed to his feet and peered stupidly about, finding himself alone. The only sound was his own ragged breathing.

Legs wobbly, he made his way across the flat to the cabin and, going around to the spring, ducked his head in the overflow. The chill shock of the water cleared his brain, dulled the pain. He stumbled into the house and fell across the bed, too beat to remove his clothes.

He slept late the next morning, not awakening from his drugged slumber until the sun topped the redrock rim behind the cabin and sent a shaft of light full in his eyes. When he looked at himself in the cracked mirror over the washbasin, he frowned at what he saw. His features were bruised, his lips split. His whole face felt swollen —he hardly recognized himself.

By the time he had stripped and had a bath below the spring, scraped his face and put on his town clothes, he was feeling better, though woefully weak.

While he cooked and ate his breakfast, his thoughts chased themselves in circles. He had a choice. He could catch the three o'clock stage, as Overton had ordered, or he could stay. He didn't want to leave the valley. This was his home now. Yet if he refused to run, he had a fight on his hands. The picture of Overton with a gun in his fist was pretty dismal. And this time it would be with guns, not with fists. He couldn't imagine he'd have much chance against the man. His lips tightened. All along, he realized, there'd been only one answer.

He got up from the table, cleaned and put away the dishes, took a last look around. He spied the heavy shotgun leaning against the wall. It had been his father's and was the only thing he had brought with him from Ohio. He picked it up and went outside. Ten minutes later he had the team hitched to the buckboard and was heading for town.

As the horses moved into the edge of timber, Adam looked back. Would he ever see this place again? And what about Terry and her supper invitation? Northward, he could see where Overton and his men had torn down a hundred yards of fence. Already cattle were beginning to work through, heading for the spring.

It was noon, then. It was half-past two when he drew the team up in front of Sorenson's Mercantile in Silver Bow. He sat there a spell looking at the town. Two short blocks of weathered false fronts bordering a rutted street. Dust lay everywhere. But it suited Adam.

Diagonally across from where he sat rose the sun-faded front of the Crystal Palace. Half a dozen saddled horses drooped dispiritedly at the rack. Opposite the saloon, directly ahead of Adam, was the stage station. Already the hostlers were busy readying the stage for the three o'clock run to the railroad.

"You ain't got much time, son."

Adam twisted about to look up at the speaker, a portly, middle-aged man with a toothpick jutting out of his wide, mustache-hidden mouth. Adam saw the silver star. This would be Henry Dobson, the sheriff.

"You're the law," Adam said. "Can't you do anything?"

"You want to swear out a complaint?"

"Would it do any good?"

Dobson's shrug was eloquent. Removing the toothpick, he spat into the dust and said heavily, "You can't win, son. Be smart."

Putting the toothpick back in his face again, the sheriff nodded and clumped off. Just short of the stage station he stopped and put a shoulder point against the corner of the building. To the still watching Adam, he seemed to fall asleep standing there.

"Hear you're leaving town," someone said beside Adam, and he brought his glance away to take in the lantern-jawed face of the owner of the livery. The man added, "You want to sell them horses and wagon, I'll make you an offer."

"I'll let you know," Adam said. Beyond the man he had spotted Terry Crane. She was coming out of the Mercantile, several packages in her arms.

At sight of him, she gasped. "You're staying?" Her eyes looked wide and frightened.

Adam nodded. He couldn't trust his voice. Dressed in white shirt-waist and colorful print skirt, she looked even prettier than she had the day before.

"But you *can't* stay!" she cried. "You'll be killed!"

Adam shrugged. "I'm not running."

"But you don't know Big Jim Overton! You won't have a chance!"

"Some things a man can't dodge," Adam told her. "If I run now, I'll be running all my life. Anyway, I like it here. I like most of the folks I've met, certain ones especially." He looked full at the girl, holding her eyes. A faint flush came over her. After a moment he added, "You'll be in town awhile?"

She nodded mutely.

"Then I'll see you later. I think you'd better get away from me now."

Out of the corner of his eyes he'd seen a man push through the Crystal Palace's batwings, throw a glance at the wagon, and duck hurriedly back inside. It had been, Adam was sure, one of the Diamond O crew.

Terry had glimpsed him too. Cheeks paling she said, "I wish you luck, Adam," and, turning, walked quickly away.

Up ahead a man called, "That's the lot, Will. Take 'em away."

A man yelled, a whip cracked. The six stage horses lunged into their traces. The coach lurched and began to roll forward, trailing a banner of dust. Adam tooled the buckboard into the space vacated by the stage. He wrapped the reins around the brake handle and turned slightly, facing the Crystal Palace, right hand resting lightly on the seat.

All along the walk men slowed, and stopped. Within thirty seconds all movement, all sound, up and down the street had ceased, every door and alleyway holding its quota of silent watchers. In the stillness, the creak of the saloon doors was startlingly loud as Big Jim Overton, flanked by his trio of gunhands, stepped through to the walk. For a moment the rancher looked fixedly at Adam, dark eyes narrowed. He stepped into the street and lifted his voice.

"You leavin' or stayin'?"

It was Adam's move. He could clear out or fight.

"I'm not running, Overton," he said flatly. "I'd like to live here in peace, but if it's war you want you can have it right now."

Overton's mouth fell open. Then he snapped his jaw shut and ripped out a curse.

"If that's the way you want it—" He went for his gun.

But Adam moved faster. His hand swept up the shotgun from the seat and leveled it before Overton's gun cleared leather. Overton's face whitened as he stared into the two round barrels of that gaping death. He dropped his Colt as though it had burnt him. One of the Diamond O hands muttered a curse and started a hand toward gun, but stopped all motion when Adam said:

"Better tell your crew to keep out of this, Overton, if you want to stay in one piece."

Overton needed no second warning to give the required order. He didn't care for the look of those ominous steel tubes. He knew what they could do to a man.

"I told you all I wanted was peace," Adam said, "and I intend to have peace one way or another. You're one of those who thinks might makes right, aren't you, Overton?"

Puzzled, Overton nodded. "Yeah. Sure."

"Then if I'm able to beat you with my bare hands, will you leave me and the rest of these people alone?"

Overton's calculating eyes weighed him briefly. "Hell, yes!" he said with a short ugly laugh. Thirty pounds heavier, a good four inches taller than Adam and with a correspondingly longer reach, the man had no doubts at all of the outcome. He had never lost a saloon brawl yet. He pulled back his shoulders and let out his breath.

Adam called: "Sheriff, will you hang onto this shotgun and keep off the rabble?"

Henry Dobson was at Adam's side in three strides. "I'll shoot the buttons off the first gent that opens his mouth," he said, taking the shotgun into both hands. "Shuck your arsenal, Jim. This is going to be square."

The rancher unbuckled his belt, looped it over the tie rail and came lunging, sensing a quick and easy victory. Adam met him in the center of the street. Overton drove a hard right to Adam's face, mashing lips already considerably damaged. But it was the last punch he landed.

It was short and savage. Adam met him, never once backing up. Moving around Overton, hunting an opening, he saw Terry Crane on the seat of his buckboard watching wide-eyed, both hands to her mouth.

He found his opening then and his fist took Overton squarely in the face. Blood spurted as the rancher's nose squashed flat. Overton, stunned, tried to hit back, but he never got a chance. Adam knocked him down with a vicious right. Waiting until Overton was back on his feet, he again sent him sprawling. After five of these upsets Overton lay there, blinking dazedly up as if he couldn't believe what had happened. He presently rolled over and, getting himself onto an elbow, wiped a shirt sleeve across the wreck of his face.

"Had enough?" Adam panted.

Overton didn't have the breath to answer. All Overton could do was move his head up and down. Adam lowered his hands and took a look at the crew. He found grudging admiration in the eyes that met his. A man at the back of the crowd said, "By Gawd! I didn't think there was a man in the Territory could do that!"

Adam brought his glance back to Jim Overton. "Be at my north line," he said, "first thing tomorrow morning with enough men and wire to repair that busted fence."

Again Overton nodded, and Sheriff Henry Dobson added, "I'll see that he's there, son."

And then Adam Baxter was smiling as he broke through the circle, his legs quickly carrying him across to the buckboard and the waiting girl high on the seat.

He grinned up at her through sweat and dust and blood and said, "That supper invitation still open, Terry?"

Timber Tough

by Noel M. Loomis

Second President of WWA, Noel Loomis has served on the Board as a director and has for several years been the organization's Secretary-Treasurer. He has edited one WWA anthology (*Holsters and Heroes*, Macmillan, 1954) and appears equally at home in all categories of this field. His novel, *Short Cut to Red River*, won the Spur for Best Western in 1958; with "Grandfather Out of the Past" he won the Short Story Spur in 1959.

☙ ☙ ☙

BIG, BLACK-HAIRED Steam-Engine Simpson stood a-straddle a ten-inch pine log and swung his broadax lustily down the sides, hoping to work up a sweat. He had almost reached the end of the log when Auvinen the Finn staggered up the snow-covered logging lane. Auvinen had blue eyes and cotton-colored hair, and he never wore a cap, even at thirty below zero.

Auvinen came to a stop, swayed for a moment with his eyes

closed, then shook his head vigorously. He opened his eyes and got Steam-Engine in focus. "The new foreman just got in camp," he said. "He went down to the river to count the ties. You think this one will crack the whip, ya?"

Steam-Engine sliced off the last bark from the side of the log. Then he pushed up his stocking cap so it hung on the back of his head. He smiled proudly at Auvinen. "I've sent three bosses back to Encampment already this season because they tried to crack the whip." He added grimly, "It's not for nothing that they call Bridger Peak camp the toughest logging crew in Wyoming Territory."

But Auvinen's brow, ordinarily as smooth as bleached leather, became furrowed. "The timekeeper says it is January yet and we are 'way behind on ties."

Steam-Engine snorted. "With you and me," he said confidently, "we can always catch up."

Auvinen looked at the trail of fresh-cut railroad ties behind Steam-Engine. "Ya, I never seen a man cut down a forest as fast," he said respectfully. "Sometimes I think you're ambitious."

Steam-Engine looked down at Auvinen fondly. Auvinen was built wide and solid like Steam-Engine, but he was forty pounds lighter. Still, he was the only man west of Laramie who could drink or fight or log with Steam-Engine. Auvinen never stopped drinking as long as there was liquor, and he never stopped fighting as long as he was conscious. So Steam-Engine overlooked his last insult.

"I'm working the akavit out of my system," he said, "and you better do the same. We got to trim out some ties." He looked faintly troubled. "I don't like any man to say I'm not doing my work. Maybe we been drinking too much of Breezy Baxter's bootleg liquor this winter. We better get going and catch up to our quota. Go back and get your ax, and tell Shorty Peterson to get up here, too. We got work to do."

"The new foreman sent Shorty down to the road to bring up his books."

Steam-Engine froze with his broadax on his shoulder. "Books!" he said with abhorrence. The ax whistled down and the razor-sharp blade was buried in the log up to the eye. He left it there, quivering, while he glared at Auvinen. "What's he bringing books into this camp for?" he demanded. "You can't cut ties out of a book. Is he trying to make fun of us?"

Auvinen stood up under Steam-Engine's accusing stare for a moment. Then he went back to the bunkhouse and got his ax and began to cut his own swath of chips and ties. He and Steam-Engine worked up the slope, alternately trimming the sides and bucking the logs into seven foot lengths. As they day went on, their axes rang louder and their cross-cut saws snored and squealed through live pine as they had not done for weeks.

Steam-Engine's conscience began to subside, and when they got back to camp that evening they both were sober, hungry and jovial. But Breezy Baxter met them outside of the bunkhouse and said furtively, "The new foreman is here." He looked disturbed. "He's been down by the river counting ties and checking the timekeeper's book," he went on. "He's told Shorty Peterson he didn't see how any camp could be fifty thousand ties short."

Steam-Engine felt a momentary qualm at the mention of fifty thousand, but after all it was just another big number, and with two good men like him and Auvinen, and maybe Shorty Peterson . . . Steam-Engine snorted as he turned to the bunkhouse door.

But Shorty Peterson, fifty-five years old and the bow-leggedest Norwegian in the Medicine Bow Mountains, was coming up from the timekeeper's shack with a sheet of paper in his hand. Steam-Engine waited, frowning.

"Here's a notice." Shorty pushed the paper under Steam-Engine's nose.

Steam-Engine looked. It was white paper ruled with faint blue lines, and filled with ink writing in shaded loops and curlicues. Steam-Engine ignored the paper. He looked down at Shorty and growled, "What does it say?"

Shorty took it back and began to read slowly but proudly: "Sunday, January 15, 1888. This is to serve notice that the Medicine Bow Logging Company has been bought by the Wyoming Tie and Timber Company. All employees will for the present be—"

Shorty paused and frowned over an unfamiliar word. By this time there was quite a crowd around, and Steam-Engine felt impelled to comment, "We got a foreman who writes letters to us."

Shorty looked up. "If you don't want to listen," he said, aggrieved, "you can read it yourself." He thrust the paper at Steam-Engine and stumped away.

Steam-Engine knew that Shorty must have hit a word he didn't know, otherwise he would have read it through. He stood staring at Shorty.

Then Auvinen said, "Well, read it."

Steam-Engine looked at Auvinen and then at the paper and drew a deep breath. He crumpled the paper in his huge fist and threw it on the ground. "I don't read no letters from no foremen," he said. "If he's got anything to say to me he can say it to my face."

Somebody looked toward the timekeeper's shack just then. In a moment they were all looking that way. The door of the shack was open, and a tall, slim man was standing in it. He met Steam-Engine's gaze without a change of expression. Then he withdrew and closed the door.

Steam-Engine was vaguely uneasy as he snorted and turned sidewise to get his shoulders through the bunkhouse door. The camp would get its quota, all right. He'd see to that. And when he'd see about the foreman.

Next morning when the crew went up to the timekeeper's shack to be checked in they met Slim Coleman, the new boss.

Slim was about thirty years old. He was tall and lanky, but he looked tough and his skin was a deep bronze. He sat at a little table as the men crowded into the cabin, and presently he opened a black-covered book, then raised his head. His calm blue eyes watched them as he said, "Carl Olson." When a thick, musical voice said, "Ya," the blue eyes moved quickly and appraised Olson. Coleman made a mark in the book. Then, "Gus Olson."

"Ya."

Another mark in the book. "Shorty Peterson."

"Ya."

"Breezy Baxter."

"Here," said Breezy.

The blue eyes studied Breezy for a moment, and a sort of glint appeared in their depths. To Steam-Engine it looked like contempt.

"You're down in the book as a tie-hack," Coleman said to Breezy, "but you've cut a lot fewer ties than anybody else—which is little enough."

"I been sick," Breezy said, lying.

Disbelief was plain in Coleman's face, but Steam-Engine knew instictively that Coleman would never ask Breezy or anybody else why his ties didn't total up right. This Coleman was beginning to look a little different from the usual parade of foremen.

Coleman's eyes dropped to the book. "Mike Auvinen."

The cotton-headed Finn said, "Ya."

Coleman looked up at Auvinen, and the way he looked made Steam-Engine comfortable again. A faint twinkle appeared in the depths of Coleman's eyes.

Then: "Steam-Engine Simpson."

"Here," came Steam-Engine's great guttural voice, and his big chest expanded proudly as he waited for Coleman's approval.

Coleman looked up. He took in Steam-Engine in all of his great length and breadth.

Coleman said, "I understand you're the camp leader."

"That's right," said Steam-Engine.

Coleman paused, seeming to speculate. There came in his eyes a flicker of the same look he had given Baxter. He looked back at his book and wrote something. Then: "John Anderson."

Steam-Engine felt squelched. He didn't like to be classed with Breezy. That fellow hadn't done one honest day's work since he had signed up in September. He made a monthly trip to Encampment and packed back a gunny sack full of akavit which he stashed in the woods and sold to the hacks. Steam-Engine reflected uneasily that, although they all had fallen down on their quotas, Baxter had kept others from working. Steam-Engine didn't like being classed with the bootlegger.

Coleman finished calling the roll, then laid the black book down. He stood up and looked them all in the eye. He was pretty tall, Steam-Engine saw, and looked wiry enough, but he underweighed Steam-Engine by nearly a hundred pounds.

Coleman said quietly, "I understand the Bridger Peak camp

takes pride in being the toughest crew in the Territory." That momentary warm twinkle came again in his blue eyes. "In fact," he went on, "I have heard some claim all of North America."

It seemed accidental that his glance settled on Steam-Engine, but Steam-Engine shifted his feet uneasily, for Coleman's glance lingered a moment too long and the twinkle was gone. Then Coleman resumed soberly, "Since you've sent your last two foremen into Saratoga with delirium tremens, I'd say you're justified in that claim."

He paused, and Steam-Engine stiffened. Now it was coming, and Steam-Engine knew that when it did he would be on familiar ground.

But Coleman said, "Drinking and fighting are your own affair—as long as you do your work. You signed up last September to cut out ties, and on that basis the company made a contract to furnish ties to the Chicago and Northwestern Railroad next July. This camp is the only one behind in its quota—and from the looks of this crew of loggers I see no reason for it. All I ask is that you do your work, and I expect you to keep up from now on. In fact, I think you can make up a big part of the deficit—if there is no disturbing influence in the camp."

His glance swept both Baxter and Steam-Engine, and again it bothered Steam-Engine to be counted off with Baxter. Also it puzzled him that he resented it, for Coleman was, after all, a foreman—a letter-writing foreman.

But Coleman was delivering his only rule: "Drinking interferes with work and is dangerous in logging. If you've got any liquor stashed away, drink it at night. No drinking on the job."

Steam-Engine knew the crew was eyeing him, awaiting a cue. So far, Coleman really hadn't said anything out of line, but the men expected Steam-Engine to speak up.

"How many ties you want us to make?" he asked.

"Any real tie-hack can trim out fifty ties a day. You get ten cents for every one, so I want seventy-five ties a day from now on by every man who can handle a broadax."

Steam-Engine raised his heavy black eyebrows. He and Auvinen and Shorty Peterson could maybe turn out a hundred a day if they were pushed. Steam-Engine was surprised that Coleman had not asked for more.

But Coleman didn't seem to understand that. His blue eyes became cold. "You're all experienced loggers," he said. "I'll see that you get good grub and plenty of it—six times a day if you want it. You see that I get ties." He waved them away.

Steam-Engine pushed his stocking cap back on his black head and said to Auvinen as they left together, "He didn't threaten to whip us."

"Not like the last one," Auvinen said.

They both remembered the last one, a big man named Harrison. He had lasted almost a month. Then he had made the mistake of challenging Steam-Engine.

The next morning Harrison managed to get out of bed unaided, but he tried to walk back to Encampment in his stocking feet. They had to tie him up.

"Maybe," said Steam-Engine, "Coleman ain't much of a fighter. He's not very heavy."

Bow-legged Shorty Peterson came up with his broadax on his shoulder. Shorty was older than most of them. "Sometimes," he said, "a boss can git your number without fist-fighting."

The next few days went fast. The men started working for Coleman. The averages went up. Steam-Engine's count hit ninety-six. Auvinen was cutting around ninety. Shorty Peterson was not far behind.

They went into February without dropping their pace. The teamsters skidded the ties away, and presently, down on the bank of North Spring Creek, the pile stacked on the ice began to reach a good size.

Every morning Steam-Engine could see Coleman go down to the creek to count ties and write in his little black book. Then Coleman would walk up the logging lane, which was now more than two miles long, to look at the timber ahead. The men were gratified by the pleased expression on his face. But the day after Steam-Engine hit a hundred ties even, Coleman went by without a word or even a look.

Steam-Engine was puzzled but not discouraged. All Coleman had asked was that they do their work, and Steam-Engine had hoped he would appreciate the extra ties he was getting. Every man on the crew felt the same about Coleman, and all were working for his approval.

All but Baxter, that is. Baxter wearied of working for a living, and one morning after Coleman had completed his usual survey and gone back toward camp, Baxter pulled from inside his shirt a quart bottle of akavit with a faded green and red label. "I'll sell this to the highest bidder," he said loudly.

It made Steam-Engine's mouth water, but he kept firm hold on his thirst. He stalked over to Baxter and took the bottle away from him. "I'll take this," he said. "No more drinking till we get caught up to the quota."

He turned to throw the bottle into the woods, but coming toward him was Slim Coleman. Coleman was too far away to have heard what Steam-Engine had said, but he was close enough to see the bottle in the big logger's hand.

He came up to Steam-Engine wearing a look of utter contempt, snatched the bottle, and hurled it deep into the forest. Then he faced Steam-Engine. "I said no drinking on the job. That means everybody."

Steam-Engine said helplessly, "I wasn't drinking."

Baxter kept still.

Coleman's eyes were like a slow fire. There was acid on his tongue. "I know about you, Steam-Engine Simpson. You broke the last three foremen in this camp, but that doesn't cut any ice with me. I didn't come up here to tell you off, but neither do I believe it necessary to take anything from a logger who is determined to make trouble."

Steam-Engine was confused. He wasn't trying to make trouble. His fists began to ball up, and he turned back to Coleman. Coleman's eyes were cold but somehow there didn't seem to be anything personal in what he said. Steam-Engine decided to let it go. He lumbered back to his broadax.

As he hacked out ties, however, he got more and more angry. He didn't mind so much that Coleman had taken the bottle, but he did resent the accusation of making trouble. He thought about it all afternoon. Nearly a hundred ties a day, and he was accused of making trouble!

After supper he went back to the bunkhouse and found his favorite black-powder keg to sit on. He pulled it up to the fire, clamped his broadax between his knees, and went to work with a razor-hone.

Auvinen was stretching, yawning. "Way we're going," he said, "we'll have a lot of drinking money when we get to Encampment next July."

Shorty Peterson said soberly, "I got ninety-four ties today. I'm going to take my money next summer and make a trip to the Old Country."

Steam-Engine's big hands at the ends of huge arms stopped honing the ax. He looked up and put all his discontent into a scorn which he did not mean for Shorty. "Three days after the drive you won't have enough money left to get to Cheyenne," he said. He studied Shorty and added sarcastically, "Or maybe you'll be buying books instead of liquor when we get to Encampment."

He was astonished at the immediate silence that fell.

Then Shorty said slowly, "There's worse things. Slim Coleman studies law books about timber every night and writes out lessons."

Steam-Engine glared around the circle of faces. "I don't read books on law," he said proudly, "but I can lick any man in Wyoming Territory."

There was no answer, and Steam-Engine realized with an abrupt chill that Slim Coleman had dominated them completely without ever fighting anybody—even Shorty. Steam-Engine moved his ponderous frame. He got up and hung his ax on the wall. He went outside, bareheaded, and stood for a few minutes morosely staring at the moon rising down the snow-filled valley, and thinking. Everything had been all right until Coleman took the akavit bottle, but now Steam-Engine's own leadership was in question.

He'd have to take care of that immediately. He had spent ten years building up his reputation, and no man was going to take it from him by reading law books. He strode off up the logging lane. It was twenty below, but the cold air felt good to his injured feelings. He remembered where he had been standing when he took the akavit from Baxter. He went into the woods and found it. The bottle had landed in soft snow and was unbroken. He opened it, took four deep swigs, put the bottle in his hip pocket, and went back to the bunkhouse.

Next morning, while he was pulling on his dry, stiff socks and his caulked boots, he took the bottle from under his straw mattress. He took two swigs and grunted. "A hundred ties a day I cut—and he says nothing. Never was a foreman you could satisfy."

Auvinen, who bunked above him, didn't answer, but Auvinen was watching the liquor. Might as well make it good, Steam-Engine figured. He passed the bottle to the Finn. Auvinen took four swigs and handed it back. Steam-Engine took four. Auvinen hit it again, and Steam-Engine finished it. By the time the breakfast bell sounded, both were roaring drunk.

The other men kept quiet around the breakfast table, but Steam-Engine and Auvinen roared at each other until finally Slim Coleman came in quietly and looked around. Steam-Engine expected the showdown then, but Coleman left without a word. He was carrying a book in one hand.

Steam-Engine growled to the Finn, "Anyone here can see he's afraid."

Auvinen looked doubtful. "Mebbe. Mebbe not."

Steam-Engine was disappointed because the crew didn't start a fight. He had seen the time when there would have been a riot if the foreman had even looked in the cook shack, but now they were a bunch of sissies. He let loose a Gargantuan snort of contempt. "Mebbe they want book-learning, too," he said to Auvinen. "Mebbe they can't fight no more."

By the time they finished the ham and eggs and fried potatoes and started on the flapjacks, the akavit was at maximum potency. Steam-Engine gulped down a pint of bitter black coffee and staggered outside. He got his broadax from the bunkhouse and started off up the mountainside.

Two hundred yards from the bunkhouse, Breezy Baxter was waiting for him. Breezy stepped out, broadax on his shoulder. "You owe me three dollars for that akavit," he said.

Steam-Engine frowned. Breezy Baxter was asking him for money, and Breezy had a broadax on his shoulder. It struck him irrelevantly that he never had seen Breezy fight. Breezy was big and his motions were quick, but he talked faster than he moved. Steam-Engine glared at him. Anger surged through Steam-Engine's brain, for he knew now that his position as camp leader had gone to pieces.

He looked at Breezy and roared through lips that felt big from the akavit. "Put down that ax, you—"

Baxter didn't move fast enough to suit him. Steam-Engine cocked an enormous fist. He didn't bother to take his broadax from his left shoulder, but held the end of the handle in the palm of his left hand. Then through the vapors of akavit he realized that Baxter had his own broadax in both hands and had it back over his shoulder and was menacing him with it.

"Touch me," Breezy said between bared teeth, "and I'll cut your head off."

Steam-Engine's indignation at being challenged by a man with a puny seven-pound ax was more than he could bear. His rage exploded, but he didn't bother to heft his ax. He jabbed at Baxter with a huge, hard fist. Baxter stepped back and swung his ax with both hands. Steam-Engine, in his amazement, stumbled just in time to hear the ax whistle over his head.

He was up then, with his broadax in both hands. Crouched like a panther, he went after Baxter, while Baxter retreated with his own ax over his shoulder. Baxter's ax was in position to swing, but Baxter, facing Steam-Engine's fury, was suddenly afraid to swing it. Steam-Engine stalked him, a low growl rising from his throat.

Then a slim figure was between them. Slim Coleman said to Baxter, "Give me that ax."

Baxter was glad to get rid of it. Coleman, with the ax in his hand, turned to Steam-Engine and said sharply, "Go on about your business." Then he sniffed. His eyes, blue and cold, looked straight into Steam-Engine's. "You're drunk," he said. "Go to the bunk-house."

All Steam-Engine could see at that moment was the picture of Slim Coleman walking into the cook shack that morning with a book in his hand. And now that same man was telling him to go home—like a kid. He looked in Coleman's eyes and remembered what Shorty Peterson had said about some men getting a man's number without fighting. That was what Slim Coleman had done. Without ever lifting a finger, he had gotten all their numbers—all but Steam-Engine's.

What he had done to Steam-Engine was worse. He had undermined his position. Even Auvinen didn't back Steam-Engine any more. The Finn was standing to one side, saying nothing. Peterson was on the other side, likewise noncommittal, and so were the rest of the crew, in a wide circle around Steam-Engine and Coleman.

A tremendous growl erupted from Steam-Engine's throat. With both big hands holding the broadax cocked over his shoulder like a baseball bat, he aimed at Coleman's shoulder a blow that would have amputated the foreman's arm.

Coleman did not have time to be surprised. He could only duck. The ax cleaved the knot off the top of his stocking cap. The knot floated to the ground. Steam-Engine grinned and waited confidently for Coleman to start backing away. Then his eyes widened. Coleman was coming after him, swinging Baxter's ax.

Steam-Engine jumped backward and brought his own ax up grimly. He wasn't in position, but he swung it in a great backhanded blow and the head caught Coleman in the side.

Coleman grunted, but the cold expression in his eyes didn't change. He swung at Steam-Engine's middle, the sharp edge first, but it was short.

Steam-Engine was feeling the ground with his feet. By now he knew what it was about Slim Coleman that had them buffaloed. It wasn't just guts and it wasn't strength. It was Coleman's conviction that he would win.

For the first time in his memory Steam-Engine wasn't sure of himself. For the first time in his life a man had faced him with a broadax and hadn't backed down—was even now attacking.

The blow came—a short, sharp cut that missed, but allowed quick recovery of the ax.

Steam-Engine put all of his force into a roundhouse sweep. The blade didn't bite in, but the knobby head skidded off Coleman's shoulder blades as he bent under it.

Steam-Engine recovered his balance. He got his eye on Coleman.

Coleman's ax was coming at him, and it was too late to duck. The ax took a slice of meat from the corner of Steam-Engine's shoulder. He hardly felt the cut, but he felt the blade scrape bone and saw the blood spurt out.

Up came the ax again. For the first time, Steam-Engine was scared. This man was trying to kill him. He shortened his grip on the ax and swung.

Coleman met it. The flat side of Coleman's ax-blade clanged on the side of Steam-Engine's blade. Then Coleman's blade sliced off the handle of Steam-Engine's ax and the nine-pound ax-head went spinning. It cut a big gash in Coleman's right thigh, and Steam-Engine lurched in for the close, head low. He knew he might get Coleman's ax in the backbone between his shoulder-blades, but he went in. Coleman stepped back. His wrist twisted and he tossed his ax away. Then he met Steam-Engine's rush.

His hard shoulder took the force off the logger's butting head. He sent swift, clean jabs at Steam-Engine's face. His fists were hard, and where they landed they cut. But Steam-Engine planted a blow on Coleman's nose that knocked him end over end, and Shorty Peterson had to move out of the way.

Steam-Engine drew a great breath and waited. Coleman got up. He came back, throwing fists. His eyes were still cold. He opened a cut over Steam-Engine's eye, and for a moment everything looked red. Then that eye didn't see at all.

Coleman took a smash to the side of the jaw but came back swinging. He landed on Steam-Engine's chin and the logger heard his own neckbones grind. He felt dizzy. There was one thing left. He closed in. He got his big arms around Coleman and pulled the slim man against him. His arms crossed in the small of Coleman's back. He got his big head against Coleman's chest. Coleman's back was arched. Steam-Engine strained for the crack.

But somehow Coleman managed to draw himself up enough to throw out his feet like the snapper on a black-snake whip. He literally threw himself out of the hold. He rolled when he hit, and although Steam-Engine tried to cover him, to pin him down, he kept rolling, and bounded to his feet. But even then he didn't run. He came back, both fists hammering.

Steam-Engine hesitated. In that second of pause he lost the fight, for Coleman knocked him out, swinging fast, deadly fists—two, three, four smashing blows to the chin.

Steam-Engine collapsed, falling on the frozen earth.

They were tying up his shoulder in the bunkhouse when he came to. He shook his head to clear away the cobwebs. He flexed his left hand and flinched. "Guess I'll have to work one-armed for a few days," he said.

Auvinen the Finn said in a hushed voice, "The boss vant to see you, Steam-Engine."

Steam-Engine got up on his big legs. He had been licked, but somehow he didn't feel so bad about it. And by the sound of Auvinen's voice he knew that even the Finn didn't look down on him for getting licked. He felt better. He walked to the foreman's shack.

Coleman was wrapping a bandage around his leg. He looked at Steam-Engine briefly and said, "Pretty good fight."

Steam-Engine swallowed. All of a sudden he was a little bit ashamed of having forced Coleman to fight.

Coleman looked at him again. This time his eyes studied Steam-Engine. Then they changed. They seemed to soften. He said, tying the bandage, "You want to work in this camp?"

Steam-Engine, surprised, said, "I sure have to work."

Coleman said, pulling on his boot, "Baxter high-tailed it. I guess he was the troublemaker—not you. I added up your totals. You've been cutting a lot of ties lately." He looked at Steam-Engine thoughtfully. "The first day I was here, I saw you throw my announcement about the sale of the company on the ground, and I figured you were at the bottom of things."

Steam-Engine felt his face grow warm. With any other man he would have said nothing, but with Slim Coleman it was different. He wanted Slim to know the truth: that he wasn't trying to make trouble.

"Everybody in this camp but me can read," said Steam-Engine humbly. "I can't even write my name." He looked at Slim Coleman, hoping for once that he would be understood.

He was. Coleman's eyes looked as if they were seeing a lot of things about Steam-Engine that most people didn't see. Then the deep twinkle came in them. He said, "I could teach you to write your name. I could even teach you to read if you want me to."

Steam-Engine nodded enthusiastically. "I'll come tonight," he said. He turned around and started to shuffle out. "I got to get a new handle for my ax," he said. "I lost an hour already with this damn fighting."

Due Process

by Steve Frazee

A Director and one-time President of WWA, Steve Frazee is one of the most original writers in this field today. Author of more than thirty novels and innumerable magazine fictions, he is a great outdoorsman, living with his family at Salida, Colorado, in a house they built themselves. This is his third anthology appearance.

☘ ☘ ☘

IT WAS MAYBE TWO WEEKS after old Ute Henderson died of the slow fever at his home place on the Little Peralta.

Spring roundup was on, which meant for four-five days crews from the five outfits in the southern part of the valley would headquarter at the big holding corrals not far from Joe Tonso's saloon and store.

Those of us who could get away in the evening after work would go up to Tonso's, which didn't mean we got roaring drunk every night. We didn't have that kind of money, and Tonso didn't give that kind of credit. We did get together for a little fun and talk.

This particular evening the fun was out. Obadiah Smith showed up and as usual he was trying to start trouble. He was a whopper-jawed, scorpion-eyed cuss who fancied himself as a gunfighter. We doubted that he was, but none of us cared to find out the hard way, and that of course made it easier for him to be a bully.

Obadiah's specialty was pushing Mexicans around. He worked for Burt Hamlin, who didn't have any Mexican riders, but there was a fair sprinkling of them in other Peralta Valley outfits. They always tried to avoid Obadiah.

This time it was Ragged Hudnall, one of Obadiah's own crew, that Obadiah was giving trouble. "Take a man like you, he don't have the guts for gunfighting," Obadiah said.

"You're right," Ragged said.

"Sure I'm right!" Obadiah swung a look around the room. "And the rest of you are the same way."

"Yep," Clum Bronson agreed, and the rest of us just tried to pay no attention. Obadiah was having one of his streaks. The best thing to do was let him run.

Not getting any rise out of us, he tried Joe Tonso. "This is a fine two-bit dump you run here, Joe."

Tonso was slopping glasses in a bucket behind the bar. "I guess you could call it that."

"I am calling it that!"

"Suit yourself," Tonso said.

Nothing makes a bully meaner than lack of resistance. Obadiah was trying to figure who to abuse next when Pistol Pete showed up, getting as far as the doorway before he saw Obadiah. Pete was a grinning, bandy-legged little Mexican who worked for the Circle T, a good rider, and about as harmless as they come. We'd nicknamed him because of the big old horsepistol he always carried. Nobody had ever seen him shoot the gun and some of his nearest friends claimed it was too rusty to go off anyway.

There he was in the doorway, grin wiped out by the sight of Obadiah.

"Come on in!" Obadiah said.

"I think maybe I have some business somewhere."

"Come on, come on! I'll buy you a drink."

Pete's big-toothed grin winked on and off as he came up to the bar. Tonso eyed Obadiah and said, "Don't start no trouble."

"Who's going to start trouble? You worry too much." Obadiah grabbed Pete's arm and hauled him over close, pouring him a drink. Obadiah raised his own glass. "To Pistol Pete, the terror of the Peralta!"

"Si," Pete said, straining to be agreeable. All he wanted was to get out the quickest way he could. He gulped the whisky.

"Another one," Obadiah said. "We'll drink to all the dirty, chili-picking greasers I'm going to wipe out one of these days."

Pete tried to grin. "Gracias," he said, and drank and started to leave.

Obadiah spun him around and threw a glass of whisky in his face. That was one of Obadiah's favorites. He liked to blind a man, gun-whip him down and stomp him into the floor.

I grabbed a singletree off the wall.

Obadiah reached for his gun. No hurry. He grinned as he watched Pete standing with his eyes squinched shut and whisky running off his face.

That was when Pete, blinded and scared, hauled out his rusty old cannon and fired. Talk about roar! Pete was blanked out by the powder smoke.

The slug knocked Obadiah back. He doubled over and hit the floor on his face, deader than a slunk calf.

We stood there with our mouths open.

Pete dropped the gun and ran. He hit the side of the door going out, bounced off and kept going. He was on his horse and away before we grasped the full fact of what had happened.

Tonso came trotting from behind the bar and got down beside Obadiah. "He's done for."

"He had it coming," Ed Glassman said.

Some of the boys carried Obadiah outside into the moonlight and put him alongside the wall.

"He was bought and paid for a long time ago," Tal Hunter said. We went back inside to talk about it.

Nate Matlock showed up a few minutes later, leading Pete by a rope around his chest and arms. "I was on my way here when I heard the shot. I met Pete, riding like a wild man. He wouldn't stop, so I went after him and roped him. What's going on?"

We told him.

Nate said, "This calls for a little investigation."

"Never mind that lawbook you stuck your nose into once," Glassman said. "There's no problem here."

Nate paid him no attention. "Why'd you run away?" he asked Pete.

Pete cut loose in Mexican so fast and furious that only Tonso could understand. "He says he was afraid the Hamlins would start a war of extermination against the Mexicans in the valley on account of it. He was going to warn them."

Pete nodded vigorously, cut loose again. "He says he thought you were bringing him back here to hang him," Tonso interpreted.

Nate took the rope off. "The facts seem clear. Self-defense—but of course we'll have to take it to a jury."

"Why?" I asked.

"Proper procedure," Nate said. "Due process of law."

Ragged grunted. "Hell! Let's just bury him."

Obadiah's pistol was on the bar. It had fallen out of the holster while we were carrying him outside, and someone had picked it up. "Is that the full extent of the search of the deceased?" Nate asked.

"That's his gun, yep," Tonso answered.

"We'll defer further action along that line." Nate was sure taking charge. "Right now, as a coroner's jury, it's up to us to determine the cause of Smith's death."

"He was shot," I said. "Dead center, by a slug big enough to knock over a buffalo."

Nate shook his head. "Hearsay. Set down, all of you, and let's have the evidence properly presented."

"You mean we haul Obadiah back in here?" Ragged asked.

"That won't be necessary. I want each man to tell carefully and honestly his version of what occurred."

"You don't talk that way all the time," Glassman growled. "What's bit you, Nate?"

"His ma used to stack lawbooks on his chair so's he could set high enough to reach table," Ragged offered. "I think his learning seeped in the wrong end of him."

Nate laughed with the rest of us, but he was some serious when he got started on legal matters. Before long he had things going his way. No wonder Pete got nervous, what with everyone so solemn, and one after another telling how he had killed Obadiah.

Pete decided we were working up a hanging, so he made a break for it. Clum tripped him. We made Pete go sit on a keg of salt pork while we completed the inquest.

Nate announced the finding. "One Obadiah Smith was killed by a bullet fired from a pistol in the hands of Pistol Pete, and the whole mess was self-defense."

"That was a heap of talking to get around to something that even Tonso's hound knew beforehand," Ragged observed. "Now, where do we get our pay?"

"Pay?" Nate shook his head.

"I was on a jury once and I got paid," Glassman argued.

"This wasn't exactly a jury, not the kind that gets paid, leastwise," Nate said. He thought for a while. "Well, I guess each man, including Pete, can have one drink."

"Who pays?" Tonso asked quickly.

"The court will take the matter of payment under advisement," Nate said.

Tonso grunted. "That means I'm stuck for the drinks." He set them out.

I didn't drink, and when I asked for a can of tomatoes, Tonso balked. "You get whisky, or nothing."

Whisky was two bits a shot. Tomatoes cost one buck a can. "All right, give me a cigar," I said. I didn't smoke, either, so I gave the dried-out black stogie to Pete.

Pete still wasn't sure that we weren't going to hang him. The cigar seemed like a last gesture. Once more he started to light out, but someone hauled him back and Tonso at last got it into his head we weren't holding anything against him.

"It's getting late," Ragged said. "We got plenty of hard work again tomorrow, so let's bury Obadiah and get out of here."

"It's not that easy," Nate said. "There's certain legal aspects yet to be taken care of. Tonso, give us your best lantern."

We assembled around the deceased. He didn't look very good in the moonlight.

Nate said, "You know, we haven't actually proved him dead."

"Huh!" I said. "I'm satisfied."

"We really ought to have a doctor say so."

"I hear there's one about seventy miles south," Glassman said. "Go get him, Nate."

"I'll have no levity," Nate studied Obadiah. "Yeah, I'd say there's no doubt about it."

"Where do we bury him?" Ragged asked. "Or does that take another court session?"

"The deceased will have to be thoroughly searched in the presence of witnesses."

"Help yourself," Tonso said.

"Get a pencil and some paper, Joe," Nate ordered. He looked at me. "You're appointed to do the searching."

"Who appointed me?"

"I did."

"I just resigned the appointment!"

"Court order," Nate said. "Get on with it before you're held in contempt."

Everybody else was quick to support him.

I rustled through Obadiah's pockets quick as I could. Found a Mexican dollar, a Piper knife and some crumbly twist tobacco.

"There's a bulge under his shirt," Nate said. "Proceed with the examination of the deceased."

"Why don't you just call him Obadiah? I'm getting sick of that deceased stuff!"

"Proceed," Nate said.

Around Obadiah's waist was a money belt of fine leather. It was heavy. When I gave it to Nate, he ripped some stitches with his knife and out popped a twenty-dollar goldpiece.

We went inside where the light was better. Sewn around the belt in little flat pockets were twenty-three more.

"By Ned, he's robbed a bank somewhere!" Ragged said.

Nate looked stunned like the rest of us. He said it would be proper, we still being a jury, to allow certain expenses from the money while deliberating.

We deliberated for three drinks around. For me it was a can of tomatoes.

By that time the jury was some loosened up and ready to deliberate in earnest, but Nate called a halt to further expenses. "How much is his horse and rig worth?"

It was a good outfit. We decided on a hundred and ninety bucks. Glassman said make it two hundred to keep things even.

"His pistol?" Nate asked.

"Twenty bucks," Clum Bronson said, "holster and all."

We agreed that it was a fair price.

"What happens to his stuff?" Ragged asked.

Nate scowled. "That's what I'm trying to figure out. Does anybody know of any relatives?"

Glassman snorted. "He never even had a friend!"

Hunter said, "We got a better idea where he went than where he come from." He hefted Obadiah's pistol. "I *would* give five bucks for this."

"I guess anyone would," Nate said, "but that ain't the way we're handling this business."

"How are we handling it?" I asked.

Nate cleared his throat. He sort of drew himself up, which wasn't hard, since he was about six feet three to start with. "Gentlemen," he said, like he was addressing Congress, "we've got an estate on our hands."

Danged if he didn't make it sound pretty important, but Ragged grunted disgustedly. "Estates are houses and a lot of land and money in a bank and that sort of stuff."

Nate shook his head. "Everything Obadiah left is his estate, money, horse, gun—the whole works. We will have to apply the due process of law to the handling of it. I'm hereby declaring myself administrator and the rest of you deputy administrators."

"Deputies?" Pistol Pete looked uneasy. As a matter of fact, none of us was much taken with the word.

"What's this here administrator thing?" Ragged asked.

"That means we take care of everything Obadiah left until it can be disposed of in a legal way for the benefit of his estate, or heirs."

"How can you benefit the estate by disposing of it?" Clum asked. "And if Obadiah ain't got no heirs—"

"Objection overruled!" said Nate.

"Sounds simple enough," said Glassman. "Let's divvy up the works and be done with it."

Nate looked like he'd been hit in the belly with a corral pole. "We've got to follow proper procedure!"

"Yeah? Well, you name it," Ragged said.

Nate hemmed and hawed. "I'll have to take it under advisement."

"How long does this here advisement last?" Tonso asked.

"Until our next session tomorrow evening."

In the meantime, Nate would be doing the same work as the rest of us, and getting just as dirty and sweaty, but he made it sound like he was going off to a high-paneled room somewhere to throw a study on all the law that had ever been written.

"I don't want Obadiah laying around out there until tomorrow evening," Tonso said.

We buried Obadiah down in the gulch, where we could do more bank caving than shoveling.

That night when we went to Tonso's, Nate said to me, "I've set four drinks per man as the expenses of each meeting. That means you get one can of tomatoes, or equivalent value in place of four drinks."

"You sure must have been thinking hard today."

"The session is in session," Nate said. "Who's got an idea about Obadiah's estate?"

"I think we ought to consider everything careful before we make any moves," Tonso said.

Glassman snorted. "You're boarding Obadiah's horse and getting paid for it, and making twenty-four cents on every two-bit glass of whisky we drink. We could set on this case all year and you'd be happy."

"I'll have no personalities!" Nate said. "What I want is ideas."

Tonso's blue hound came in and lay down with a sigh near the door.

Hunter said, "Let's sell the whole estate to Tonso here, and—"

"Fine!" Glassman nodded. "What do we do with the proceeds?"

"Lemme finish, damn it! Turn the whole works over to Tonso. Then he provides free drinks for any cowboy that shows up, until the estate is gone. Of course he don't say beforehand that the drinks is free."

Offhand, that sounded like a fine idea. Tonso was nodding agreeably.

"What happens after everybody in the valley finds out about the free drinks?" Nate asked.

"Be quite a rush," Hunter admitted. "But—"

"I know who'd be leading the rush," Glassman said. "What with you staying on the Bragg place all summer, and the rest of us out in the hills in cow camps."

"Calling me a drunkard, huh?" Hunter came around and took a swing at Glassman.

Glassman jumped back and fell over the hound, which let out an awful howl. Nate grabbed Hunter. "Order! Order! We ain't going to have none of that around here!"

"He called me a drunkard!"

"You wanta be cheated?" Glassman yelled.

We didn't get nowhere that night.

As a matter of fact, we didn't get nowhere the following night either. There were some pretty fair ideas about getting rid of Obadiah's estate, but Nate put the kibosh on all of them. We began to call him Old Proper Procedure, and we were getting about as disgusted with him as we were with Obadiah for getting himself killed.

When we were going out to the horses, Ragged proposed, "Let's take the estate and send Nate somewhere to study law."

"Yeah," Hunter said. "Maybe to Europe."

"She is a long way from here," Pistol Pete ventured.

We rode back toward camp.

Ragged said, "You brought on this whole thing, Pete. There ought to be some way we could make you responsible."

"No, no!" Pete said.

"I got it!" Hunter yelled. "All that money Obadiah had proves he was wanted somewhere for robbery. There's a reward out for him, sure as shooting, and it's a cinch it amounts to as much as the estate. Pete killed him, so Pete gets the estate."

That sounded like straight thinking. But Tate said, "There's no proof there was a reward. Even if there was, rewards ain't paid out of a man's estate. Motion overruled."

Hunter got sore. "I quit!"

"You'll be in contempt," Nate warned.

Hunter paused. "What's that?"

"Not showing proper respect for a court and legal procedure."

"Where the hell is the court? You mean us arguing and gabbing every night in Tonso's?"

"We're law, every one of us. We've got to act like it. We're responsible for our actions to the Territorial Courts."

"I quit," Hunter said, but it sounded pretty weak.

"Bury the money in a hole," Pete said. "We shoot the horse. Bury him too. On top we put the lariat so it will turn into a snake if anyone makes to dig."

"Yeah," Ragged said, "and we throw Nate in with the rest of the stuff."

"We ain't burying nothing," Nate said. "We're going to settle this thing all legal and proper."

We had one more night to go. After that, we were going to be scattered all over the Peralta until fall. I didn't see much chance of getting the estate settled.

When we went back to Tonso's that last evening, there was a six-horse team in the corral and a wagon with a hunk of rock on it that must have weighed six tons. My back ached just from looking at that stone.

Tonso introduced us to Jake Foley, a rawboned fellow with a face about like the rock on the wagon. We'd heard about Foley. He'd taken up a claim near Dirty Billy Springs and spent his time blasting.

"Mr. Foley here," said Tonso, "is on his way to sell a gravestone to Ute Henderson's widow."

Ragged began to laugh. Nate rammed him in the ribs.

"What's so funny?" Foley asked.

"I didn't tell him," Tonso said.

Nate took the floor, naturally. "Ute Henderson was married to an Indian, Foley. She and her family got up and left when he died. Far as we know, they took Ute along to bury him somewhere in the rocks up high."

"Why, I'd heard he was one of the leading citizens around here!"

"Reckon he was," Nate said, "but that's what happened to him. You won't be selling no rock down there, Foley."

"Stone." Foley eyed us all with suspicion.

Tonso set out the first round of our expenses. "I persuaded Mr. Foley to wait until you boys had a chance to talk to him about buying his rock for—"

"Stone," Foley said. "For whom?"

"Obadiah Smith," Tonso finished.

"Buy a rock!" Clum said, outraged. "What for? The country's full of rocks."

Nate set his glass down. "A stone for Obadiah! Tonso, I think you've got it!"

"Got what?" Hunter asked.

"We'll use the money to buy a stone for Obadiah," Nate said. "That will settle our problem."

Naturally, he didn't want Foley to know it was an estate because the price of everything always goes up where an estate is involved.

Foley said, "Was this Smith a leading citizen?"

Hunter choked on his whisky.

"You could say that," Nate admitted.

You could, sure enough. It was a hell of a lie but you could say it.

"I never heard of him," Foley said.

"You hadn't heard that Ute Henderson was married to a squaw," I said. "There's probably quite a lot you ain't heard."

"Sure!" Tonso said. "If you ever got away from your quarry you'd have heard of him. It'll be a fittin' monument—"

"They don't make the kind of monuments Obe ought to have," Glassman said. "But maybe Foley's rock will do."

"Stone."

Nate asked, "How much were you figuring on getting from Ute's family?"

"Maybe seventy-five dollars."

"Maybe we can come close to that," Nate sighed.

"The price is not everything." Foley showed considerable doubt. "My stones are not just something to be sold. They're cut to last for centuries, and I'm rather particular where they get put."

Trying to run the price up, I thought.

"Fine a piece of granite as I ever quarried."

"We'll pay your price," Nate said.

Foley got a stubborn expression. "It'll have to be a worthy place."

"Right down in the gulch," Hunter said.

Foley looked horrified. "Down in a gulch!"

"We'll work it out," Nate said hastily. "How much?"

"Who was this Obadiah?" Foley asked.

"What's the difference?"

"I'm not placing a stone on the grave of some drifting gambler." Foley was a Vermonter, we found out later. He had narrow views.

Foreseeing the end of court expenses, Ragged was crowding the bottle. "Obadiah was no gambler. He was a loud-mouthed, no—"

"One of us, one of our friends," Nate cut in.

You could see Foley wasn't much impressed with our bunch. That man had a whale of a pride in his granite.

"How did this feller die?" Foley asked.

"I shoot him!" Pete said.

Foley scowled. "I don't like the sound of this. I don't think this corpse was the kind I'd respect."

"What's that got to do with us buying your rock?" Ragged shouted. "We got the money."

"Stone," said Foley.

"I can show you a million tons of the same just by going to the door!"

"Not like mine," Foley said. "Mine is a piece of the finest blue granite. Not a flaw in it."

"Whatever it is, we'll buy it," Ragged grunted. "All you want for it is money."

Foley's blue eyes turned angry. "Money is never the most important consideration in the placing of monumental stones," he said coldly. "My father and his father before him refused large sums to set their stones on the graves of immoral people."

"Who said Obadiah was immoral?" Nate sounded indignant. "You insulting his memory?"

Foley didn't back up. "How did he happen to be killed by him?" He jerked a chin at Pete.

"I will show you how I killed him," Pete said. "He—"

"Never mind that!" Nate smiled at Foley. "Pete's like a kid. Kinda excitable. Might even say he's not quite all there. Why, he wouldn't shoot a magpie."

"Not Pete!" we all cried.

Pete looked a little confused. He started spluttering Mex.

"What's he saying?" Foley asked.

"Telling how he killed twenty-two Injuns single-handed," Nate said. "See what I mean about him being a little off?"

Foley said, "If he's crazy, why do you let him carry a pistol?"

"A toy," Nate said. "Worthless." He stepped over and grabbed Pete's gun. We'd examined it after Obahiah was killed, and found only two caps on the nipples.

The odds were a hundred to one that Pete hadn't even cleaned it since the shooting.

Nate tipped the cannon up and began pulling the trigger. It clicked three times. "See there?" he said, and should have quit right then, but he went one click too far and the gun like to lifted the roof off.

Tonso's hound let out a howl.

"How could a man kill another man with a gun that hits once out of five times?" Nate snorted. He tossed the pistol back to Pete.

"Four times," Foley said. He coughed in the powder smoke, eying the roof. "I guess you've proved your point."

"So you'll sell us the rock—the stone?" Nate asked.

Foley frowned. "How *did* Obadiah die?"

"Caused by something that he was born with, I think," Nate said.

"Sure, he had that trouble all his life," Ragged said.

Foley eyed us narrowly. "He wasn't a sinful man?"

"Good to his horse," I said. "Always took off his hat around women." Those were facts, everything on the good side I could remember.

Some could lie better. They built Obadiah up considerable. He'd been polite, thoughtful, helpful and honest. Before they went too far, Nate shut them off, and just in time, for Foley said dryly, "I never put a stone on the grave of a saint before."

"We'll have to admit that on occasion he did use swear words," Nate said.

"I do a mite of that myself," Foley admitted.

"He was thrifty," Tonso said. "He saved money."

"Ah!" said Foley.

"How much for the rock—the stone?" Ragged asked.

"I won't go less than seventy-five dollars."

"A measly seventy-five bucks for a stone for a man like Obadiah?" Hunter said in an outraged tone.

"I can get a larger one, but that will take time."

"The one outside will do," Nate said, "but we feel that we'll have to spend more for it. One hundred dollars."

"Two hundred," I said.

"Three hundred bucks!" Glassman yelled.

Tonso whacked the bar with his hand. "Four hundred!"

"Four fifty!" Ragged shouted.

"One thousand boocks!" Pete howled.

"Told you he was crazy," Nate said.

Foley figured we all was. He walked out.

"We're not joking!" Nate yelled. "This is serious."

We followed Foley outside, all of us trying to make him believe us. In all my life I never found a man so hard to give money to.

After Nate got us shushed, he talked to Foley over by the wagon. Tonso figured up the bar expenses and a buck and a half for boarding the horse, and came up with a figure that was the entire estate of Obadiah.

"It's our final offer," Nate said. "I can't be responsible for what the boys might do if you don't accept."

We looked tough as we could, although I'm sure that didn't influence Foley in the least.

"Is there something sinful or unlawful about this?"

"Believe me," Nate said, "we're straining ourselves to be as legal as we can."

"It's a damn funny offer." Foley thought a long time. "But I'll take it."

We all breathed with relief.

"I'll show you where the grave is, so you can start setting the stone tomorrow," Nate said.

"In a gulch?" Foley shook his head. "No stone of mine will be placed on loose ground."

Dead or alive, that Obadiah was nothing but trouble.

"You've already made the deal!" Ragged raged.

"Oh, no! The sale of a stone includes the setting, and if I don't have solid ground I don't sell."

Ragged threw his hat on the ground. "It's fifteen feet down to solid ground in that wash!"

Foley said stonily, "No deal."

"What *do* you want?" Glassman asked.

"Rocky ground." Foley glanced at the point of the hill above Tonso's. "That looks a good place."

"The guy ain't buried there," I protested.

"Move him," Foley said.

Hunter groaned. "By God, up there's all solid rock!"

"Good. My stone will set well in a place like that."

Nate said, "Your stones ain't more important than the people themselves."

"They are to me."

We went back into Tonso's to argue about it. There was no shaking Foley. He wasn't going to set his stone on loose ground, and we couldn't dig a hole in rock.

"You move him, Foley," Ragged suggested. "You're getting enough for the stone to move all the graves from here to the mountains."

"I'm a stonemason, not an undertaker."

Nate had been thinking like sixty. "Foley, ain't it proper to set monuments on land to someone lost at sea."

"Yes."

"All right, put Obadiah's monument on the hill."

You could see that Foley was pretty favorably taken. "You claiming his grave is lost?"

"Yep!" Ragged said. "We buried him at night. I doubt that any of us could say where he's at."

Hunter tried to mess that up. "I know right where he is."

"Not me," I said.

"Me neither," Ragged grumbled. "First big rain—"

Hunter was stubborn. "I kin find him."

Foley shook his head. "The man is right. There's deceit in this. I won't be a party to it."

There we were, stuck fast against Foley's pride and hard morality.

We looked to Nate, but all he said was, "I think I'll remove all restrictions on the expense limit."

The expenses began to flow pretty fast. Foley was right in there, holding his own. His face got red, but I couldn't see that he was loosening up much.

The conversation had got pretty loud and it had extended to about everything under the sun. It was then that Nate brought us back to business. "We'll have a vote to determine whether the grave is lost or not."

Everyone of us except Hunter voted that it was lost beyond reasonable finding, whatever that was.

"No, sir!" Hunter said. "I'll show you where it is."

He lurched away from the bar and started out. He fell over the doorsill and lay there groaning.

"I accept that as evidence that he was incompetent to vote," Nate declared. "Therefore, the grave of Obadiah Smith is lost by unanimous action of this group."

"Second the motion!" yelled Pistol Pete. He was learning something, though not much, about democratic procedure.

We looked at Foley.

"I agree," he declared, solemn as an owl.

"It is, therefore, fitting and proper that Obadiah's stone be erected on a suitable hill in the vicinity where he was last seen," Nate said. "All those in favor—"

"Aye!" we yelled.

"No more expenses," Nate said.

"Hell, I was just beginning to understand law," said Ragged, who could hardly walk by now.

"And what do you want as the inscription?" Foley asked. He took two cuts at the last word before he got it right.

Nate said, "Obadiah Smith, 1881. That's enough."

We all wanted to add something. "In Memory of" or "Rest in Peace" or "He Was a Good Man." I thought "He Died Game" would be pretty good.

Hunter staggered up and came back to the bar. He'd skinned both shins on the high log sill and was feeling ill used. "Just put 'To Hell With Him'!"

Nate had his way. Nothing but the name and date.

We sold Obadiah's gun to Tonso for twenty bucks, and added that to the gold. It was somewhere close to four hundred and fifty bucks, a heap of money for a stone, but getting that estate settled was a big relief.

We'd overlooked something. There was still the horse and the rig, which we'd appraised at two hundred. Tonso called that to our attention.

"You know, of course, Foley, that a horse is involved in the deal," Nate said.

"No, I don't know it." Foley had all the gold before him on the bar. The way he was staring at it, you could tell that his conscience and principles were having a real rough time. "I don't know nothing about a horse. I don't want nothing to do with it."

"You have to take the horse," Nate said.

"I don't even have to take this money." Foley weaved a little, but his eyes were hard and steady. "It's too much."

"The horse is extra for cutting the inscription," Nate said.

"No! That's included."

I had a feeling that it wouldn't take much for Foley to shove that pile of gold back at us.

"I'll buy the horse and rig," Tonso said, "but I won't go any two hundred. I'll go seventy-five."

"It's a deal!" Ragged said.

"No, it ain't," Nate said. "We set the price at two hundred, and that's what we'll get."

Tonso shook his head. "Not from me."

"You ain't shoving the horse off on me either," Foley said.

I tell you that Foley was a hard man to deal with.

But Nate wagged his finger at Foley. "In payment for services to the estate of Obadiah Smith you have just accepted one bay horse, with saddle and bridle, for two hundred dollars."

"Not me," Foley said. "You'll have to do something else with the horse."

"Would you deprive the late lamented of the esteem the world should render by leaving him in an unmarked grave?"

"The grave is lost," Foley said. "I ain't depriving him of nothing."

"You just sold the horse," Nate said.

"Huh?"

"You just sold it to Tonso here for seventy-five dollars. Give him the money, Joe."

Tonso counted out seventy-five dollars and added it to Foley's pile.

"There," Nate said. "Nobody can say it's sinful to lose money on a deal."

"Hah!" said Foley. "That's even more sinful than making too much." Way he stared at that pile of gold on the bar, the more he looked like a dog with a mouthful of bad meat and no place to spit it.

Suddenly he heaved up tall as he could and glared like we was the scum of the earth. "I confess to greed," he said. "I was swayed by the power of gold, but now I renounce the whole deal."

We stood drop-mouthed.

"I will not be a party to deceit and trickery!"

"Nobody asked you to shoot your grandmother," Ragged growled. "Just take the money."

"No!"

Nate cut in smooth and fast. "Of course on transactions of this kind, we do expect a contribution to our cause."

"The wages of sin— What cause?" Foley said. The way he tightened up, you could tell he was not only a hard man to give money to, but a tougher one to take it away from.

"Church fund," Nate said.

"There ain't no church."

"Of course not," Nate said. "That's what our fund is for, to build one." He looked Foley hard in the eye. "I suggest that you contribute all but seventy-five dollars of that money to the fund."

Foley wrassled with that. "I haven't the right."

"Now you're obstructing justice and law."

"That's the first I've heard of any law around here."

"We've got it. You're obstructing it."

Foley counted out seventy-five dollars, put it into his pocket. "For the stone." He shoved the rest away from him. "Do what you wish with it."

"No," Nate said. "We gotta have your statement you're contributing it to the church fund."

"It wasn't mine! I've refused it."

"You took it once. Now you're giving it to the church."

"All right!" Foley yelled. "I'm giving it to the church!"

Nate shoved the money at Tonso. "Deposit this with the rest of the church funds."

"How much have you got?" Foley asked.

"I haven't counted lately," Tonso said, "but it's coming along."

A sudden quiet fell over us. The thing was done.

Smith's monument is still on the hill where Foley set it. You'd be surprised at some of the yarns told today about how come it to be there, about that great pioneer Obadiah Smith.

Hell, maybe he was! His money built the church.

Jackass Judgment

by *Kenneth Fowler*

A former Yonkers newspaperman, Ken Fowler has edited for both Street
& Smith and Popular Publications, served in the Air Force and reviewed
books for the *New York Herald Tribune*. He has written more than two
hundred short stories and half a dozen novels in this genre. Currently he
lives in Florida.

❦ ❦ ❦

I WAS FEELING PLUMB DISMAL when me and my pardner, Charlie
Snow, headed into the camp powwow at Blackjack Henebry's Sun
Dance Bar. Two, three hours earlier some curly wolf had broken into
our cabin on Spanish Creek and tailed out with our cache of four
thousand dollars in dust and nuggets. We'd called the powwow to
elect a Vigilante Committee, which I told Charlie was locking the
barn after the horse was stolen. But Charlie said no, the Lord would
give us a "Sign."

That was the way he talked. He hadn't changed the tune even
when we'd come into our cabin and found just an empty hole in the
floor where we'd cached our dust. "Who diggeth a pit," Charlie had

said, staring down at the hole, "shall fall therein. Let not your heart be troubled, Zeke. The robbery of the wicked shall destroy them, because they refuse to do judgment."

My pardner had a power of knowledge on the subject of sin. That would have been all right, if he'd just been satisfied to be saved himself. But Charlie honed to lead our whole Yanktown diggings up the Glory Trail, and the way the boys hoorawed him was a wicked shame.

I put him up for chairman of the Vigilante Committee, but Shorty Dwyer hooted, "Reverend Snow will now lead us in prayer!" and that brought on such a caterwauling and boot-stomping as like to cracked the back-bar mirror.

After the rumpus died down Bide Tadlock nominated his brother Mort, and Ed Beasley, a camp roustabout, seconded the motion. Mort was a tall, dark hombre with a slick gift of gab, and he got elected. He was the camp politician and glad-hander, and quick as the votes were counted he proved how smart he was by making Charlie a member of his eight-man Vigilante Committee.

When we got back to our cabin I started shucking off my boots to get ready for bed, but Charlie allowed he would stay up for a spell and read. "I will do good to them that despise me," Charlie said when I tried to tell him the boys hadn't meant no harm by that joshing they'd given him. Then he put on his specs. "The Lord is far from the wicked," he said, "but He heareth the prayer of the righteous."

Stretched out on my bunk, I watched Charlie bent over his Bible in the candlelight. I'd run into Charlie on the trail, and we'd teamed up. I didn't know much about him except that he'd lost his wife and daughter in an Indian massacre, and once, in his younger days, he'd been a gun marshal in some little jerkwater town called Siringo Wells, back in Kansas. I figured he'd bummed around a lot before he'd got religion. But it wasn't till we made our strike that I learned what he planned to do with his share of our dust. He aimed to give it to a little waterfront mission in Frisco—the place where he'd first seen "the Light."

Charlie had me up before daybreak and we rode out on the trail from camp, hoping to cut sign. And at Ripple Box Gulch, four, five miles from the diggings, we ran into something. There was a jackass grazing along the edge of the trail and we could see where a saddle-bag strap had left a broad welt in his hide. To the left of the jack was a shale ledge, and poking around there Charlie found a spot where two bullets had snipped splinters out of the rock.

We put it together from that. A jackass had been toting a load, likely our two pouches of dust. The thieves had been high-tailing out of camp when a highwayman had opened up on them. They'd put him on the run, but then they'd decided to wait for safer weather before smuggling out the gold. They'd fogged it back to the diggings with the pouches, leaving the slow-footed jack to take care of itself.

Back in camp, Charlie tied the mule to an iron spike behind the cabin and I went out to snoop around and see if anybody had reported a jack lost, strayed or stolen. Nobody had. One jackass looks pretty much like another, and finding the owner of this one began to look like one of those needle-in-a-haystack propositions.

But the next day I had a change of luck. Looking around, I found that Ed Beasley and Shorty Dwyer had owned a mule, but didn't own him any more. They said he'd died. I hotfooted to Charlie with the news, but he wagged his head and said it wouldn't do to be hasty. "Judge not according to appearance, Zeke," he said. "When the Lord is ready, He will give us His Sign."

"The Lord," I snapped, "helps them who help themselves. We wait any longer and one of these nights them two'll be sloping out of here, lock, stock and barrel."

"Patience, Brother," Charlie said.

And that night patience got a kick in the pants. Somebody tried to steal the jackass. In our little cabin the slam of Charlie's Sharps sounded like a cannon, and the way I jumped out of bed I like to busted a gusset.

Charlie had his Old Betsy braced on the ledge of our back window, and as he lowered it, gentlelike, to look around at me, I got a creepy feeling.

"Zeke," Charlie said, looking like the cat that swallowed the canary, "the Lord has given us a lamp unto our feet and a light unto our path. Tomorrow He will lead us against the Philistines."

But when I went out for a look-see I didn't find any corpses. If anything looked dead, it was that jackass. And Charlie's palaver about "Signs" and "Lights" was getting on my nerves. After breakfast next morning I lit out for our claim, leaving Charlie to ride herd on the jack.

When I got back to the cabin, along towards the shank of the afternoon, I had a surprise. Charlie stood at the front door, holding the jack by a rope, and with him were Bill Storrs and Andy Grau of the Vigilante Committee.

The sight of that poor dumb mule did something to me. Its long ears drooped like a pair of wilted sunflowers, and you could almost count the ribs sticking out of its mangy hide. That was one of the few times I ever let go at Charlie.

"You and your highfalutin' palaver about kindness and Christian charity," I said. "When's the last time you fed that poor fly bait, Charlie?"

"Peace, Brother!" Charlie said, and he gave the mule a whack on the rump. "Walk while ye have the light," he told me sternly, "lest darkness come upon you."

There's nothing to do with a man like that but humor him. I fell into line behind Bill Storrs and after a couple minutes had to hump it, to keep up with the parade. By the time we got to the foot of Skunk Hill, that slat-ribbed mountain canary was running. Charlie was tugging on the rope to hold it back, his snowy beard fluffed out like a sail to the wind and a kind of avenging look in his blue eyes.

The burro made a beeline for the first shack at the top of the hill, heading for the feed crib out back of it. At that moment there was a creaking sound and the cabin door swung open.

"Evening, gents," Mort Tadlock said, casually. "Something I can do for you?"

"Ye can," said Charlie in his deep-bottom preaching voice, "and ye will. We have come for our dust, Mort Tadlock."

Mort grinned, but there was a kind of iciness in his gunflint eye. Suddenly he threw back his head and guffawed.

"Better take him home, Zeke," he said to me, "and sober him up."

I had it then—that mysterious "Light" Charlie was always yawping about. And now I knew why he hadn't fed the jackass for two, three days.

"Mort," I said, "I taken a sudden notion you and Bide been trying to get rich too quick."

Charlie's voice rolled out like a deep organ. "And he that maketh haste to be rich," rumbled Charlie, "shall not be innocent."

Andy Grau began, "Mort, you'd better—" and that was as far as he got. Andy, Bill and me had been so busy watching Mort we didn't hear the footsteps behind us. But Charlie did. I saw Charlie whip around, and then I saw Bide Tadlock, with the gun arching up in his fist.

The shots slammed together, sounding like one big wallop on a bass drum, but Charlie was a hair quicker than Bide. My eyes were glued on Bide as he staggered and slumped over, and then I heard another shot and when I jerked around there was Mort backed up to the doorjamb and sliding down against it, and smoke was feathering from the muzzle of Andy Grau's big Peacemaker.

Well, we found the dust buried right in the Tadlocks' cabin, and next day Yanktown had a new Vigilante Committee chairman—Charlie Snow. And I guess it won't be long now before the boys are getting religion mixed in with their law.

Because, naturally, there was just one place where Charlie could have got his notion to starve that jackass and make it lead us to the Promised Land.

"It is written," Charlie explained, "where all may see who who will hearken unto the Lord, in Isaiah, one, three. 'The ox knoweth his owner, and the ass his master's crib.' "

Hired Gun

by *William R. Cox*

A former newspaperman, Bill Cox authored sports, crime and mystery fiction before appearing in the Western field in 1939. His novel, *Comanche Moon*, topped Western Ratings last year with the highest number of votes ever recorded, eighteen. He has twice been a Director of WWA.

❦ ❦ ❦

CHARLIE LANG GOT OFF the train in Sirocco and looked curiously around the station. The last time he had come to the burgeoning town it had been aboard a stagecoach. The West was changing and in Charlie there was a slight unease.

He was a small man in striped trousers and a dark jacket and a white shirt somewhat soiled from flying cinders. He carried a large carpetbag adorned with sad roses. He saw Daniel Shay at once and went toward him.

Shay was too stout, his head looked smaller than ever. He looked prosperous, but then Shay could always make money; his trouble was in consolidating his gains. There was a woman with him and Charlie removed his cream-colored Stetson, his vague discontent growing. He did not like women in on a job.

A man with a badge pinned to his vest sauntered past. This was Trowbridge and Charlie was glad he had not worn a gun. Shay had guaranteed Trowbridge without subduing Charlie's deep distrust of all lawmen. That was the way it had always been, they didn't like him and he didn't like them. If it had been different, somewhere in the past, maybe there wouldn't have been the killing and the hoorawing and all that went with it.

Shay said to him, "Knew you'd make it, Charlie. By God, you always make it. This here is Violet Corrivan. She works for me."

The woman was not young, she was medium sized and rather plump. She had fresh skin and she looked directly at Charlie, bowing with the formal elegance peculiar to dance-hall gals in public places. Charlie found himself looking straight into her eyes.

There was something odd about her eyes. They were very blue, with shadings and they looked at Charlie, not through him. They searched inside him and then she smiled, with good teeth and he found himself smiling back and this unsettled him, because most women were afraid of him, distrusted him on first sight.

He said to Shay, "We'd better get out of here. I need to wash. You got everything lined up?"

Shay motioned toward a carriage at the platform. "Certainly I got it lined up. Me and Violet been for a drive, so I come over in the rig."

Charlie put his bag in the carriage. Watching the way Shay held the woman when he helped her onto the seat he knew all he needed to know about them. He felt a twinge of sorrow for the woman.

There were more people in the town, but the street was still dusty. Shay drove to the hotel and bar and gambling joint which bore his name in huge letters and they clambered down in the alley between the place and a livery stable. Shay couldn't keep his fat hands off the woman. They walked around to the veranda.

Through long habit, Charlie used his eyes to cover every detail of the scene. He spotted the H-Bar-H brand on horses at the rack and lagged behind, his hands cold as always. He almost stopped and opened the bag but he knew that was no good and kept on walking.

Three men came down the steps of the hotel porch. One was dark and incisive and reeking with power, the other two were hard-bitten, carefree range riders. The leader was Ring Hatton and he wore his strength like a cloak. His voice was oddly fuzzy but clear enough and not loud, merely dangerous.

"You strung the fence, didn't you, Shay? You had to cut off the water hole. You asked for it."

"The water hole is on my ranch. I bought that land fair and square and I got a right to the water hole."

"You run off the nesters and you got Loco Barnes to homestead it for you," Hatton said. "He was quite somethin', Loco." He paused, grinned briefly. "You heard me. Was. He ain't, not now no more. We cut the fence, too. That's why I'm here. To tell you we cut the fence and remind you how it could be with you. Like the Loco. Was —but ain't."

The two riders guffawed. They were not experienced, Charlie thought, tough enough, maybe too brave, but not honed by gun war. Hatton was different. Shay had been right when he wrote that his enemy was poison. There was murder in Hatton's furry, slurred tones, in the hands that opened and shut above the gun butts. Charlie had seen his kind all over the frontier and had avoided them whenever possible. They were the kind who liked to kill, and Charlie was rather glad to see this. It made the ending easier.

Shay was clinging to Violet, safe in the tradition that Hatton would not start anything to endanger the woman. "I got the law on my side."

"Town law. And Trowbridge wouldn't scare me if he was honest. I'm givin' you the warning, Shay. Just once."

He stepped aside and for a moment his eyes rested on Charlie, flaring a little, then steadying, studying. Charlie plodded past him, patently unarmed, toting the bag, demure as he could possibly manage and Hatton seemed satisfied that he was another drummer. Still, Charlie thought, this was not an ordinary man. It would be necessary to be very sure of it with Hatton.

The barroom of the hotel was huge, with two faro tables, four poker tables and a wheel in the rear of the place. The bar ran to the gaming space. There was a dais for a piano against the far wall. The woman went over and sat at a table alone. Shay ordered a double whisky.

Charlie said, "You get drunk and I'm hauling my freight. You picked a dandy this time."

"You can handle him." Shay was sweating. The fear that was always in him did not deter him from his ambition for money and power but it made him sweat.

"Maybe I can and maybe I can't. Bear that in mind. You can't handle liquor. Lay off."

"They killed Loco."

"You leave a simple halfwit out there alone, he's bound to be killed. If you weren't so cheap, you'd have hired some guns. Hatton —I've seen them like Hatton."

"You can pick your time and place."

"Yeah. Tell you what, Shay. Send word to him that you don't buy his warning. That you're going to restring the fence."

"Now? Right now? You're crazy, Charlie."

"Send word or I'm taking the afternoon train."

Shay poured another drink. "But why? Can't you look around, pick some place and lay for him?"

"You heard me. Send the word." He got a key from the desk and carried his bag upstairs to a large room overlooking the street. Shay was scared but he would obey because he recognized that it had to be quick, he might not last if it wasn't over soon. There was no sense giving a man like Hatton any time.

He took off his coat and shirt and washed with care. Shay, he thought, a crook with a yellow streak. Always trying to make it big, never quite succeeding. Always running up against real men and yelling for help.

Well, he couldn't shy off from Shay. He had been hired by worse men. Shay paid off, that was for sure. There were times, before he had gone completely cold, when he had not collected his money.

He opened the capacious bag. He took out a .38 revolver and

harness and the parts of a stubby, sawed-off shotgun, which he assembled with swift hands. He found a clean shirt and knotted a loose tie at its collar and slid into the harness, which settled the revolver beneath his left armpit. He donned a light alpaca jacket with a single button, a loose garment. He slipped spare shells into his pocket, made sure of both weapons.

There was a tap on the door and he admitted Violet Corrivan, not surprised, anticipating her so that she looked curiously at him.

She said, "Shay sent the word. They'll be coming pretty quick."

"Sure, they will."

The woman's gaze was searching. "Can I help?"

"Yes. I was sort of counting on you."

"You were?"

"Why do you think Shay sent you up here? Shay knows about these things."

"Shay knows too much, sometimes. I'm getting sick of Shay, Mr. Lang." Now her eyes opened, bolder. She had been a lovely girl, once.

"He's a good meal ticket."

"You don't know that side of him. You don't know how he is with a woman."

"Maybe I do. Maybe I can guess."

"Shay's no good for a woman."

Her meaning was clear enough. Charlie waited for her to get to the point. She moved toward him, touched his hand. Her fingers were very soft. She exuded a powerful force. Two of them in one day, he thought, Hatton and the woman. Why hadn't they combined to swallow Shay?

She said, "Suppose you were a little slow? Just slow enough? Suppose Hatton got Shay?"

"Who'd pay me?"

She laughed, a carefree sound. "Honey, I know where his poke is hidden. There's an afternoon train. Going west."

"Happens I'm heading that way. California." He hesitated, then said, "Maybe I shouldn't be telling you this. I'm making this my last job."

"California. I've never been there." Now her eyes changed, be-

came hopeful, losing the gleam of avidity. "Life is sudden, sometimes. California."

"Might open a little place, sell booze, deal a game. It's warm in
California all year 'round."

"I can sing. I could handle the cash. I'm quick at figures. And
I can cook, Charlie, if only somebody would let me cook."

Charlie took her hand, held it. He said, "Can you hide the shotgun under your dress? Can you hand it to me when I give you the
signal?"

"I can do it. I'm not one of your red-skinned, shiny nose ranch
women, but I can do it." She was excited but she was calm under-
neath, Charlie saw.

"You're sure you had enough of Shay? No strings?"

"I had plenty of Shay." She snorted. "He's scared of everything
and everyone but me. I get it, everything he can't do to other people.
I've been sick of him for some time."

He gave her the gun. Her skirts swirled up and it vanished, held
in place with one hand. She was as tall as Charlie and once she must
have had a wonderful body.

She said, "Make it good, Charlie Lang. Make it real good. You
got two reasons, now."

Out in the street a man spoke loudly to a horse. She was staring
at him and he was aware of the silence in the room. He could have
kissed her, he could have made some demonstration but he did not
stir.

She said, "I've heard plenty about you, Charlie Lang. Not only
from Shay. Don't think this is all on the spur of the moment. I know
about you."

"Don't let anybody see the gun. Stay close at my end of the bar."

"I'll know what to do. Make it good, Charlie Lang." She went
out, moving lightly, quickly into the hall. She paused one instant,
audaciously winked at him, then was gone.

The man in the street yelled again and the horse whinnied. A
carriage squeaked by. There wasn't much time. Charlie thought
about the woman.

It was a long time since he had been involved with a female
except upon the purchase plan. His wife had run away many years

ago and he had let her go and thought to profit by the experience. This Violet Corrivan had something, all right, something extra. She must have been working Shay for all he was worth.

Well, he thought, fish or cut bait. He had told the truth about California, where he was unknown. He was weary and he had some money in a San Francisco bank. It was time to quit the rat race before he began thinking like a rat.

He went down the steps, past the desk, noting that the lobby was empty save for the clerk and an old man reading an ancient newspaper. He went into the bar and stood at the far end. Violet slid past him, ignoring him, and sat at a table nearby.

At the other end of the bar Shay was drinking despite everything, the perspiration pouring down his cheeks. The bartender was a middle-aged man and Charlie could see that he was not in it. There were no customers but outside in the street there was a murmur of subdued excitement and then Hatton's odd voice and the sound of hard heels.

Charlie looked once at Violet, about four feet away from him. Hatton and the two men came through the swinging doors. Shay drained his glass, put it down and tried to straighten himself. The bartender dropped the glass he was pretending to polish.

Hatton said to his men, "Like I was saying, a shoat only's got one purpose. To be butchered for the good of people."

This was the moment Shay should have chosen, Charlie knew, before they were set. It never happened that way. If only once some-one made the right move at the right time, things would be easier. But Shay just stood there, a big, fat target.

Hatton put both hands on the bar, arching his body away from it, balancing on the narrow toes of his boots. Still Shay did not make his move, fearful of the two riders who remained in back of Hatton, flanking him.

"I don't like the whisky in here. Gimme some of your special stuff."

"We—we only got one kinda whisky," said the barkeep.

"I'll take that bottle." Hatton pointed toward Shay. "The one the shoat's drinkin' out of."

Shay inhaled and stepped away from the bar. He was wearing a gun on his right hip. Hatton took his hands from the bar and the riders moved to give him room. They gave him a lot of space, covering the entire bar from where they made their stand.

They would let Hatton take Shay without interfering, Charlie knew. They were witnesses. On the other hand, Hatton was taking no chances. He looked at Charlie.

"How about a drink for you, stranger? Some of the good stuff?"

" 'Scuse me, I only take sarsap'rilla," said Charlie. He tried to make his voice colorless and vacuous. "Got something wrong with my stomach."

"Then don't wait on us. We got a little business with Mr. Shay."

Charlie grinned weakly. "Oh, that's all right. Don't mind me."

One of the riders laughed. Hatton said, "Couldn't you go somewhere else? Any place, so long as it ain't here."

This could be serious, Charlie thought, unbuttoning his coat with his left hand, trying to appear stupid and without understanding. "I'm all right, thank you."

"Yeah," said Hatton. "You're all right for now." He wheeled around on Shay. "Did you say somethin', Mr. Shoat?"

Charlie stole a quick glance at Violet. She had not moved. She held her hand on the shotgun beneath the skirts. Her face was smooth and quiet. She really did have nice skin.

Shay said, his voice faltering but shrill, "You've got no call to come in here bullyin' people around. Our business is on the range. You got no rights here."

"Why don't you call your town law, Shoat? Why don't you call Mr. Trowbridge, the marshal?"

He was laying a lot of stress on his words, Charlie thought, wasting time. He began to wonder if Hatton was so smart after all, or if he was just murderous. It was hard, sometimes, to tell the difference. He thought Hatton was smart, he thought it better to play the thing that way.

Shay had got up his nerve at last. "I don't need Trowbridge nor anybody else. This is my place. You got no rights here and I'm callin' your bluff."

Charlie made his eyes wide and innocent and tried to look frightened. As a matter of fact he wasn't feeling too brave at the moment. He didn't like the setup. He wished Violet could handle the shotgun, that would do it. He shrank into the corner, managing to get his right hand where it needed to be even as he appeared scared.

Hatton was still talking. Too much palaver, Charlie thought, and the riders weren't acting right.

"You got big and brave all of a sudden, didn't you, Mr. Shoat? You're callin' me out, is that it?"

Maybe that was for the witnesses and maybe it was not, Charlie thought. Talk, talk, talk, he never remembered one where there was so much gab. He stepped away from the bar.

Then Hatton said sharply, "All right. Make your play."

The two cowboys moved again. Charlie's thoughts became clear and sharp and well defined. They knew he was in on it, Hatton was smart after all.

Like all cowards, Shay's fear drove him to action. Hasty, injudicious action, of course, his hand slow in going for the gun. He was counting on Charlie to beat the count.

The two riders were converging, reaching for their weapons. Charlie got out the .38 with a slick, sleek motion. They were a little late or he would have been dead where he stood. He got one in the shoulder, then knocked the woman to the floor and upended the table. A bullet hit Charlie.

Hatton shot Shay twice, but Shay fell behind the end of the bar. Then Hatton turned and his eyes were fox-red. Charlie shot the other cowboy.

Hatton was advancing, gun pointed, hand steady. Charlie couldn't walk but he shoved himself away from the table. He had been hit in the hip. Hatton fired once. The bullet nicked Charlie's left shoulder, spinning him, so that Hatton's next bullet missed his head by an inch.

Charlie said, "Ah, there, killer," and held his gun low, pumping three fast shots, emptying all chambers.

Hatton took them in the middle. He folded up like an empty overcoat as they slammed into him. He lay curled on the floor.

Shay was howling, "Charlie, where are you, Charlie? He got me. I'm dying."

People came in, now that the shooting had stopped. Charlie was on his knees, hurting a lot. He had the empty gun in his hand, he stared into the eyes of the woman. He said, "Unload that shotgun."

She was kneeling on the floor, the weapon in her hands. She said, "You—you knocked me out of it."

"You know it."

"You're hurt. You're bleeding."

Shay was pleading and a voice said, "Here's Doc. Shay is over yonder. Looks like Hatton finally jumped him."

Another voice said wonderingly, "Did Shay get the whole kit and kiboodle of 'em?"

They could not see Violet and Charlie behind the table. Charlie said, "How much did Hatton pay you?"

"Are you crazy, Charlie? You knocked me out of it." She reached toward him. Her eyes were bright with tears. "You need the doctor."

"Before I got to town. You went to Hatton. You wanted to get away from Shay. You weren't sure about me, but you tipped them just now. They were ready for me."

"No! I didn't. Hatton figured it out. You know Hatton was smart."

"Honey, you played it every way from the middle. You figured to win no matter what happened." The pain was getting bad. He smiled at her. "Hatton would've killed you just as quick as Shay or me. Good thing I shoved you over."

She said, "Charlie, so help me, I didn't. If you hadn't knocked me out of it, I'd have used the greener."

"I saw you knew how to handle it." He took the shotgun from her, then handed it back. "See if you can get it out of here."

"You won't tell that story to Shay? He'd kill me. He could kill a woman."

Charlie felt himself slipping to the floor. He said, "Honey, what the hell. No harm done. I like a smart woman."

So long as he lived, if he lived, he would never forget the look in her eyes at that instant. They lighted up like a Fourth of July fireworks. She slid the gun back beneath her skirts. She leaned forward and kissed him on the mouth.

She stood up. She said, "There's a man here. He's hurt bad. He saved Daniel's life. I think he's a lawman of some kind. You better get over here, Doc."

She moved behind the bar, hid the shotgun. Shay was moaning. People were milling about. Two men carried Hatton out onto the veranda. Violet went back to Charlie.

She whispered, "I've got some money of my own. We can't make today's train, but one comes through here every day, Charlie Lang."

He closed his eyes. If he lived, Shay would have a story to convince the tame marshal. The pay would be there, Shay always paid off.

Maybe he wouldn't take the money. Maybe he would take the woman, call it a trade. This was his last job and he sure did take to a clever woman.

She could have killed him with his own shotgun.

Best of all, she hadn't admitted the truth. If you're stuck with a lie, hang onto it, Charlie always believed. The doctor came and shook his head and men lifted Charlie and put him on a faro table and the doc said he was a brave man and that his friend Shay was all right, he would live.

They gave him whisky and murmured as he lay there, letting the doctor probe, grinning a little. They didn't see Violet, hovering, tipping him that sly, promising wink.